Breakdown on Blowhard Mountain

A Travel Mystery

Carolyn Jourdan and
Ludger Dominic Bracht

Map and custom road signs by Bran Rogers - http://www.bran.ink - Instagram @branrogersart

ISBN-13: 978-1-946299-11-6 Softcover
ISBN-13: 978-1-946299-10-9 Ebook
ISBN-13: 978-1-946299-12-3 Audio

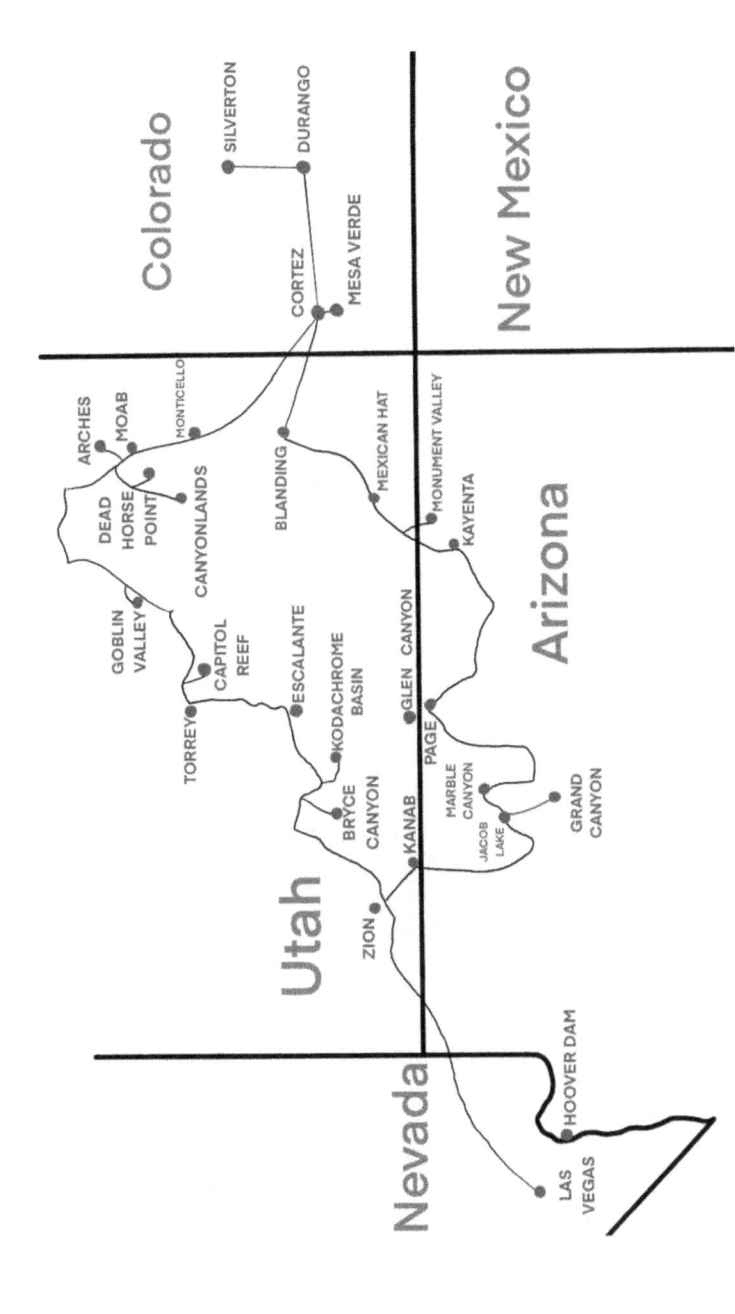

Prologue

The coyote heard humans shouting. They were always yapping about something, but this was even noisier than usual.

He didn't like being around people. They were dangerous. But they always had food. Their scraps were tasty and he needed all the calories he could get, so he crept over the rocks to take a peek.

He saw a big white car and a little black car. Two men near the black car were pointing guns at the white car. The doors on the white car popped open and several humans got out and stood with their hands up in the air.

There was some more shouting.

He got a whiff of bacon. *Mmmmm.* Possibly some chicken and maybe a bit of ham. He'd have to act fast or one of his competitors might make a move. There was a lot of competition around these days.

He crept closer. His natural coloring and stealth made him hard to see. The humans were focusing on each other and yapping back and forth, so they might not even notice him.

He tilted his snout and tested the wind until he homed in on a delicious odor emanating from a canvas bag on the ground between the two groups of humans. They seemed to be fighting over it.

He could understand why. That smell was irresistible.

He had a clear shot. He could do a dash 'n grab and keep running until he'd lost 'em. He took one last look around to make sure the coast was clear, then he leaped into action.

He went straight for the bag at top speed and grabbed it in his teeth. It was a lot heavier than he'd anticipated but he was too far into this to let go now, so he bit down hard and ran as fast as he could.

The bag was dragging on the ground and snagging in brush but he didn't drop it. Two of the shouting guys, the ones from the black car, came after him, but nothing on two legs had a chance of catching him.

He heard some loud pops and puffs of dirt went flying up all around him. *Uh oh*, they had guns. He'd seen guns before. They were bad news.

He ran faster.

There was more shouting and then he heard car engines start. The men chasing him heard it, too. They stopped running and turned around to see what was going on.

That's when he doubled down and made his getaway.

As soon as he was out of sight, he dropped the bag and did a quick search for the meat. He found half a sandwich and gobbled it three quick bites.

It was one of the tastiest treats he'd ever had in his short life. The dangerous gambit had been worth it.

The two guys were after him again, though. He could see them scrambling over the rocks, coming his way, but he was on his home ground and knew all the tricks.

He took off again. They'd never get him now.

Chapter 1

Eleven Days Earlier

Alex Weiss had the knack of being able to go to sleep anytime, anywhere—and stay that way—but even he couldn't sleep through the high-volume howling coming from a set of unhappy twin babies in the economy section of an airplane.

He opened one eye.

An ear-splitting duet of screaming and shrieking was emanating from two tiny red-faced infants a few feet away. He was in an aisle seat and the children's mother was in the aisle seat across from him. Her progeny shared the seat next to her.

The woman's efforts to hold and comfort one baby and then the other were totally ineffective. The painful racket went on for a few more agonizing minutes, then the mother started crying, too.

Alex took this same flight several times a year. He'd always been able to sleep as the plane made the transatlantic hop from Germany to Georgia. It was a special torture to be trapped for hours in a confined space with screaming children.

The noise was tremendous. He glanced over at her again. Both babies were inconsolable over some mid-flight misery. Much grumbling could be heard coming from the other passengers as well. He knew everyone was suffering.

The flight attendants had vanished.

The poor mother was at the end of her rope. Something needed to be done.

Alex reached across the aisle, touched the woman's arm, and said, "Let me help you. My wife says I have a way with small children."

The desperate mother immediately thrust one of the twins toward him. At this point she didn't care if he was an ax murderer. He reached out and took hold of the squirming, yowling baby and settled the tiny child against his chest.

The crying stopped immediately.

The mother stared at him in open-mouthed shock. "How did you do that?"

He smiled and shrugged.

The noise was reduced by half, but there was still the other furious twin to deal with. But even when trying to cope with only one of the babies, the mother couldn't stop the crying. Hers or the child's.

"If you'll switch seats with me," Alex said. "I think I can get them both to sleep."

The young woman leaped up immediately and he moved over into her seat without waking the infant he held. When he was settled, he lifted the other twin and held them both, one in the crook of each arm.

Suddenly the plane was quiet.

"Thank God!" said someone, loud enough to be heard. This was followed by muffled laughter throughout the cabin.

A stewardess suddenly appeared through a curtain and strode down the aisle to his seat. "Whatever you want for the rest of the flight," she said, "just name it and it's yours."

As the hours wore on, the twins slept peacefully, as did their exhausted mother.

Passengers moving up and down the aisle gave Alex a grateful smile, a thumbs up, or some of other gesture of appreciation. He gave them a smile or a wink in return.

This was his job after all. Comforting unhappy travelers. He was a professional tour guide. And he was very good at his job.

***

Alex was restless by nature. He was happiest when in motion, like a dog riding with its head out the window of a speeding car. But as he'd grown older, gotten married, and had two children, he'd needed to find a way to monetize himself—and he had.

He'd become a professional traveler.

When the plane was about to land in Atlanta he gave his seat and the twins back to their mother, then stretched to loosen stiff muscles and joints. Unfortunately a lot of modern travel involved being wedged into uncomfortable seats for hours in planes, trains, trucks, buses, vans, cars, ATVs, dog sleds, you name it.

Alex worked freelance. When he wasn't busy shepherding people around on their vacations, he worked with local crews as a Mädchen für alles, a *jack of all trades*, for touring musicians who gave concerts near his home in Münster, Germany.

After sixteen hours in the air from Düsseldorf to Atlanta as a nanny, or a *manny* as they called it in the U.S., he'd need to go through immigration and customs, change planes, then try to get some sleep from Atlanta to Las Vegas.

He shuffled along in the typically sluggish conga line out of the airplane, up the jetway, and into Hartsfield-Jackson International Airport. He adopted a brisk gait and headed toward the Global Entry kiosk, passing dozens of slower passengers.

He expected to breeze through the entry process since he'd paid extra for the privilege, but *nooo*. When he reached the kiosk, he was singled out for what the agent said was a *random extended interview*.

He wasn't sure how random it actually was, but it was certainly extended. So much for getting ahead of the crowd. But by the end of his terse exchange with the hard-eyed agent he'd been successful in convincing the U.S. government that he was indeed Alexander Maximilian Weiss as his documentation proclaimed.

He was released from the immigration area, retrieved his luggage, and joined another line at customs where he was singled out yet again for more personal attention than anyone else was getting.

He tried to stay calm and cooperative. Doing anything else would've been counterproductive. Eventually he cleared the secure area and headed toward the domestic gates for his flight to Las Vegas.

Once he'd made it to Las Vegas and picked up his luggage, he headed for ground transportation. He knew the way. He'd made this same trek many times before.

Alex was young, athletic, friendly, and bilingual—and pretty good looking if he did say so himself. Years ago he'd decided to capitalize on his particular constellation of attributes by becoming a tour leader for German speakers who were vacationing in the U.S.

He led high-end off-piste and heli-skiing trips, guided national park wilderness and adventure tours, and did some location scouting for European film and television producers, as well.

Germans *loved* to travel and they did it more frequently than the citizens of most other countries—possibly because Germans got more paid vacation time than the inhabitants of other countries.

For reasons that Alex never questioned because he himself was German, Germans loved to hike, and they were particularly enamored with the romance of the American Wild West. And bison.

Who could resist bison? Not Germans.

This meant that Alex flew over the Atlantic several times a year to lead tours that involved clambering on eerie formations of red rocks, gawking at geysers, peering down into expansive canyons, or staring up in wonder at the sheer walls of narrow ones, gaping at vast open spaces that extended to the horizon in every direction, and otherwise beholding as many iconic

Western sights as possible in the time allowed—typically one-to three weeks.

If Alex needed any further stimulation to combat his jet lag, he got some as he encountered tourists playing slot machines before they'd even made it out of the airport. He loved gambling, but dared not partake in it. He and his wife were saving for a larger apartment. They needed every penny he could earn.

He got a second jolt when he walked out of the air-conditioned building and into the blast furnace of the desert. It was nearly ninety degrees outside even though it was only May.

The sun was blinding.

Of course, being blind in Vegas wasn't all bad.

It gave you a layer of protection from the proliferating plethora of tacky marvels like the petite Paris with a half-size Eiffel Tower—a full-size one would've been a hazard to airplanes landing at McCarran—an indoor Venice with chlorinated canals, and a plastic and pleather Caesar's Rome complete with valet parking.

These things didn't ruffle Alex. He had a natural tendency to focus on the positive. Las Vegas was a convenient hub for visitors to arrive and depart from. And it made a wonderful contrast to the national parks. Actually it made a stupendous contrast to pretty much everywhere.

Vegas grows on you, Alex thought. It was a nice change from Münster, referred to by residents as a Regenloch, a rain hole, on account of it tending to rain buckets in the city while clear blue skies encircled it.

But the biggest contrast between Vegas and Alex's home town wasn't the weather, it was that Münster was a very Catholic city. Another of the local sayings was, *It's either raining or the church bells are ringing.*

The only church bells heard on The Strip were cheesy recordings emanating from one of the fifty or so wedding chapels. Speaking of which, various sounds had been emanating from Alex's phone ever since he'd turned it back on. While he waited in the taxi queue, he switched his SIM card to AT&T to save money and to get reception in areas where his German carrier would have none.

He scanned his calls, emails, and texts.

A neighbor had called to ask if he would pick up her kids from school at the same time he retrieved his own two daughters, Amilia and Vianne. He'd have been glad to do it, but he'd been six miles above the Atlantic Ocean when that task needed to be performed. Alex hoped his wife, Sonja, had explained to the neighbor why he didn't respond to her request.

He texted Sonja to let her know he'd arrived safely. He missed her and the girls already, but he shrugged it off manfully. This was his job. It was how he supported his family.

He had to be on a different continent to do it, which wasn't a perfect solution, but it paid better than some of his other part-time gigs like erecting circus tents, catering, or cooking on a *Plattbodenschiff*—a 19th century Dutch sailing vessel repurposed for hire.

Leading tours involved long exhausting days, but so did working concerts and festivals where he often had to put in fourteen hours or more at a stretch. He was grateful that cell phone and internet enabled him to keep in touch from pretty much anywhere, except for some of the remote areas he'd be passing through on this trip.

He reminded himself that there were worse jobs than going on other people's vacations. He knew this for a fact because he'd had a lot of them.

Alex took a cab to the hotel where his tour group was convening for departure in the morning. He reviewed his paperwork and saw that the American driver for this trip was a fellow named Steve Jackson.

Steve had a Commercial Driver's License and he'd be the chauffeur while

Alex acted as guide and translator.

If things were going according to plan, Steve and the van would already be at the hotel. He'd have driven over yesterday from his home. Alex had a vague memory of being told he was from a wooded hamlet in Oregon. Steve didn't speak much German, but that was fine. Alex spoke good English.

During the cab ride Alex texted Steve to let him know that he'd made it to town and was now on his way to the hotel. Steve replied immediately with his room number.

When Alex knocked on the door Steve opened it within seconds and they both got their first look at their new roomie for the next three weeks.

Steve smiled in greeting and a quick glance revealed him to be fit and tan. He was kitted out like a model in an outdoor outfitter's catalog. He wore high-tech khaki pants featuring zippers placed at rakish angles, and a pale blue long-sleeve shirt that Alex recognized as being the kind that would provide at least 50 UPF sun protection and came from the manufacturer pre-loaded with bug repellent.

Alex suppressed any knee-jerk internal commentary on his co-worker's getup. He knew that Americans aspired to be fully protected at all times. To ensure their personal safety, they relied on a dazzling array of prophylactic measures from assault weapons to superfoods to sunscreen.

On the plus side, Steve's attire was obviously not new. That was a good sign. Alex wore his usual outfit of well-worn jeans and a misshapen t-shirt. The men simultaneously estimated each other's age as mid-forties for Alex and mid-fifties for Steve.

They introduced themselves and shook hands. Steve called Alex, *Al*, but that was okay. People in the tourist industry were generally outgoing and easy to get along with. All in all, Alex decided he was pleased with his new co-worker. He hoped Steve shared his view.

"I was just about to go to the grocery store," Steve said, "I need to get a case of bottled water, some fruit, and a couple of boxes of energy bars."

"You want me to go with?" Alex asked.

"Nah, I got it," Steve said. "You'll wanna unwind from those plane rides."

Good, Alex thought, because at the moment what he wanted more than anything in life was to leap into the hotel's swimming pool.

"If I don't see you beforehand," Steve said, "we're scheduled to meet our guests at seven o'clock tonight in the hotel lobby."

"Gotcha," Alex said, swinging his suitcase inside and throwing himself onto the unoccupied bed.

Chapter 2

Alex and Steve left their room and walked together to the central hub of the Alexis Park Resort. It was a sprawling place. They arrived in the main lobby a few minutes before seven to meet and greet their small group.

Alex hoped it would turn out to be a compatible bunch because they'd be spending the next couple of weeks together. Long hours of that would be inside a van as they travelled a fifteen hundred mile loop through as many of the spectacular national parks as possible. Then most of the group would stay together for another week for an add-on tour to California.

Alex scanned his roster of seven guests to see who he should be keeping an eye out for. There'd be a couple in their seventies from Zürich, a man from Vienna in his fifties, a guy in his sixties from Barcelona, a woman in her sixties from Paris, and a couple from Berlin with an age gap of more than forty years, the husband being the elder.

The guests who'd given home addresses in Spain and France had German names, so Alex assumed they were native German speakers who were living as expats. It was easy for EU citizens to choose to live in a different EU country. No approval was needed from the new home country.

As the group began to congregate Alex was able to identify most of his flock from the basic information he had. He spoke German as he introduced himself. He was happy to learn that his assumption had been correct, the guests from Barcelona and Paris spoke German as their first language.

Steve introduced himself in English. The guests shook hands and nodded politely and mumbled English greetings of varying intelligibility. Most of them spoke at least a little English. Alex checked each person off his roster as they were identified.

When everyone was accounted for, Alex announced that they'd be making a short drive to The Orleans Hotel and Casino for a buffet dinner. He led the group out to the company van. It was white and emblazoned with a rust colored logo featuring a cowboy on a bucking bronco and the name *Wild West Adventure Tours.*

He watched how each guest behaved as they chose their seating. The driver and guide had dibs on the front seats. Behind them were three rows of seats for guests. The first two rows consisted of a pair of seats on the left and a separate jump seat on the right with an aisle between them. The third row had four seats that took up the full width of the van.

Alex watched to see who wanted the front, who wanted the back, who was pushy, and who wasn't happy with what they got.

The mismatched German couple, Klaus and Tina, went to the back row. The Swiss couple, Georg and Elisabeth, went to the front row.

The three solo travelers were lucky. The van's configuration with two jump seats gave them seating options, so they wouldn't be forced to spend every minute of the tour sitting beside a stranger.

The Austrian fellow, Peter, took the second row jump seat. The woman from France, Frida, took the one near the front, and that left the man from Spain, Gerd, with a pair of seats in the middle row. He sat next to the window and plopped his heavy camera bag onto the empty aisle seat.

Instead of heading straight for the buffet, Steve took the group on a detour to show them The Strip. Along the way Alex pointed out some of the most famous hotels and casinos. The timing couldn't have been better. On their way to dinner they'd see the city in daylight, and then on the way back to the hotel after dark they'd get to experience the transformation to a spectacular public art gallery of colorful LEDs and vintage neon.

"The American nickname for this town is *Sin City*," Alex said, as they cruised through town. "The name Las Vegas is Spanish and it means The Meadows," he said. "It refers to the natural artesian wells here that produced some rare patches of green in the middle of a vast desert.

"The wells attracted native people, then ranching pioneers, and eventually the railroad. People, livestock, and steam engines all needed the water and it was hard to find out here."

"What about the Mafia?" asked Klaus, the German man with the young wife.

"We'll talk more about that tomorrow when there's more time. But the short answer is the Mob played an important role here at one point, but these days it's mostly gone."

On the way to dinner the guests introduced themselves, chatted about their respective home cities, where and when they'd arrived in the U.S, and their plans for the days immediately after the tour ended.

None of them had been to Las Vegas before and, except for the couple from Zürich, none had been to the U.S. before. There was a flurry of commentary about what they were seeing.

"These casinos are much larger than the ones in Monaco and Venice," said Georg, the husband in the couple from Switzerland.

"That's true," said Alex, "But there are some in Macao and South Africa that can compete with these."

"Why are the cars so big?" asked Frida, the lady from Paris who was traveling by herself.

"Americans love big cars, especially SUVs and trucks," Alex said. "It's the same all across the country."

"The people are so fat!" said Elisabeth, the other half of the Swiss couple. "That's why they need big cars and big casinos. So they can get their giant rear ends inside."

People smiled politely, but now Alex had his first clue about who the complainer would be. There was always a risk of getting one. Some people were chronically unhappy. Others didn't deal well with the unpredictability and discomforts that came with traveling. Those people should stay at home, but they frequently ventured out in the midst of other people's vacations.

He'd make the best of whatever happened, though, because that was his job and he was really good at it.

A few minutes later Steve guided the van into the parking garage adjacent to The Orleans. It was a Mardi Gras-themed complex. As usual for Las Vegas, the layout forced them to walk through the gambling area on the way to the restaurant.

As they passed through the cavernous space their senses were assaulted by blinking lights, ringing bells, flashy and/or trashy attire of the patrons, and the overall hustle and bustle of the place. It was intentionally designed without clocks or windows so there was nothing that would give any indication about whether it was day or night, or how much time had passed since you'd entered.

They paused at the cashier on their way into the food area to order a couple of buckets of ice, and made beer and wine orders, then the hostess led them to the table. Once they all found a seat they followed Alex to the buffet. He stood back to observe their reactions to the vast food selection. This was the irresistible bait Las Vegas had relied on since the earliest days to lure people to the casinos—good food, and lots of it.

Steve staked out a table while they loaded their plates. When they were seated and digging into their dinners, nearly everyone was having wine or beer. Everyone but Peter, the quiet solo traveler from Vienna, and Steve, because he'd be driving them back to the hotel.

Drinks flowed and the atmosphere loosened up. Later, as dinner was winding down, Alex shared some brief safety advisories. "We're going to be in a wilderness area," he said, "and we're going to be hiking across some rough terrain. We're likely to encounter wild animals and scenic overlooks that are adjacent to dangerous cliffs.

"Tourists die every year out here from encounters with wild animals, or by falling off of high places, or from heatstroke, or drowning. There are poisonous snakes, also, so be on the lookout for them. Don't stick your hands into any crevices without checking first to see if they're occupied.

"Later we'll be seeing elk, deer, pronghorns, bighorn sheep, and bison," he said. "Remember that these are wild animals. They're accustomed to seeing humans and cars, but they don't tolerate humans at close range. You *must* stay well away from all of these creatures. They're quite dangerous.

They can and will hurt you, or kill you. Even the ones that look peaceful and slow are deceiving you. Every year wild beasts in the national parks kill or gravely injure multiple tourists. So be very careful.

"I also want to warn you about predatory humans," Alex said. "There are criminals who prowl crowded areas where tourists congregate. Keep an eye on your valuables at all times. Don't leave anything of value where it's visible in the van unless one of us is staying with it.

He was pleased to note that they seemed to be paying attention to the warnings, but he'd still keep a sharp eye on them.

"Well, that's all I wanted to say for tonight. We'll gather in the hotel lobby at seven in the morning and head into the red rock areas. The breakfast service at the hotel starts at six, so if you like, you can grab something before we leave.

"If anyone wants to see more of Las Vegas tonight, Steve and I will be happy to drop you off wherever you'd like, but when you're ready to return to the hotel, you'll have to walk back or take a taxi."

Despite their jet lag, the couples from Zürich and Berlin, as well as the solo woman, asked to be dropped off at the Bellagio fountains. Steve drove them to the South Strip and let them out, then he drove Alex, Gerd, and Peter back to the hotel.

"Gute Nacht," Alex said, to the two guests.

Gerd nodded, Peter raised a hand in farewell, and the two men disappeared toward their rooms.

Chapter 3

When the guests were out of sight, Steve turned to Alex, and said, "I'm gonna gas up the van for tomorrow, wanna come?"

"Sure," Alex said.

They got back in and drove to a gas station where Steve pulled into the fueling plaza. This was Las Vegas, so even at this late hour the place was busy. The only available pump was in a far corner, next to a ramshackle fence that separated the gas station from an alley.

Steve got out and started filling the tank. Alex opened all the van doors and used a small stiff broom to brush the carpets. Then, while Steve went through his checklist of fluids, filters, lights, and tires, Alex wandered into the little convenience store to take a look around.

Vegas was a prime jumping off spot for *Grand Circle* tours that tended to focus on seven of the most famous western national parks— Zion, Bryce, Arches, Canyonlands, Mesa Verde, Grand Canyon, and Capitol Reef. Tourists tended to travel along the same scenic routes through Arizona, New Mexico, Colorado, Utah, and Nevada.

If you wanted to see Yellowstone, you might fly in and out of Salt Lake City, but otherwise, domestic and foreign companies offered a vast array of tours through the major parks you could drive to and still make it back to Vegas in time to fly home.

Steve was crouching down between the pump and the van, checking tire pressures on the driver's side, when a man quietly slipped through a hole in the fence.

The fellow looked around nervously and fixed on the van with all its doors thrown wide open, parked barely twenty feet away. He moved silently toward the side with the double doors passengers used to get in and out. He reached into a pocket and removed his wallet. He glanced around to see if anyone was coming, then opened the wallet and extracted a small black object.

He crept to the van, leaned inside, and shoved the gadget down into one of the small side compartments of the camera bag which Gerd, blithely ignoring the safety instructions, had obligingly left on the floor between the first and second rows of seats.

As the man was straightening up he noticed a dark-colored windbreaker lying on a jump seat. He was reaching for it when Steve made a noise that startled him. He grabbed at the jacket, then lurched back away from the van, and silently retreated into the darkness.

Before the man left the fueling plaza he used his phone to snap several quick photos of the van, being sure to capture clear images of the logo on the front passenger door and the license plate. Then he retreated through the hole in the fence.

He'd done his best. Now all he needed was a little bit of luck.

He didn't realize it yet, but in his awkward scramble to snatch the windbreaker and get away from the van, he'd dropped his wallet. It was now lying in the shadows on the floor behind the front passenger seat.

The man knew he was being followed, but he felt relatively safe now. He was no longer carrying what they were looking for.

He shrugged into the windbreaker and pulled the hood over his mass of curly blonde hair, looking overdressed for the weather, but at least he was partly disguised. He didn't realize that the men assigned to capture him had caught a glimpse of him slipping through the gap in the fence toward the gas station and also seen him pop back out a minute later wearing the stolen jacket.

The men surveilling him quickly circled the block in an absurdly flashy black Mustang Shelby GT350R to try to head him off. With 500 horsepower and a top speed of 175 miles an hour, they figured they ought to be able to catch a guy on foot in a couple of minutes. The $75,000 ride was over the top, even for a couple of wise guys working out of Las Vegas, but the Boss had a reputation to maintain, so he always provided his foot soldiers with cars that made a statement.

The goombahs didn't know what this guy had done, but they knew the Boss wanted him—and that was all they needed to know.

Steve completed his meticulous survey of the van's mechanical condition, removed the dispensing nozzle, and screwed the gas cap back on. Alex walked around the van closing the doors as he went, and they returned to the hotel, oblivious to the drama that had been played out a few feet away.

***

Steve parked at the hotel and he and Alex got out.

"I'm gonna grab a beer," Alex said. "You wanna come?"

"Thanks, but I better not," said Steve, "I wanna be sharp for tomorrow."

He gave Alex a brief wave, then walked away holding one of the key cards to their shared room. Alex patted his back pocket out of habit to make sure he had his key card and his billfold on him instead of in the briefcase where he sometimes left valuables.

His pocket was empty, so he used his duplicate key to open the van and reached into the ballistic nylon bag that sat between his seat and Steve's. No billfold. He must've lost it when he was sweeping the van.

He glanced into and around his seat and saw the plain black wallet lying in the floor just behind it. If he hadn't been jet lagged and had so much beer with dinner he might've noticed the subtle differences between this wallet and his own, but he didn't. Instead all he felt was relief. He grabbed it and jammed it into his back pocket without thinking twice.

To stave off the inevitable sadness of spending that first night of a long trip away from his family, Alex intended to briefly join the perpetual beer fest taking place a hundred yards away at a Vegas-style replica of a German bar. As he turned to go, he noticed the tip of a cigarette glowing in the darkness. It was Gerd, the solo traveler from Spain, smoking alone outside his room.

Alex repeated his invitation to get a beer, this time in German, and Gerd nodded his acceptance.

When they crossed East Harmon Avenue Gerd was startled to catch a glimpse of a building that looked like the Hofbräuhaus. It was, in fact, a copy of the famous beer house in Munich. He pointed to it and smiled.

"Have you ever been there?" he asked Alex.

"I've never been to the original one in Bavaria, but I've been to this fake one a few times. It's okay."

Gerd nodded and they went in.

It was a kitschy pastiche that only superficially resembled the real thing. This *Biergarten* was indoors and air-conditioned with a ceiling painted to resemble the sky. Vegas was simply too hot for it to be open air as it would've been in Germany.

The place was packed with customers. Alex smiled at Gerd's befuddlement over the mishmash of decor, and said, "We're probably the only Germans in here."

They sat on one of the wooden benches that lined the wooden tables. The band was playing a mixture of Bavarian and Austrian music, accompanied by bizarre, randomly-placed blasts from a Swiss Alphorn. Gerd was dumbfounded.

"The Americans have tossed all the countries of the Alps into one big pot and stirred them around," Alex said. "It's a cultural jumble. I saw the same thing at the so-called *Swiss Days* in Midway, Utah. They had beautiful young girls wearing dirndl dresses, performing a Schuhplattler!"

Gerd laughed out loud at that.

The Schuhplattler, or *shoe slapper*, was a Bavarian and Austrian dance from the north eastern Alps designed to be performed by men to impress women. It involved a lot of rhythmic hopping and stomping and slapping of thighs and knees and shoes. It was very athletic German version of Irish step dance.

But this was … the Las Vegas version.

When a waiter came to their table Gerd ordered a *Helles*, a blond Bavarian beer served in a liter-sized mug. It was more than he wanted, but Alex decided to go along with him to show solidarity as a real German in a fake bar.

"Would you like something to eat?" the waiter asked.

They shook their heads on account of their recent gorging at The Orleans buffet, though the *Schweinshaxe mit Klössen*, pigs' legs with dumplings, certainly sounded appealing to them both.

The men sat bemused as they were treated to yet another flabbergasting scene that one would never see being performed outside of Las Vegas. A waitress dressed in a traditional folk dress like the one Julie Andrews wore in *The Sound of Music* went from table to table offering the customers shots.

Each person who drank a shot, mainly drunken men, would stand up, bend over the table, and allow the woman to spank them with a large decorative paddle. She was hitting the men hard, too, but they seemed to enjoy it, and they were even tipping her for it.

Alex and Gerd found this demented, but surprisingly entertaining.

It didn't take long for the waiter to return with two huge beer mugs which he slammed onto the table in front of them. They toasted each other saying, *prost*, meaning *cheers*, and each took a huge pull of their beer.

They sat there companionably, content to look around at the vast, high-ceilinged room. It was a beautiful place. The plastered walls were painted a clean white and the vaulted ceilings were a cheerful sunny yellow.

As was traditional in Bavarian beer houses, strangers sat together at the tables. After guzzling their first *Mass*, the Bavarian name for a mug containing a liter of beer, they each ordered another.

While they waited, Gerd said, "For many years my wife and I could not afford to travel. Then, after reunification, when we could have afforded to go, she was sick. She wanted me to stay home with her and I did.

"She died a year ago."

Alex murmured sincere condolences.

"I am old now," Gerd said, "but I am not getting any younger so I decided to take the trip I had always dreamed of—and this is it."

Alex was moved by Gerd's story. He loved to travel and had done a lot of it in his life. He couldn't imagine what he'd do if he lost his own wife. He said with deep feeling, "I am very sorry to hear about your wife."

"Today was her birthday," Gerd said, and took a huge drink of his beer.

Alex did the same, in respect.

"Thank you for inviting me to this place. It is just what I needed," said Gerd.

They toasted to that.

The two men were somber after that, but the mood was rising among the rest of the patrons as the night wore on. The crowd began to *schunkeln* by hooking elbows with the person sitting on either side of them and swaying side-to-side in time with the music.

In a normal situation neither Alex nor Gerd would've enjoyed traditional Bavarian music very much, but after a liter and a half of German beer it began to exhibit an unexpected appeal.

They ordered some pretzels.

On top of the alcohol they'd had with dinner, by the time they finished their second *Mass*, they were both feeling quite the buzz.

"Maybe we should go back to the hotel now," Alex said. "We have to get up early."

Even though he had the wits to make the suggestion, he lacked the willpower to carry it out. They were both already past the point where reasoned decision-making was possible.

In addition, by this point, neither man could recall the other's name. The guest reintroduced himself as Gerhard, and added, "You can call me Gerd."

"And I am Alexander. You can call me Alex."

They shook hands.

To celebrate their renewed acquaintance Gerd was able to convince Alex to have yet another beer. This offer highlighted one of Alex's recurring problems. When he reached a certain point of inebriation he couldn't resist offers to become even further foxed.

He and Gerd manfully downed a third *Mass*, which meant they'd consumed the equivalent of nine American beers. Both of them were really drunk and more than ready to go back to the hotel. Alex reached for his wallet, but Gerd said, "No, no! Let me get it. You have helped me on a difficult day and I will never forget it."

Gerd's act of generosity prevented Alex from discovering that he'd left his wallet on the counter in the gas station convenience store after paying for snacks and sundries. But even if he had realized it, it was too late to matter. His wallet was long gone.

The people who shared their table tried to convince them to stay just a little longer, but both men were now firmly resolved to get out while they could still walk.

Together they made it to the street corner and stood, wobbling, waiting for the traffic light to change. Gerd glanced across the busy road and noticed a man on the other side wearing a jacket that looked almost exactly like the one he'd brought on this trip.

He started to laugh, finding it funny. The guy was fidgeting and looking around, obviously in a hurry to get across. He looked like he needed to find a restroom. That made Gerd laugh even harder.

The light on the main thoroughfare finally turned red and the guy on the other side broke into a run. Slower moving people flooded into the crosswalk from both sides of the street. When Gerd and Alex were about to come face-to-face with the fellow running toward them, the driver of a black car gunned the engine and blasted right through the red light.

He almost hit the guy.

Alex and Gerd were amazed. That was *close*! It looked like the black car was *trying* to hit the guy. The man continued running and in a few moments he'd been swallowed up by the crowd and was able to slip unnoticed down a side street.

Traffic was heavy but the black car made some more extremely aggressive moves that telegraphed the fact that the driver was trying to follow the fleeing man. Alex and Gerd were so shocked at almost being run over in the crosswalk it sobered them up a little, but after that much beer nothing could've sobered them up completely.

A couple of minutes later they reached their hotel. They mumbled their Gute Nachts and went into their respective rooms to pass out.

Chapter 4

Steve was sleeping like a baby when his roommate staggered in during the wee hours. After that he got no sleep at all on account of Alex's loud snoring. He'd lay there listening to the tremendous racket until his alarm finally went off at 5:30.

He got up immediately, switched the coffeemaker on, and went into the bathroom to get ready for the day. While he showered, shaved, brushed his teeth, and dressed, Alex remained facedown, dead to the world, and continued snoring.

Steve made as much noise as possible as he packed up and prepared to vacate the room. Alex still didn't move.

In revenge, Steve opened the package of donuts Alex had bought at the gas station the previous evening. He took a bite out of one and went into the kitchen area of the suite to get coffee and slam as many drawers and cabinet doors as possible while preparing and consuming his breakfast in the hope that his roommate would regain consciousness.

When he'd finished his coffee and two of Alex's donuts he carried his suitcase out to the van to start the pre-check he was expected to perform every morning before they left. By the time he'd finished it, Alex still hadn't appeared, so he went ahead and hooked the luggage trailer to the van by himself.

It would've been a lot easier with help. This new guy looked like he was going to be a problem.

Steve loved to be ready ahead of time and to be fully-prepared for the day to come. Alex was apparently the opposite. Steve sighed and checked his watch. It was 6:30.

By 6:45 the first guests were bringing their luggage out of their rooms. He sorted the pieces and set them in separate zones behind the van so he could balance the load of hard-sided cases, duffels, and backpacks as he placed them inside.

At 6:55 Alex still hadn't appeared so Steve decided to go check on him. He was annoyed and frustrated to find his coworker still asleep in the same position, and still snoring.

Alex was having a complicated Hofbräuhaus-related nightmare involving being paddled by Julie Andrews while she sang *My Favorite Things*.

"Alex!" he said, but got no reaction.

He glanced at the clock on the night stand and saw that it was already 7:02. He shoved the sleeping man's shoulder, then shook him hard, calling his name even louder and at point blank range.

Alex twisted his head to look at Steve with unfocused eyes.

"Come on, let's go!" Steve said, "Everyone's waiting to leave!"

"What time is it?" Alex mumbled.

When Alex realized he'd overslept, he rolled over and sat up, grabbing his head in both hands in an unsuccessful attempt to lessen the headache, nausea, and vertigo of a horrible hangover. He cursed in German.

Steve's German wasn't that good but he was able to make out the gist of what Alex was saying.

"Tell them I had to take an urgent call," Alex mumbled. "I'll be down in fifteen minutes."

Steve went back to the van and decided to focus his attention on packing the trailer, alone. He found luggage interesting. He was lucky in that because he had to handle a lot of it. Mostly other people's, but he didn't mind. He enjoyed reading the guests' bags for clues to their personalities and histories.

As he organized the pieces and loaded them into the trailer he made a mental review of the guests, their names, their ages, their home country.

The Swiss couple, Georg and Elisabeth, were the oldest members of the group, but they seemed physically fit. They had two identical aluminum rolling suitcases. Rimowa Titanium Pilot cases. *Very nice*, Steve thought, *nearly a thousand euros apiece.*

The German couple, Klaus and Tina, were as different in their choice of bag as they were in their ages. Klaus was carrying his own well-worn brown leather duffle, as well as Tina's white leather Valextra suitcase.

"Beautiful," said Steve, smiling at the gorgeous woman with long blond hair cascading down her back. She was wearing a skimpy athleisure outfit that left very little to the imagination.

She smiled back, which made Klaus frown.

"Your … bag, … I mean," he stuttered. "Jackie O carried this same style."

Tina moved a little closer than necessary, put a hand on Steve's arm, and said in a sultry tone, "I just *love* a man who values beauty."

She carried a large hot pink Valextra tote like a purse and took it into the van with her. Steve knew that those two Italian bags were some of the most expensive pieces of luggage on earth. The suitcase would cost ten thousand and the tote another five.

He sincerely hoped Klaus was getting his money's worth. He smiled and reached to take Klaus's far more modest and practical bag, saying, "Now *this* is more *my* style."

Klaus gave him a long appraising look that had a bit of an edge to it. The older man's hostile body language made Steve wonder if his remark had given the impression that he was gay.

It was the first morning of the trip and already he couldn't win with this couple. He decided to keep his mouth shut whenever he was around them.

Frida, the lady from Paris, smiled and handed him a jaunty yellow canvas duffle that said more about a cheerful and practical personality than her net worth. He smiled back and was pleased that their exchange carried no toxic subtext.

The Austrian, Peter, was a quiet, serious, unremarkable fellow who had an unadorned black nylon rolling case. A perfect match for his demeanor.

Gerd, formerly of Berlin, more recently of Barcelona, and even more recently of the Hofbräuhaus, was next. He stood before Steve empty handed.

"Your bag, sir?" Steve said with a smile.

Only then did Gerd realize that he'd left his luggage next to the wrong van. He went across the parking lot to get it. Steve stifled the urge to laugh.

Gerd returned with a battered gray hard-sided plastic case that was held closed by a red seatbelt around its middle. "Sorry," he mumbled, as he set it on the ground behind the van.

When Steve leaned forward to take the suitcase he caught a strong odor of beer and cigarettes. Gerd was wearing sunglasses but it was still obvious from the careful way he was moving that he, like Alex, had over-imbibed the night before.

Steve attempted to explain to the group in a mixture of English and badly pronounced German that Alex was on the phone dealing with an emergency, but would join them soon. There was some back and forth among the guests as the better English speakers relayed the news to the others.

The Swiss lady, Elisabeth, said, in German, "This is a very poor show. A very poor show indeed. Staff should not be late and certainly not on the very first morning. We will miss ….." Steve couldn't understand anything she was saying, but it was easy to catch her drift.

He assured her in English that they'd be leaving very soon. He, like Alex, made a mental note. You didn't always have a complainer on a trip, but when you did it usually took a few days for them to reveal themselves. This one had already started on the first morning before they were even out of the parking lot.

He decided he'd kill her with kindness even though he knew she'd be grumbling from now until he waved goodbye at the end of the last day, three weeks from now. He suspected he'd be relieved to watch her disappear over the horizon.

Alex, in his panicked, deeply hungover scramble to wash, dress, pack, and get out to the van, swept his personal belongings off the desktop and into a bag and, again, failed to notice that the billfold was not his own. At 7:25 he finally made it outside. He apologized profusely.

And just as the group had immediately perceived the nature of Gerd's problem, it was obvious that Alex was hungover, too, and that he was suffering mightily. George shot his wife a glance warning her to keep her thoughts to herself and miraculously, she did.

Gerd and Alex took one look at each other and exchanged grimaces. They knew just how each other felt.

By 7:30 Steve was able to slam the trailer door on nine people's luggage, a couple of coolers, one for food and the other for bottled water, and a tote bag full of nonperishable snacks. He buckled himself into the driver's seat and looked around. There were seven guests, a guide-translator, and himself, all present and accounted for. They were good to go.

Alex tried to catch his eye to apologize, but Steve avoided meeting his glance. Alex wanted to explain that his drinking had been to commiserate with Gerd for the loss of his wife, but he couldn't do it within hearing of the guests. He'd have to wait until they had a moment alone.

Steve chauffeured the tour group away from the city and toward the wilderness. Alex pulled himself together enough to narrate a concise history of the city.

"Indians came to this area about 2,000 years ago," he said. "In the late 1800's this was part of a ranch occupied by a young couple. Life was really rough. When the wife was only thirty years old and expecting her fifth child a neighbor shot and killed her husband. She managed to survive and later sold part of her land to the railroad.

"A rail line was built that connected Los Angeles to Salt Lake City in 1902 and the city of Las Vegas was founded shortly afterwards. It's been able to thrive because of Hoover Dam.

"In the 1930s the Colorado River was dammed as it came through a canyon. It was a massive construction project and the laborers created a surge in the local population.

"Nearly all the workers were young men, so women and casinos came next to entertain the thousands of guys who were stuck out in the middle of nowhere with nothing to spend their money on.

The guests looked out at the glass towers that sparkled with the reflected sunrise and tried to imagine what the town had looked like more than eighty years ago.

"All this reflective glass has caused some unique problems. The curved glass front of the Vdara Hotel was reflecting and concentrating the sun on the concave side of the building, especially at the pool area, in what the media called the *Vdara Death Ray*. It gave people severe sunburns and even melted plastic objects, so they had to install special protective umbrellas.

"Is prostitution legal here?" Tina asked.

"It's legal in parts of the state, but not in Las Vegas."

"What about the mafia?" Frida asked.

"At first the gambling establishments were owned by Las Vegas families. But in the 1940s Bugsy Siegel and Meyer Lansky laundered enough money through Mormon-owned banks to build The Flamingo. A few months later Siegel was murdered in a flashy public spectacle in Beverly Hills. The story was made into a movie called *Bugsy*.

"In the 1950s, many of the most famous casinos were built with money from the Teamsters Union and Mormon bankers. The money was still tainted by the Teamsters' association with the Mafia, but it was cleaner than outright Mafia proceeds.

"Then, in the 1960s Howard Hughes came to town."

That provoked laughter. Some of the guests had heard of the bizarre aviation genius.

"At first he was at the D.I., the Desert Inn. He reserved the top two floors for ten days. The D.I. was a fabulous place. Prime Minister Churchill, President Kennedy, and President Truman stayed there. The chef came from the Ritz in Paris. The entertainment was world class. They had singers like Frank Sinatra and Dean Martin, and comedians like Jerry Lewis.

"When his ten days were up Hughes decided he didn't want to leave, so he bought the hotel. And then he bought the local television station so he could have them run whatever movies he felt like watching. He was *extremely* rich.

"He stayed at the D.I. for four years, with blackout curtains drawn, running his empire in the nude, in a room where he'd sealed the doors and windows with tape. Housekeepers weren't allowed in either.

"He spent $300 million buying famous hotels. He focused on the ones with ties to the Mafia. By doing this he transformed the city's reputation from a criminal enclave to a legitimate vacation destination."

Minutes later they'd left the densely populated area, and Alex said, "Over a hundred atom bomb tests took place about sixty miles from here at the Nevada Test Site, starting in the 1950s. People used to go out into the desert to watch the mushroom clouds for entertainment."

That information got a lot of attention, but no commentary. Germans tended to stay away from war-related topics.

Steve focused on driving. To him, Alex's German narration sounded like a mixture of barking and throat clearing. He could catch some of the names and a few words like *mafia*, but he tuned most of it out and stayed lost in his own thoughts as he drove them farther and farther into the wilderness.

Chapter 5

The sun had been up for a couple of hours when they arrived at the Valley of Fire, but it was still early enough that the place hadn't become the inferno it could be by afternoon.

"This area used to be under a sea," Alex said. "Then for a long time it was a desert. This particular park is known for its Aztec Sandstone created from the sand dunes that were here 150 million years ago. In many places the rock is an orangey-red. In others it's red with white and gray limestone stripes."

Soon after they passed the park entrance they made their first stop. "This is Atlatl Rock," said Alex.

Steve pulled into the parking area and everyone got out. They were glad to escape from the vehicle, but Gerd and Alex were particularly happy to be able to move around and breathe fresh air.

Steve handed each guest a brand new water bottle and a small LED flashlight. Then he led them to the back of the van and filled each person's bottle from one of the gallon jugs of spring water he'd stocked up on the night before.

"Now you're ready to go," he said, smiling.

"An *atlatl* is a tool used by ancient hunters to help them throw a spear farther and faster," said Alex. "That made it possible to kill dangerous animals from a safer distance.

"Modern day re-creations of the throwing sticks make experts think the hunters could toss their spears at nearly a hundred miles an hour."

He pointed at a nearby wall of red rock. "The petroglyphs here were carved by Ancestral Puebloans, sometimes called Anasazi people, who in some cases were working fifty feet above the valley floor! We have it a lot easier. We have stairs. Let's go up and take a look."

Alex suspected that the carvers were able to stand on sand dunes that were there long ago and didn't need ladders or ropes to do their work. He hoped that was true, for their sake.

The group set out climbing the long series of metal stairs. Later in the day the handrails would get too hot to touch. Even in May, afternoon temperatures in the area could exceed 100ºF. But at the moment they were still usable.

"See the way the rock face has blackened?" Alex said. "This patina takes a long time to develop. The color comes from iron and manganese oxides, and it's called *desert varnish* or *rock rust*."

Out of consideration for the guests' ages, Alex slowed as they climbed higher. When they were about half way up, he stopped to assess everyone's condition. He and Steve casually scanned the group, looking for anyone having trouble. There was some huffing and puffing, but nothing that looked problematic. Frida was coming last, but keeping up with the rest.

The two men exchanged glances of approval at how things were going. It would take a couple more days for the visitors to adjust to the altitude and get more comfortable walking on uneven terrain, climbing over boulders, hiking in sand, and tolerating the afternoon heat, but so far, so good.

The group chattered about the carvings and photographed them as they climbed. There were human stick figures, horned animals like elk or sheep, and shapes like circles, crosses, and spirals.

Alex continued to the top of the stairs and stood with the guests enjoying the view. It was very different from Europe.

Alex and Steve had each made the Grand Circle Tour loop several times, but they'd never made it in the same van until now. It was hard work, but they enjoyed it because they loved the parks. They planned to enjoy this circuit, too, but of course they had no way to know what was already headed their way.

***

"This is Balanced Rock," Alex said, gesturing, as Steve drove slowly by the strange formation. It was a huge irregularly-shaped boulder resting at a precarious angle atop a tall sandstone base.

It looked like the smallest of tremors or a strong gust of wind would be all it would take to knock it off its base. When that happened the stone would roll across the ground, flattening whoever and whatever was in its path.

That is creepy, Peter thought, but didn't say. He remained quiet out of long habit.

***

"Next we'll take a look at the petroglyphs at *The Mouse's Tank*," Alex said. "To see those we'll have to hike down a canyon wash. A *wash* is an area that's usually dry, but where water runs after it rains. Washes are notorious for collecting and channeling runoff and flooding after a storm.

"*The Mouse's Tank* is said to have been named for an outlaw Paiute Indian called *Little Mouse*. He was wanted for murdering a couple of prospectors. Legend has it that he used this area as a hideout in the 1890's. He was able to stay alive out here in the desert because he found a natural rock bowl where water accumulated after a rain. Today that rock is called *The Mouse's Tank*.

"This area, the Valley of Fire, has been used as a filming location for several well-known movies," Alex said. "The racing scenes at the end of the Elvis film *Viva Las Vegas* were shot here, as well as the Mars scenes in the Schwarzenegger movie *Total Recall*.

Star Trek Generations used it for the planet Veridian III. One spot in the valley is a particular cult favorite with the Trekkies because it's where Captain Kirk died and was buried."

Steve had been through there enough times to know what Alex was likely to be saying. Nevertheless it was amusing to hear names like Elvis, Schwarzenegger, and Captain Kirk pop out in the middle of all the otherwise incomprehensible guttural mutterings.

To entertain himself while waiting, he imagined a revised spiel using the parts he could understand. In his scenario Schwarzenegger had gotten hopelessly lost in the valley and totally by accident he discovered that Elvis was still alive and living in a primitive cabin nearby.

Arnold was introducing himself to Elvis, when Captain Kirk suddenly appeared due to a transporter malfunction. Elvis was happy to receive the unexpected guests, even though he had no idea who the men were because he'd been living in a canyon that was too narrow to get cable or satellite service.

Being a polite southern boy, he invited the strangers to stay for lunch and promptly fried up three of his special peanut butter, bacon, and banana sandwiches.

***

After they left the Valley of Fire, the group stopped at a grocery store in Overton, Nevada, to buy some food for lunch and afternoon snacks. This first shopping foray always took quite a bit longer than the subsequent ones would—and it required a lot of assistance from Steve and Alex—because the travelers were unfamiliar with American foods and packaging.

Although each member of the group could speak at least a few words of English, only two of them were fluent. But even fluency wasn't enough when trying to locate foods that were known by different names in different countries. Alex jokingly pointed out the Münster Cheese from Wisconsin and the Swiss cheese from Ohio.

No one wanted to get sick on the first day of a long trip, so they were cautious with their choices. It took several passes for all of them to find something they were comfortable trying to eat.

The most popular items turned out to be cured sausages, sliced ham, fruit, fruit juices, and ready-to-eat pre-packaged salads.

"American bread is disgusting," Elisabeth said. "*widerlich, ekelhaft!*"

This set off a spirited discussion about whether or not it was possible to get good bread in the U.S. Alex explained in a neutral tone that a small town grocery in the middle of a vast desert wasn't the best place to find European perishables, or even American perishables.

When they'd all done their best to acquire a palatable cache of snacks, they trundled over to the picnic tables at the town park.

***

"There's so much open space here!" Gerd marveled.

"It's too hot," said Elisabeth, removing her wool sweater.

"This park is quite nice," Georg said, reflexively trying to sooth his chronically ill-tempered spouse. "Such a little town, but they have these nice grills, and tables, and benches for the public to use."

"And this pavilion," said Frida, "and restrooms, and neatly trimmed grass."

The group speculated briefly about how the people of Overton could make a living, then quickly switched to discussing American politics.

Steve had observed that European attempts to fathom the U.S. political situation often started at about five minutes into the group's first meal together. As usual, it had begun at dinner last night, and now the guests were picking up where they'd left off.

He was thrilled to be able to stay out of it. Consensus was difficult enough to manage among the citizens of a large, diverse country founded and populated by refugees, heretics, and protestors of every stripe, many of whom had been forcibly ejected from more ethnically pure surroundings.

It was hard to govern a country of eccentrics who prized individualism. Mercifully he couldn't follow the conversation except for a few names uttered in an outraged tone of voice, accompanied by violent gestures.

After everyone had eaten, enjoyed a lively debate peppered with brutal commentary on their host country, and stretched their legs, they were ready to hit the road again.

"We're going north now, through *The Arizona Strip*," Alex said. "It's the part of Arizona that lies north of the Colorado River. This area is isolated by the harsh topography. The Colorado River and the Grand Canyon block ingress and egress. It would make more sense for the place to be part of Utah or Nevada, but it's not. A side-effect of the isolation has led to its survival as one of the holdout areas for Mormon extremists who practiced polygamy."

The mention of polygamy sparked off another lively debate that continued as they passed the *Utah, Live Elevated* sign.

***

Southern Utah was Alex's favorite place on earth. It had forests, deserts, lakes, rivers, slot canyons, snow, heat, high mountain ranges, flattop mesas, and countless other variations in topography and climate.

When Alex had made his first trip to Utah, he'd already seen a lot of the U.S., but after that visit he decided Utah was the best place to be. He was an avid outdoorsman and Utah was the outdoor capitol of the world. Almost any outdoor sport imaginable could be pursued in the area.

He'd taken a job at a ski school in the Wasatch Mountains of Northern Utah, near Salt Lake City. If he hadn't had a girlfriend waiting for him in Germany, he'd never have returned. But he did go back and the girlfriend was now his wife and the mother of their two young daughters.

Even now, years later, each time he crossed the state line into The Beehive State it felt a bit like coming home. He was bemused by the fact that although he considered himself a liberal person, he felt comfortable in and welcomed by this extremely conservative area where over half the population followed the beliefs of The Church of Jesus Christ of Latter-day Saints, otherwise known as LDS, or Mormon.

"Our first stop in Utah is the town of St. George," he said. "This is the home of the oldest continuously operated LDS temple in the world."

They parked near a splendid tall white building jutting up out of the desert and walked around the beautifully maintained grounds.

"St. George is famous for being the hottest city in Utah," Alex said.

"Then why would anyone build here? These people are stupid," Elisabeth sneered.

"Climate data for the area wasn't available in the 1860s," Alex said, struggling to keep a neutral tone. This guest was going to be a pain. "One reason for building the temple in this area was that sandstone was readily available. The stone for the temple in Salt Lake City had to be hauled in from the Wasatch range."

Chapter 6

By mid-afternoon the guests were having difficulty staying awake. They were desperate for coffee, partly from jetlag, and partly because it was customary in Germany to have coffee at this time of day, like tea time in England.

It was odd to them to be drinking from paper cups while sitting in a café. In Europe, paper cups were only for takeaway drinks.

Steve made a stop at a coffee house in an outlet mall next to I-15. He and Alex stood off to one side as the guests put in their orders. "I owe you an apology," Alex murmured. "For this morning."

Steve didn't say anything, more from shyness than animosity.

"That will never happen again," he said. "Tomorrow morning will be totally different. I promise."

Steve gave him a brief smile and a quick nod. All was forgiven.

***

When the group had recharged their batteries with caffeine they were ready to continue on their way.

Alex called ahead from the road to make dinner reservations at Rusty's Ranch House, a great steak house on Highway 14 that they'd pass as they made their way up the Colorado Plateau.

During the drive Steve noticed dark clouds gathering. He shot Alex a concerned look, but didn't say anything for fear of worrying his passengers. By the time they reached Cedar City, a town famous for its Shakespeare Festival, it was early evening.

The van had gradually gained altitude as the day progressed and by the time they stopped at the steak house it was much colder than it had been in the lower elevations.

***

Alex convinced everyone to order a steak.

"*Mein Gott*, look at the size of these plates, and these portions," Elisabeth grumbled. "No wonder Americans are so monstrously fat!"

Georg quickly cut a piece of meat and popped it into his mouth. He looked at his wife and said, "Mmmm, delicious!"

Most of the guests had beer or wine with their meal, and that loosened everyone up again, just as it had the evening before, and the conversation began to flow more freely. Alex and Gerd were noticeably restrained in their consumption.

At the end of the dinner when it was time for the waiter to present the checks, Alex fished around in his briefcase to pay for his meal. The restaurant was poorly lit, but even so, in his sober condition, he realized the billfold he was holding didn't feel right.

He held it on his lap below the level of the table and inspected it.

On the outside it looked almost identical to his, but when he opened it he found only a few small bills in American currency. That was nowhere near as much cash as he'd had with him. And a quick glance revealed that the rest of the contents were not his.

He was bewildered, wondering how he could've lost his wallet. He was even more baffled at how he could've possibly gotten hold of someone else's without realizing it.

He remembered having it at the gas station in Las Vegas the night before and then finding it later in the floor of the van. But now he realized he hadn't found *his* wallet. He'd found someone else's.

That made no sense. Maybe he had one of the guests' wallet.

He looked around the table and each of the men. Gerd, Peter, Klaus, and Steve all had billfolds in hand and were brandishing credit cards. So he didn't have a guests' money.

He was freaking out, but there was no time to delay payment without making a scene so he extracted a Visa card. He glanced at it. The card was issued in the name of *Jason James Stanfield.*

He flipped through the rest of the billfold and found a Nevada driver's license with the same name. Then he studied the photo on the license. He didn't recognize the name or the face.

The guy was a few years younger than him and had a head of wild blond curls. Some of the contents rendered his name as *J.J. Stanfield.*

He needed to use the card, but he had no idea if it would work. Perhaps the owner had already cancelled it. He knew he would've done so the instant he realized his own billfold was missing.

Oh no! His own billfold *was* missing! Good grief! He needed to cancel his credit cards ASAP.

He was still wondering what he should do and was distracted when the guests inquired about the procedure for paying with a credit card in the U.S., how much they should leave for a tip, and whether they should leave the tip in cash.

Alex forced himself to focus on his job enough to explain the procedures. The guests were confused by the fact that they were supposed to give the waiter their credit card and allow him to walk away with it, and take it somewhere out of sight.

They feared the waiter would charge more to their card than they actually owed. And filling in the amount of the tip after the waiter returned with their cards was particularly bizarre to their way of thinking. The system in Europe was totally different.

Alex explained as best he could and assured them this was normal and that it was relatively safe, but he could tell the process was making them uneasy.

He rapidly finished his below the table survey of the contents of the wallet, and confirmed that he wasn't going to get very far with the cash Stanfield had on hand.

Uh oh. He was already in the doghouse with Steve over being late and hungover. He'd made a terrible impression and deserved Steve's ire. Now this.

Alex was afraid to try to explain it. He couldn't even explain it to himself.

He decided not to say anything. Maybe he could get things sorted before anyone noticed anything was wrong.

He sat at the table, trying to appear calm. He briefly wondered if one of his passengers had brought the wallet into the van. But that didn't seem very likely.

Surely if one of them had found it they'd have said something. Could a guest have stolen it? If so why would they leave it lying around to be discovered?

Then he wondered if it might've been left behind by a guest from the previous tour. But that didn't seem likely either because he'd personally cleaned the van since then. And the tour company had cleaned it before he had.

"Do you know anyone named J.J. Stanfield?" he asked Steve.

Steve shook his head, "Should I?"

"No, just wondering if the name meant anything to you," Alex said.

The tour company would certainly have searched the van thoroughly and mentioned it to Steve if a guest had lost his wallet on a previous tour. The guy on the driver's license was younger than the typical age for guests on small-group tours, though, so that wasn't likely either.

Whatever the case, Alex needed to pay for his dinner *right now*, so he handed the waiter the Visa card with a barely noticeable tremor in his hand. When the waiter returned, Alex scribbled an illegible signature on the check and put the card back into Stanfield's wallet.

He was so nervous he couldn't formulate a coherent plan for what to say if the charge was declined, but miraculously the transaction went through just fine. *Whew*, he thought, *bullet dodged.*

He promised himself he'd reimburse J.J. Stanfield, whoever and wherever he was, for every penny he spent, plus something extra in gratitude.

He excused himself and went to the restroom to make a call to the American bank that issued the debit and credit cards he used when in the U.S. He needed to see if there'd been any suspicious activity on either of them, and report them lost or stolen.

He wasn't extremely worried about being delayed in his reporting because his credit card was almost to its limit and there was very little money in his bank account. But he'd had an uncashed paycheck for a thousand dollars in his billfold.

Steve had brought it from the tour company office. Now that was gone, too. Somehow he had to find a way to pay for meals and any other incidental expenses on a three week trip.

His bank came back on the line after checking his account balances and assured him that no charges had been made and no cash had been withdrawn since before the wallet was lost. That was another bullet dodged. For now.

He examined the contents of the billfold again and noticed an ATM card. He hadn't focused on it before, but he did now. It was no help, of course, unless he had the PIN.

He carefully examined every item in the wallet. The only thing that could possibly be of use was a small scrap of paper with a phone number scrawled on it.

He'd learned from his work as a runner for touring musicians that carrying something that looked like a phone number was a common way to disguise a PIN. A phone number with no name identifying it would either start or end with the tour manager's PIN.

More than once busy tour managers who couldn't leave a concert venue had given him a number coded this way on a slip of paper, and sent him to make a withdrawal for them. If his suspicion was correct and this was the ATM code, it was a very foolish thing for J.J. to do. But Alex would be grateful to him for it.

He decided to try to withdraw the limit at the first opportunity. Unfortunately there was no ATM where they were, so he'd probably have to wait until they reached Ruby's Inn near Bryce Canyon.

What a bizarre situation. He hadn't actually *stolen* the credit card, but it wasn't actually his either.

When he'd completed his phone call and at least superficially organized his thinking he went back to the group.

Chapter 7

Alex was glad the guests were in a good mood. Experience had taught him that most guests tended to relax gradually as the trip went on, but this group seemed to be relaxed already.

As they walked out to the van the sky was spitting snowflakes. Steve and Alex exchanged a worried look at this unexpected change in the weather, but neither of them said anything. There was nothing they could do either. They had to reach their cabins before stopping for the night.

Steve hated to drive this particular road at dawn, dusk, and dark—even in good weather—because there was a lot of wildlife in the area. Wildlife tended to be most active during those times. Many species were known for suddenly bursting out of the vegetation alongside the road and appearing in the headlights.

Animals, like humans, preferred to travel on roads if they had a choice. Their lives were hard enough already. Mother Nature could be very cruel. So why would they waste energy bushwhacking cross-country if they didn't have to?

When it snowed, travel was much easier on a paved surface. And some types of animals were notorious for bedding down on the pavement where even a light covering of snow made them hard to see at night.

Most worrisome of all, though, was that this road was taking them to even higher altitudes where the weather conditions were likely to be much worse.

The nearby Cedar Breaks National Monument, an area with red rock formations similar to Bryce Canyon, hadn't even opened for the season yet on account of the winter snow accumulation.

By the time everyone was back in the van and settled in to resume the ride, the snowflakes were significantly larger. It took only a few minutes before Steve could see in the rear view mirror that they were leaving tracks.

He couldn't hide the fact that he was nervous. He hunched over the steering wheel and frequently glanced over at Alex.

Steve had a degree in Meteorology. In his younger days he'd done a stint as a television weatherman for a station in Oregon. His degree, his on-air experience, and the massive amount of travel he'd done in the West added up to a lot of knowledge about weather patterns in the area, especially *bad* weather.

He clutched the steering wheel and leaned forward to see better. This wasn't supposed to be happening. When he'd checked the forecast that morning a storm had been predicted, but it was supposed to be taking place fifty miles away.

Things had obviously changed.

Before they reached the highest point of Highway 14 between Wood Knoll and Blowhard Mountain there was already six inches of snow on the road. It was late in the year for a storm of this magnitude, especially when the day had been warm and cloudless.

The van had all-season tires, which were fine for most conditions, but they weren't ideal for driving in snow—and they hadn't brought chains because they'd never anticipated a need for them.

Towing a trailer wasn't helping either.

It was white-knuckle driving until they made it to the ten thousand foot summit and started down the other side. After that they knew the temperature would begin to rise. They'd cleared a major hurdle.

Steve leaned back in his seat, relieved, but almost immediately a group of elk leaped out of the woods and onto the road. They kept going when they saw the van, but there were several of them and it took a few seconds for all of them to cross.

Steve braked and steered into the oncoming lane to avoid a collision. A seven hundred pound animal coming through the windshield with four thrashing hooves was never a good idea.

He was successful at evading the elk, but the maneuver sent the van into a skid. It went sliding along the icy pavement, then left the road on the slight curve and slammed into a tree, damaging the body of the van on the driver's side, and breaking out two of the large passenger windows.

When the van had come to a rest, Alex turned in his seat and called out, "Is everyone okay?"

He couldn't accurately assess the situation visually because the interior was dark. He'd told everyone to buckle up, but it seemed that not all the guests had done so.

There was some grumbling as people regained their seats and rearranged themselves and their gear. Certainly there would be some bruises tomorrow, and maybe some sore places, but mercifully, no one seemed to be injured.

"Thank goodness," muttered Steve.

"You said it," Alex agreed.

The engine had died on impact and the headlights were out. Steve turned the key in the ignition, but the motor wouldn't crank. Then he tried to activate the flashers, but they weren't working either.

Steve shot Alex a look, then he raised his eyebrows and gestured with a wave of his hand to indicate that Alex needed to get out of his seat. Alex got out first, then Steve climbed over the console and got out behind him.

They inspected the damage. It was obvious that the van wasn't drivable. Alex examined the various sets of tracks in the snow, with hooves and tires, and it was clear that the elk had made it across unscathed.

Steve wanted to scream.

"What are we supposed to do now?" he said, softly, so only Alex could hear him.

The two men walked around the van. They were stranded at high altitude and the snow was getting worse. It was already drifting to knee deep on the shoulders.

The passengers were suddenly cold. There were large openings on the windward side where two windows used to be. The van could no longer provide shelter from the elements. Everyone was feeling it, too, even as they gingerly brushed the exploded glass fragments off their clothes and seats.

If the engine wouldn't start, they had no heater.

They each checked their cell phones for service and discovered that, just as promised in the description of the tour, they were indeed travelling through wilderness. They were surrounded by so much bloody wilderness nobody could get a signal.

Alex knew that with this amount of snow falling, the authorities wouldn't plow the road until tomorrow morning at the earliest. And they couldn't realistically expect help from fellow travelers because there was very little chance that anyone else would be foolish enough to try to make it across the summit tonight.

In fact, the authorities had probably closed the road behind them.

***

"*Mein Gott*, what are we supposed to do now?" Elisabeth wailed. "We will all die in this terrible place!"

"We'll be fine," Alex said, in the voice he used for soothing irate tourists in unpleasant situations. "We'll open the trailer so everyone can get their cold weather gear. We'll all want to dress as warmly as possible."

Steve went to unlock the trailer.

Elisabeth was wailing nonstop.

Frida leaned across the aisle and offered her a chocolate cookie from her purse. "*Schokolade? Schokolade!*" Elisabeth screeched. "Are you mad? What will that fix? Nothing I tell you!"

"You might be surprised," Frida said. "Give it a try."

Georg took the cookie and popped it neatly into her mouth when she opened it to spew more gloom and doom. That would shut her up for as long as it took to chew and swallow.

Steve tugged on the trailer door. The wind snatched it out of his hand and it opened with a bang. He began setting bags out into the snow.

The guests rummaged through their possessions and donned hats, gloves, and whatever wind and/or waterproof gear they could scrounge.

"What next?" Gerd said. "Do we just wait here in the van?"

"I don't think we should wait in the van," Alex said. "The windows are too large to cover. It's already below freezing in there. We'll have trouble surviving the night in these conditions. There's a reason this is called Blowhard Mountain."

This sobering assessment got everyone's attention.

"I suggest we stay in the trailer. We can use our leftover clothes to pad the floor and insulate the sides. We can stay warm if we sit inside there together with the doors closed."

At first nobody said anything. They were each contemplating how nine people were going to fit inside the small space.

"It'll be snug," Alex said, "but a great way for us to get to know each other better."

At this Tina gave Steve a predatory smile. He was shocked and looked away.

"I'm not going inside there," Elisabeth said.

"It's your decision, of course," Alex said, totally disingenuously. He'd hog tie the witch and drag her inside if she balked. "But if you don't, we'll all sleep comfortably tonight and when we wake up in the morning you'll be dead."

At this, the guests were silent. They'd all been raised in Northern Europe. They knew about mountains and cold and snow. They knew he was right.

"We can expect help to arrive early in the morning," he added.

Steve shot him a bland look that said, *Oh really?*

Alex shrugged in response.

***

The guests weren't pleased to find themselves spending the night together in a luggage trailer instead of a hotel room, but they were all experienced travelers and reasonably good sports, except for Elisabeth, so they agreed to the plan. Consensus was ever so much easier to achieve when there was no viable alternative.

So with Alex's urging, they immediately went about trying to make the best of the situation.

"This trip is already becoming a Wild West adventure just as we were promised!" said Frida.

Alex smiled at her. She was one tough broad.

Chapter 8

Meanwhile, back in Las Vegas, the predators in the glamorous black Mustang had circled the block several times and driven up and down side streets stalking their prey, but they'd come up dry.

"What wuz he doin' at the station anyways?" said the driver. "Let's go back ova there and take a look at their security camera footage. That might give us an idea as to where this clown's disappeared to."

The men went into the gas station store and flashed wallets containing fake IDs. The clerk didn't get a decent look, but he decided to go with the program since there were two of them and only one of him.

The men claimed to be from the Las Vegas Metropolitan Police. "We're lookin' for a perp who mighta got captured, so ta speak, on your surveillance."

"Knock yourselves out," the clerk said, gesturing toward a tiny office which held a desk and a monitor amid a tsunami of unfiled paperwork.

With the attendant's help, they scrolled through the footage taken by the different cameras at the approximate time their target had gone through the fence. They found what they were looking for and were able to study the scene from two different camera angles.

They watched their prey appear from a poorly lit area on the edge of the fueling plaza and use his right hand to take something out of the back pocket of his pants. He came out with what was obviously a wallet.

He opened the wallet and removed a small black gadget from it, then used a knee to balance himself as he stretched forward into the passenger area of the van through the open sliding door on the side.

He placed the item into a gear bag that was resting in the floor, then got out of the van.

He'd obviously put something inside the bag. It was easy for the men to guess what it had been. It was, in fact, what they were chasing him for. The Boss wanted that portable memory thingamajig.

Then they saw the guy do a double-take, then lean in to the van again and reach for something. He came out with a lightweight hooded windbreaker.

Then something apparently scared him, because he suddenly hopped backward and took off, disappearing into the darkness he'd come from.

"Is this a setup?" one of the fake policemen said to the other. "Has he made a deal with 'em to do a handoff?"

"Dunno," the other man said. "Those guys look clueless, though. My gut says he's usin' 'em."

They copied down the name of the tour company on the logo on the side of the van as well as the number on the Oregon license plate, then watched the videos several more times until they were satisfied that they'd learned as much from the footage as they could.

The fake cops drove a couple of blocks, turned onto a side street, and pulled over. The guy in the passenger seat got out his smartphone. A Google search of the name of the tour company returned a website as the first listing.

The company specialized in one-to-three week small group tours of the American West for German speakers. "They're not American."

"Sicilians?" the driver asked, astonished.

"Nah, Germans."

"Germans? What's their angle?"

"No idea."

The man drilled down through the website, skimming the various tours on offer, then homed in on the ones that went through Vegas. There were several that either started there, or finished there, or both. After that, it was easy to narrow the possibilities to one by searching the exact dates.

He held his phone so his co-worker could see the itinerary. The particular tour, entitled *Canyonlands*, was two weeks long and followed a huge loop through several western states. On this first leg they'd be heading from Vegas to Bryce Canyon.

Neither man was what you'd call a nature lover. They both preferred indoor nighttime action, the sorts of entertainment that Vegas excelled at. They knew approximately nothing about wilderness areas and would never have ventured into one on their own.

"We gotta figure out where this Bryce Canyon place is, and how long it's gonna take to get there," the guy in the passenger seat said. "Gimme a sec."

The driver sat quietly, fingers lightly tapping the steering wheel.

"Google Maps says the joint's four hours away by car."

"Make that three in this beast," the driver said, and they both laughed.

It would be easy to catch up with the van. They needed to find it, *or else*, to quote the Boss.

So they would. Somehow.

They'd do whatever it took.

***

Alex rigged a bungee cord to hold the doors almost, but not quite, closed. He left a little gap for oxygen.

Inside the trailer the temperature had risen to a tolerable level from the body heat given off by nine people in the confined space. It turned out that there was more than enough room for everyone to sit, and some could even lay down, if they fitted themselves like sardines in a tin.

Elisabeth shouted out a barrage of accusations in German, so Steve wasn't as upset as he would've been if he could've understood her. She followed this with few more minutes of moaning and sniffling but then she fell asleep and was mercifully silent. That was an unexpected development, but much appreciated.

During the night moisture from their breathing accumulated on the ceiling and eventually condensation began to drip. Alex was awoken by a drop hitting him in the face. He sat still and silent hoping everyone else was able to remain asleep. The indoor rain wasn't pleasant, but it wasn't like you could ask anyone to stop breathing.

***

Inevitably some of the guests needed to find a restroom, or in this case, some shrubbery. The occupants readied themselves for an Arctic blast, but what they weren't prepared for was how bright the landscape was when the doors were thrown open.

Technically it was still full dark outside, but the snow had stopped falling, and they'd been enclosed long enough for their eyes to fully adapt to night vision. A full moon had risen high in the sky and it was illuminating their white surroundings to what seemed almost like daylight.

They sat squashed together, stunned and blinking at the winter wonderland, like a nest of owl chicks.

"It's gonna be difficult, if not impossible, to make it to any kind of cover, so here's the easiest way to handle it," Steve said. "Women to the left side of the van," he pointed to indicate which left he meant, "and men to the right. Don't go far. This is no time for modesty."

Alex translated his instruction but left out the last part. Germans didn't need to hear it. They were famously immodest.

The guests who had to relieve themselves or who wanted to stretch their legs crawled to the doors and stepped out of the trailer into the snow. The men went into the deeper snow of the shoulder and the women into the easier to manage center of the road.

The guests with large bladders complained about the cold air blowing into the trailer and pulled the doors almost closed until time to let their companions back inside.

When everyone had returned, the interior began to warm up again, but it was still so cold that the group was forced to move even closer together to stay warm. Especially since some of them now had damp footwear and pant legs from wading about in the snow.

Gerd offered everyone a sip from a bottle of whiskey he'd bought at the duty free shop in the airport. He had a lot of takers.

Alex sent Steve a glance that was barely discernable in the sliver of light illuminating the dark interior. It said, *This is either going to be the most bonded group we've ever had, or the worst trip we've ever been on.*

Steve shrugged and raised his eyebrows, meaning, *Maybe both.*

Seconds later he felt Tina's hand on his thigh.

The Vegas henchmen blasted down I-15 and made it to St. George in record time. Since they were ahead of schedule they decided to stop for a quick coffee.

They were both tired. They'd had several busy days in a row and now they were gonna have to operate all night on zero sleep. But they'd done jobs like this before. They were expected to handle tough situations. In their line of work they had no choice but to man up.

Several strong coffees later—with one more in a take-out cup for each of them, they resumed their chase. Fifty minutes and one speeding ticket after that they made it to Cedar City.

They stopped at a gas station to top off the fuel tank and get information about the best routes to Bryce Canyon. They bought even more coffee. It was now raining hard, but that wasn't the worst problem.

"Highway 14 and Highway 143 are both closed due to heavy snow accumulation in the higher altitudes," said the station attendant. "Neither of those roads are gonna get plowed before six in the morning."

"Ah, geez," one of the men mumbled.

"Your only option to get to Bryce tonight is to continue on I-15 north, until the exit for Highway 20 east," he said. "After that you'll take Highway 89 south, then head east on Highway 12. That's the one they call the *All American Highway*. From there it's a short stretch along Highway 63 to get to the park."

The two men studied a map on a cell phone and wrote down the series of turns as the station attendant dictated them again more slowly. Then they returned to the car where they loaded the directions into the Mustang's GPS.

On account of their challenging working conditions they decided to snort a little coke before pulling out, just so they'd be able to stay alert during the drive. Then they took off again. They'd have preferred a hot pursuit, but what they got was a cold and wet one.

Just as the gas station guy had warned, once they left I-15 and gained some altitude climbing the Colorado Plateau, the rain turned to snow. The drive became surreal. The pitch black darkness, too much coffee, the coke, the thrilling power of the muscle car. The huge white snowflakes flying toward the windshield made it seem like they were traveling at warp speed.

To make things even more dreamlike, the '70s satellite radio station they were listening to began playing David Bowie's *Space Oddity*.

It wasn't safe to be driving spaced out like that. They needed to focus. So, to bring them back to earth, the passenger changed the channel to Sinatra. It took them a moment to realize the song was *Fly Me to the Moon*. That cracked them both up.

Neither of the men had ever travelled on such an isolated highway. It was spooky at night. There were no indications of human habitation anywhere. The place looked eerily like they might actually be on another planet.

The drive seemed endless and the snow was getting deeper. Even coked up they were forced to lower their speed. By the time they reached the town of Panguich the euphoria had subsided and a profound tiredness crashed in on them.

It was a bone deep exhaustion combined with the inevitable results of too much caffeine in a near lethal cocktail with two kinds of snow—Utah powder and Colombian. The good news was that the temperature had risen slightly, so the Utah snow was turning back into a slushy mix. That made the driving a little easier.

The guys made it farther along on Highway 12 to Red Canyon, but they were really suffering by this point and agreed that they needed a quick nap.

They caught a glimpse of a dirt track and turned off the main road. They drove just far enough to be out of sight and parked among Ponderosa Pines and some really strange piles of rock. The darkness made the formations seem even more bizarre than they were in broad daylight

But neither man was in any shape to be worrying about anything. They both fell into a deep stupor almost immediately. They snored and twitched and dreamed for a few hours, utterly unaware of the irony of their location.

Chapter 9

A monster was coming. It made a thunderous roar, and the ground shook. Alex wanted to run away, but he seemed to be paralyzed. He broke out in a terrified sweat and thrashed to break loose from whatever it was that was restraining him. Someone made a grunt of disapproval and he woke up.

He'd been dreaming.

He was indeed trapped, but it was by a tangle of limbs inside the trailer. He managed to sit up straighter and lean over for a peek through the narrow opening between the trailer doors.

He thought he'd been having a bad dream, but the roaring was real enough. It was coming from a snowplow.

Alex roused the group from their states of everything from a light doze, to deep sleep, to gray-faced borderline-asphyxia. He crawled over some bodies to undo the bungee cord. Then he shoved the doors of the trailer open wide and leaped out to flag down the plowman.

The gigantic machine paused in the road, but the driver kept the engine running. "Unlucky last night, huh?" the plowman shouted down at Alex.

"Yeah!" Alex shouted back. "A half dozen elk jumped out in front of us. They got away without a scratch, but we had to spend the night in the ditch!" He gestured toward the trailer, "We've been trying to stay warm in there!"

"At least you survived!" the plowman said. "Shoulda steered straight into an elk, buddy. Woulda made ya a nice dinner!"

Alex seriously doubted that any of the guests would've enjoyed skinning, butchering, and roasting several hundred pounds of fresh roadkill over a damp twig campfire in a snowstorm, but he knew the man meant well and he needed his help, so he shouted back over the noise of the machine, "You're right about that! I sure wish I had me an elk steak for breakfast this mornin'! I'm starvin'!"

They shared a manly laugh about breakfasting on illegally-obtained barely-barbequed meat.

"Well," the plowman said, "I could tow ya outta that ditch, no problem, but that iddn't gonna help ya much, right?"

"Right," Alex agreed. "The van's totaled."

***

Meanwhile the guests had crept out of the trailer in slow motion, stiff with cold, hobbling on cramped legs. They watched Alex's faux mountain man conversation but were spared understanding the nuances of the exchange.

The snowplow driver used his radio to report their situation and request help. A couple of minutes later the local sheriff responded with a promise to send a bus to get them once the kids had been dropped off at school. He promised to send a tow truck, too.

"I think we can get the bus to you by ten," the sheriff said.

Alex looked at his watch. That meant they had three hours to wait.

No one was happy about it, but only Elisabeth said anything. By this point everyone had her number, so they ignored her. Her lips moved, but they'd mentally adjusted the volume to mute.

The driver gave a wave and the mighty snowplow continued on its way, heroically clearing the road as it went. A few minutes later they were alone again in the frigid, silent, high-altitude wonderland. Alex knew it was a wonderland because he couldn't stop wondering how he was going to salvage this disaster.

Steve kept the guests busy locating their luggage in the snow, retrieving the clothes they'd used to pad and insulate the trailer, and repacking their bags.

"I think now we are *trailer trash*?" said Peter in his gentle voice.

Steve laughed at his joke, and said, "Absolutely."

Privately he was impressed at the group's toughness.

***

55

It was time to pool whatever they had in the way of snacks and try to get some calories into everybody. Alex scrounged up some energy bars and cookies, a little cheese, and a few pieces of bread, and shared the modest food resources with everyone amiably. The others contributed what they had as well. It was enough to stave off hunger for a few hours.

Steve had the foresight to bring the gallon jugs and individual bottles of water into the trailer with them during the night, so their drinking water hadn't frozen solid.

About an hour later another vehicle came by. It was a much used work van emblazoned with the logo of a plumbing company. He paused and rolled down his window. "Are you guys okay?" he said.

The guests were jogging in place and flapping their arms, trying to stay warm.

Alex explained their situation, then added, "It's cold, but we're alright. The sheriff's office is sending a replacement vehicle. It should be here in a couple of hours."

"It doesn't take long to get frostbite," the man said. "I'm on my way to Hatch. I'll be happy to take you. It won't be a luxury ride, but I got room in the back."

Alex translated the offer to the group, and explained that they'd have to sit on the floor in the back.

Everyone agreed readily. "Danke. Thank you. Ja gerne!" they called up to the driver.

"You go with the group," Steve said. "That way you can translate for them and, if you get to an area with cell service you can call the boss to report what's happened.

"I'll stay with the van and ride to town with the tow truck driver." He put on a ski mask, wound a heavy wool scarf around his neck, adjusted his cap and thick gloves, then pulled up the hood on his jacket. Steve was always prepared for contingencies.

There were lots of tools and plumbing supplies in the back of the van, so the group had to squeeze together, but they were accustomed to it now and appreciated the warmth each other provided.

Their rescuer said that one of them could sit in the front. They decided it should be Alex since he spoke English and knew more about the area than they did.

Before climbing into the passenger seat, Alex looked back at Steve and hoped he wasn't seeing a captain who would end by going down with his ship. His last view of his co-worker was of him stoically reloading the luggage into the trailer, stranded alone on Blowhard Mountain.

Once they were inside and settled, the driver continued on his way using the path freshly carved by the snowplow. Steve watched the plumber's van disappear, thinking that in weather like this, a lot of pipes would be bursting. That guy was gonna have a busy day.

Chapter 10

Meanwhile back at Red Canyon the goombahs from Las Vegas were startled awake by someone knocking on the driver's window.

It was a local fellow in a high-ground-clearance pickup truck who'd noticed them apparently sleeping in broad daylight with their car's engine running. He was concerned that they might've been overcome by carbon monoxide.

The driver rolled down his window.

"Hey there, Butch and Sundance!" the man said, "Just checking, are you guys alright?"

They nodded and mumbled groggy responses to show they were still alive.

"Why're ya callin' us those names?" the driver asked.

It wouldn't do to be identified as criminals on a job like this. And now this guy had seen their faces.

"This is where *The Wild Bunch* used to hide out! You know—Butch Cassidy and the Sundance Kid. This place is a maze, but Butch knew how to outsmart the law by hiding in the canyons."

"Oh, gotcha," the driver said.

Okay, so he wouldn't need to clip this joker who'd had the nerve to bang on his window. In fact it was a cool coincidence. He liked the names. And it would make a great story to tell the Boss when they got back.

"Thanks," he said, "it's time for us to get goin' anyway."

As they watched the pickup truck disappear around a bend, the driver said, "I wanna be Butch. You can be Sundance."

They got out of the Mustang to stretch their legs and relieve themselves. They were disappointed to see that what had been a dirt road yesterday was now a muddy, slushy track on account of the overnight mix of rain and snow.

Seeing the changes that nature had wrought while they were asleep—and in Butch's case, asleep at the wheel—gave them a powerful incentive to get going.

Sundance looked at the time. "Ah geez!" he said, "It's already 7:30! Let's go! Let's go!"

They hopped back into the car, Butch cranked the engine, stepped on the gas and the Mustang's 526 horsepower engine, which would take the car from zero to sixty in 3.7 seconds, took even less time to embed the rear wheels in mud.

Much cursing echoed off the canyon walls.

Sundance got out to push, but the combination of a driver with no experience in these conditions, the low slung design of the car, and the overpowered engine worked to dig the car in deeper with every rpm until the undercarriage was resting on the ground.

Sundance gave the car one last mighty heave which did absolutely nothing for the car but caused him to slip and fall face down into the cold, sloppy mud.

Even more cursing bounced off the canyon walls.

Sundance managed to drag himself upright by using the car for support. When he could stand, he brushed at the mud on his clothes, but succeeded only in smearing it around. It coated his shoes, socks, and the front of his pants, shirt, and jacket.

***

"Walk out to the road and get some help," said Butch.

"Nobody's gonna stop for a guy lookin' like this," Sundance said, gesturing at his clothes.

They decided to flip a coin to see who'd have to go.

Butch lost.

He opened the driver's door to get out. The muddy ground was nearly level with the door jamb so it was incredibly awkward to heave himself up and out at the same time. He put both feet into the deep mud, levered himself up using the top of the car door, then immediately slipped and fell onto his back.

He lay there in shock, not moving. His back was soaked with the sopping goop. He got up slowly, climbing the side of the car as Sundance had only moments before.

Once he was upright, he behaved as if nothing had happened and began to walk toward the main road with as much dignity as he could muster. He didn't even try to argue. All the filth was on his back instead of his front. Sundance still had the high ground in the dispute.

It took all his years of training in manly self-control for Sundance to keep a straight face. When Butch was gone he got into the passenger seat carefully so as not to spread the mud any farther than necessary.

Butch stood beside the road in the bitter cold, waiting for someone to come by. The first vehicle was a Jeep Grand Cherokee. Butch waved, and even though his presentable front was all they could see, they didn't stop.

The vehicle went right by him without slowing down, but then pulled over and he watched, incredulous, as a family got out to take pictures in front of some stupid rocks while still within sight of a stranded man.

Butch couldn't believe it. He wondered what the tourists were pointing their cameras at. And then, when he looked again, he noticed that the weird looking rocks were actually sort of amazing.

It had been dark when he and Sundance had reached the canyon and it had taken him a while after a rude awakening and a few action-packed minutes to notice his surroundings.

He jogged toward the Jeep and called out to the family.

They seemed to be afraid of him.

Butch tried to explain that he needed help getting his car out of the mud nearby.

It turned out that they were French and spoke very little English. Butch spoke some Italian, but that was no help. The father nodded as if he'd help, but once he had his family back inside their Jeep he locked the doors and sped away.

Butch was even more angry now. He stamped and shouted and ran around in the roadway cursing like Rumpelstiltskin. That at least had the effect of warming him up a little. He wasn't dressed for snow. He was dressed to be an Italian-American hoodlum in a hot, dry urban area, i.e., Las Vegas.

And now his expensive outfit, the only one he'd brought on this trip, was ruined. He couldn't wait to cut it off himself and burn it.

***

A few minutes later a Chevy Suburban drove up and stopped at the pullout where Butch was standing. Half a dozen Asians got out to take pictures of the same rocks.

Butch walked over casually, hoping that he'd be able to convince them to help. If he'd been awake enough to bring his pistol he could've forced them, but he hadn't thought of it. He was really slipping in more ways than one. This creepy place had thrown him off his game.

The first members of the group he tried to talk to were a bit older than the others, and they didn't understand a word he was saying. He couldn't understand them either, but they bowed and made elegant hand gestures. He thought they might be Japanese.

They indicated that he should speak to the young people taking pictures about twenty-five yards away. Butch jogged over to the teenagers and asked for help. They replied in a very friendly way in excellent English.

Of course they would help. The Japanese were the politest people on earth.

What a relief. The outlaws were rescued. American thugs would be saved by foreigners with good manners.

When the kids finished taking their photos they led him back to the Suburban. One of them pulled a couple of shopping bags out of the back and used them to cover the front passenger seat upholstery, then offered Butch the seat.

Their kindness was amazing.

Butch directed them back to the Mustang with the young people acting as translators.

Neither car had a tow rope but Butch hoped that if they'd push the Mustang gently, bumper to bumper, they could get the car back on the road.

The Japanese didn't like the idea, because they were in a rental, but Butch managed to convince them, mostly by begging and bowing.

They were lucky they decided to do what he said. Sundance was prepared to offer some encouragement. They were moments away from getting a gun to the head if they balked.

Butch took the floor mats out of the Mustang and put them between the two vehicles to avoid any scratches and encouraged the driver to approach.

The Suburban carefully closed the distance and gently shoved against the car. In seconds the Mustang was on solid, level ground.

But at the same time the Mustang was getting onto level ground the Japanese driver was bucking across the deep ruts made by the car and he accidentally touched the gas pedal harder than he meant to. The Suburban bounced against the back of the Mustang.

There was no damage to the Suburban, but the back bumper of the Mustang got a serious dent. The Japanese driver was devastated. He'd damaged the other car. He was mortified by his mistake.

Butch pretended everything was okay. He thanked the man and assured him that it was not his fault. He lied and said it would be easy to fix. He thanked the family for rescuing him and bowed. Then he jumped into the Mustang and he and Sundance sped away.

Chapter 11

Alex finally got cell service at Duck Creek Village and immediately called his boss, the tour company owner, Ellen.

"I've been worried about you guys," she said. "The owner of the cabins where you were scheduled to stay last night called me when you didn't show up.

"I tried to reach you and Steve, but I couldn't get in touch with either of you. I didn't know if you were in an area with no service or if something awful had happened."

Alex explained the situation.

Ellen was upset to hear about the van being totaled, but happy that nobody had been hurt. She thanked Alex for his ingenuity in having the group spend the night together in the trailer.

Companies that hosted small group tours into the wilderness occasionally encountered unexpected problems, but this disaster was the worst ever for Wild West Adventure Tours.

"I'm so relieved to hear that the group sees the experience as an adventure," she said. "I can send you another van from Las Vegas, but it'll be four days until I have a driver available to bring it to you."

That wasn't what Alex wanted to hear, but he had to accept it.

"In the meantime I'll try to come up with a Plan B," she said.

***

Alex hung up. He didn't want to share the bad news with his guests until he'd explored all his options.

When asked for a status report he said only that they were still working on it.

Next he called the Sheriff's Department to update them and say that the group no longer needed to be rescued.

"My co-worker is still up there with our van and we still need a tow truck to bring him and the van to a garage for repairs," Alex said, "but the guests have all been taken to Hatch by a passing workman.

"He dropped us off at Miss Lori's Coffee House on the way to his job site."

***

The guests enjoyed the warmth of the coffee house and had hot drinks and a hot meal while Alex stayed on the phone calling contacts in Utah, Arizona, and Southwest Colorado, to see if any of his friends could suggest where he might be able to get a replacement vehicle.

That was the highest possible priority. The guests would be extremely disappointed if they weren't able to see Bryce Canyon. It was one of the main reasons people chose to come on this particular tour.

Alex called Tim, an old friend in Park City, Utah. He'd gotten to know Tim well when he'd lived in Park City years ago. Alex was still grateful to him because when he'd first arrived, Tim had helped him survive until he got his first paycheck.

Tim organized a Christian Center—a joint project of the different churches in the area that took turns inviting seasonal workers from the ski resorts to join them for a free dinner together.

It had been great fun to attend those dinners. The South American workers always managed to turn the meals into a party. He'd never encountered so many different types of people from so many different countries as he did in Tim's group.

There had been young people from Chile, Argentina, Peru, Brazil, New Zealand, and Australia. And they'd had such fun times together. When he'd left Utah to return home to Germany he donated most of his belongings to Tim's group.

Alex got lucky and Tim answered the old number Alex had for him—and sounded happy to hear from him, even though they hadn't been in communication for years.

"Happy to help," Tim said. "I'll make some calls and get back to you ASAP."

When he'd done everything he could to set Plan B into motion, Alex called his wife to update her and check on how she and their two little daughters were doing. He was sorry when the call ended, but then, at last, he finally had time to get breakfast.

***

He was scarfing down eggs, bacon, toast, jelly, and his third cup of coffee when Tim called back. "I talked to a Baptist church in Cedar City. They have a fifteen-passenger van they'll let you borrow for a few days, but they'll need it back on Sunday."

"That sounds great!" Alex said.

"A volunteer will drive it up, followed by a friend in a car who'll ferry the driver back to Cedar City.

Alex thought for a moment. Today was Tuesday.

It had to be back by Saturday night. That meant they had the van for five days!

Alex could hardly believe it. "Tim," he said, "you're the greatest!"

Then he called Ellen to give her the good news. She was amazed.

"Alex, you're a miracle worker," she said. "Be sure to let the Baptist church know that I intend to make a big donation for their help."

Alex promised to relay her message, then said, "The guests are upset about missing Bryce Canyon."

"I'll try to move your hotel reservations back by a day, until you get to Moab," she said. "We'll cut a night from the itinerary in Moab. That way you can get back to the original schedule. I can't promise anything yet, but I'll try."

He forgot to ask Ellen to reissue his lost paycheck or bring him some cash, but maybe that was for the best. He needed to deal with the biggest problems first. He'd just have to tough it out somehow.

***

The group continued to wait for the replacement van in the cozy café. Several coffees later Ellen called back with good news. She'd managed to change their reservations.

Alex conveyed the happy news to the group. They were so relieved they went into party mode. The night in the wilderness had worked on them like a drug.

Alex had seen it before—adventures could change people forever.

***

Butch and Sundance raced the Mustang to Bryce Village and got there by nine. They cruised every hotel parking lot in the area looking for the van, but didn't see it anywhere.

"Looks like they've already checked outta wherever they were stayin'," said Sundance. They gotta be at the park."

They drove into Bryce Canyon—the very first national park either of them had ever entered in their lives. They passed the sign and looked for something recognizable as entertainment, but didn't see anything.

They methodically checked every pullout and parking lot they could find, as well as all thirteen scenic overlooks along the thirty-eight mile road. The vehicle they were looking for wasn't in any of them.

"Where's the fun stuff?" Butch asked. "I don't get it."

Sundance shrugged.

The ranger had given them a simple map at the entrance kiosk where they paid to get in, but now they backtracked to a Visitor Center to study a more detailed map.

It only confirmed that they'd checked everywhere already. But while they were there they saw a shuttle bus stop in the parking lot. They hadn't realized there was a shuttle service through the park. "Maybe they're usin' that shuttle," Sundance said, pointing, "and the van's somewhere else."

"Geez," Butch groaned. "I bet they're hikin'."

The hoods checked a couple of scenic pull offs and didn't see the van. Then they encountered a ranger. "When people go hikin'," Sundance asked, "where do they go?

"The three most popular trails are Navajo Loop, Queens Garden, and Peekaboo," the ranger said, and he pointed them out on the map.

"Be careful out there," he said, nodding at the caked red stains on their black city clothes. "The footing can be treacherous."

The men didn't like engaging with any type of law enforcement for any reason. They certainly didn't like being teased by some joker in a goofy Smokey the Bear hat, but they thanked the guy and kept a lid on it as they returned to their car.

Most of the park trails originated near Sunrise Point, Sunset Point, or Bryce Point, so they retraced their route checking every parking lot again.

When they reached Sunset Point and walked out to the canyon rim, the wise guys were astonished. They'd never seen anything like it. The Manhattan skyline from Staten Island was great, the Vegas Strip at night was great, but this—this wasn't too shabby.

Sundance felt himself actually getting tears in his eyes.

After a few moments of awed silence they turned their minds back to business and scanned the trails as well as they could from where they were. They saw a group of people walking along the Peekaboo Trail in the far distance and thought that maybe it was the group they were looking for.

They decided to drive over to Bryce Point so they could hike down and intercept the hikers to be sure.

***

Although they'd both been told to *take a hike* countless times, neither Butch nor Sundance had ever actually hiked on real dirt before. The only canyons they'd ever walked in were made by skyscrapers. Walking the slushy, muddy trails in their expensive Italian leather street shoes was a royal pain. They took turns skidding and windmilling their arms to stay upright.

They quickly realized that there was no way for them to get down the trail in the shoes they were wearing and, if they couldn't get down, they certainly wouldn't be able to make it back up.

They decided to return to the rim.

***

They eventually made it back up top after a great deal of slipping and sliding. Hikers passing them on the trail exploded with unrestrained laughter watching the two filthy creatures stumbling back to civilization. The men were so spectacularly dirty, they were stealing the show from one of Utah's most stunning landscapes.

By the time they made it back to the car, their attire was basically destroyed. The finely woven and tailored garments of wool, silk, cotton, and leather were now a miserable mess of *Bryce camo*—covered with random smears of red, brown and beige dirt.

No mafioso could allow this state of affairs to continue.

They got back into the Mustang totally exhausted, and transferred a fresh layer of filth to the interior.

They needed a new plan.

Chapter 12

While he waited for rescue Alex steeled himself for another test of his borrowed credit card by using it to pay for the breakfast he'd ordered without thinking. Miraculously it was still working.

At noon the van from the Baptist church pulled up in front of the coffee house. The group's rescuers came inside and called out for Alex.

Alex greeted them happily and introduced them to the guests. "Please let me buy you guys lunch," he said, and used the card again.

Shortly afterwards he got a call from Steve. "A tow truck came to get the van and I hitched a ride back with him. He dropped me off at the cabins where we're staying tonight, so I'll just wait here for you guys."

Alex updated Steve with the good news about the home office changing their reservations and about the loaner van they'd been given until a replacement arrived from Las Vegas.

"That's amazing," said Steve. "Whew! What a relief."

It was still early enough in the day to drive into Bryce Canyon and take in some of the views. Commercial tours needed a CUA, a Commercial Use Authorization, to enter a national park, though, and Steve had their documentation with him in Tropic, a small town east of Bryce.

Alex didn't want to waste time driving there to retrieve the document and the driver with a commercial driving license, so he decided he'd take them on a quick tour of the park as members of the Mountain View Baptist Church.

He explained the situation and suggested the ruse to the group. They were game to give it a try. Because of the language issue, he told them to remain silent during check in and until they were well clear of the entrance gate.

Although Alex spoke with an accent, his free-wheeling manner and excellent command of American slang was good enough to convince a ranger that nothing was amiss.

The tour group had no way of knowing it, but at the same time they were entering the park from the north—warm, dry, well-fed, highly-caffeinated, and ecstatic to be on the road again, Butch and Sundance were leaving, headed south—cold, wet, filthy, hungry, frustrated, and exhausted.

***

Alex took the group to Sunset Point. It offered a magnificent view of the fantastical Bryce landscape of eroded spires, bizarre hoodoos, sandstone monoliths, and striped badlands.

They decided to take an hour-long hike along the rim of the canyon. Alex was relieved to note that everyone, even Elisabeth, seemed pleased with the beautiful walk.

This was a resilient bunch, for sure. He was impressed with their recovery from a very unpleasant night.

***

Butch and Sundance parked in front of the office at Ruby's Inn and were relieved to hear that there were still vacancies. They booked a room and Butch went to unlock the door while Sundance made a quick stop at the car to retrieve what little gear they'd brought along on what they'd thought would be a quick trip.

The theme song to *Gilligan's Island* came to mind, "… For a three hour tour…."

Unfortunately, he wasn't able to get the trunk open on account of the damage from the push that had freed them from the mud in Red Canyon. The lock was jammed.

He couldn't believe what a fiasco this job was turning into.

Sundance swore, then shouted, "This job is cursed!"

When he shared the newest bit of bad news with Butch, his partner was livid, but first things first.

"We gotta get outta these," Butch said, plucking at his post-apocalyptic clothing.

***

They walked over to Ruby's General Store to buy something clean and stock up on toiletries and snacks.

The store was huge and offered a wide array of souvenirs, groceries, outdoor equipment, and clothes. The only problem was that the style of the attire on offer was confined to Bryce Canyon t-shirts sporting slogans like "Utah Rocks" or clownishly elaborate pseudo-cowboy attire.

Italian-American men in their line of business were expected to exhibit a certain sartorial finesse at all times. It was a fundamental aspect of the wise guy world.

They were forced to concede that this was an emergency situation that cried out for them to grant themselves a waiver.

They gingerly poked through the distasteful offerings. On account of the harsh weather they decided their only realistic option was to go with the western look. It was also considerably more macho than the t-shirts.

They acquired heavily embroidered jeans and shirts with pearl snaps instead of buttons and curved chest pocket designs that bore a distressing resemblance to leering smiley faces. Fortunately, they were able to get a decent fit in the black option of the hideous shirts. This was good because the red and white checked ones would've made Butch suicidal, if not homicidal.

He selected a shirt with a horseshoe motif and Sundance chose one with bucking broncos.

Next, they needed footwear. The choice was between sandals and cowboy boots—in other words, no choice.

The array of leathers, colors, and decoration was mind-boggling—plain or embroidered cowhide, horsehide, goat, ostrich, alligator, lizard, and snake in every color of the rainbow.

The unfamiliar higher heels caused some mild vertigo and would take practice to move about in confidently. The tall shaft would also require some getting used to, but the boots were certainly durable.

They even tried on cowboy hats, but decided that would be taking things a step too far. If they'd understood about the desert sun, they would've gotten hats. But it would take some more hard knocks to gain that bit of wisdom.

The final decision was to splurge on warm, waterproof, and windproof sheepskin jackets. The coats were beautiful and extremely expensive. By unspoken agreement they pretended not to notice the lavish fringe and beading.

They were almost to the register when Sundance snagged a *Hoodoo You Love?* t-shirt. Butch laughed and picked up one that said, *Take a Hike!*

They weren't totally averse to being forced to adopt a dude ranch aesthetic, although they'd never admit it to each other. They both secretly thought the new style was pretty cool.

They hoped the gear made them look like off-duty bull riders or bronco busters. Less charitable people might've suggested rodeo clowns.

They went to the men's room to change into the new clothes and cram their old duds into the trash.

When they left the store they walked a little slower and a little more bowlegged, in a way they thought might help them fit in. Amazingly, it worked. As they sauntered back to their car, a guy gave them a polite nod. It was the first respectful interaction they'd had on the hideous trip.

So, who knew? Maybe their luck was changing.

***

Gerd asked Alex to stop on the way to their hotel because he wanted to buy some alcoholic beverages for the group to celebrate their amazing day together. "Sure," Alex said. "We go right by a store."

As they were entering Ruby's Alex paused to hold the door open for a couple of guys in ridiculous looking cowboy outfits. He nodded in a friendly way and they gave a quick nod in reply.

The guests shopped the amazing store and got back into the church van. The fact that a church group was loaded down with an impressive array of booze did not go without notice. A woman stood nearby in the parking lot frowning at them. Alex restrained himself from saying, *It's for the poor.*

***

Alex drove the group to the town of Tropic where Steve and their accommodations awaited. The guests were delighted by the charming row of individual log cabins. Without even thinking about it they helped get their own luggage out of the trailer that was parked nearby.

Steve handed out keys and they all went to their rooms to take long, hot showers and change clothes. They'd regroup in the parking lot an hour later to walk to a restaurant that stood a few dozen yards down the road.

*****

After they'd scrubbed the mud out of their hair and off their hides, the men hesitantly changed into the new duds. Then the Sicilian cowboys hopped into their motorized Mustang and rode off into the sunset to make another check of hotel parking lots.

They rode the range, such as it was, looking for strays, but came up dry. They drove to the town of Tropic and took a look, but they couldn't find the van there either.

At this point they'd checked every parking lot for miles to no avail and they were exhausted, so they decided to give up for the night and get a couple of steaks at Ruby's Buffet before putting the Mustang in the corral, heading to the bunk house, and hitting the hay.

Despite everything that had happened to them, the guys felt optimistic about finding the van. It was bound to be somewhere along *The All American Highway*. Where else could it be?

*****

After dinner the tour group went to Gerd's cabin to have a couple of drinks together. Again, Gerd and Alex were modest in their consumption.

Steve and Peter, as usual, had no alcohol, but Alex had made certain that they could share in the party atmosphere by buying them some fizzy water and carbonated grape juice to toast with in celebration of their survival and rescue.

Chapter 13

The reasonably refreshed cowpokes saddled up at 6:30 the next morning. As former night owls they hated having to wake up early, but they needed to get this thing over with. They estimated that the tour group's journey would resume at around eight.

Their plan was to get ahead of the group, then wait for them at their first stop of the day which, according to the online itinerary was Kodachrome State Park. So, in the predawn darkness, they took hot showers, got dressed like a coupla buckaroos, and headed out.

The men had no way of knowing that the group's itinerary had shifted on account of the wreck or that they were now travelling in a church van.

They made a brief stop at Clarke's Country Market in Tropic to get some coffee and donuts, oblivious to the fact that the objects of their search were blissfully asleep in private cabins only half a block away.

Butch and Sundance drove slowly along the road through Tropic, scanning the vehicles as they went.

***

Alex wanted the guests to be able to get a good rest after the crazy night and day, so he set the departure time to ten.

Klaus, Elisabeth, Gerd, and Peter were early birds, though, so they were up well before then and sitting together eating breakfast at a table next to a window in the hotel coffee shop.

Elisabeth happened to be looking out the window and saw the muddy

Mustang slowly cruising by. "Look at that," she said. "Why would anyone drive in such a car filthy with mud! Americans are pigs."

Out of politeness, Klaus, Peter, and Gerd glanced toward the car, then quickly turned their attention back to their muesli and yogurt.

After creeping through Cannonville and performing parking lot checks, Butch and Sundance reached Kodachrome Basin State Park. They paid the entrance fee and were unsettled by how engaging the ranger was at the small building next to the gate.

"People so friendly out here," Butch said. "It creeps me out."

They turned into the parking lot adjacent to the entrance because they wanted to make sure they wouldn't miss a single vehicle that came through. Nothing would distract them this time. A coupla hours at the most and they'd be headed back to Vegas.

Neither of them said anything, but no matter how much of a rush they were in, they both knew they'd be stopping somewhere on the way back to get some respectable threads before presenting themselves and the memory gadget to the Boss.

They positioned the car for the best view of the entrance and started munching on their donuts in earnest.

After a while the ranger came out of his kiosk and walked over to their car. This made both men instantly wary. When he reached the car, Butch rolled the window down.

"Are you gentlemen looking for something?" the ranger asked.

"Why're ya askin'?" said Butch.

"You drove in here twenty minutes ago," he said. "You're still here and neither of you have gotten out of your car. Do you need directions?"

"Uh, ... yeah! That's it!" said Sundance. "Ya know any hikes?"

The ranger did a double take, then smiled, and said, "Of course I do. I work here! What kind of hike are you looking for?"

"Whaddya mean?" Sundance replied.

"I mean do you want a long or short hike, easy or difficult terrain, landscape views or wildlife?"

The ranger was actually extremely familiar with this level of cluelessness and was sincerely happy to help people who'd spent their entire lives on concrete and asphalt. He considered it his calling in life to serve this demographic in particular.

"Uh, ... nice views would be great!" Sundance said.

The ranger asked for the map he'd given them and pointed out the Panorama Trail.

"Can we see the entrance from there?" Sundance asked.

The ranger had never been asked this particular question before and it confused him. "Why would you want to see the entrance from there?"

"He's just scared of gettin' lost," Butch said. "Fuggeddaboudit. Thanks for your help officer."

Butch fired up the 'stang and drove away.

The ranger stood, bewildered, watching them drive slowly down the road in a preposterous sports car. *Those are two really strange guys*, he thought— northeastern accents, touristy cowboy clothes, driving an expensive vehicle that was being destroyed by the terrain.

***

Butch and Sundance drove to the parking lot near the Panorama Trailhead and stopped again. Sundance offered to hike the trail while Butch waited in the car, in case the ranger came to check on them.

Butch agreed to stay and keep watch.

"Honk when you see 'em," Sundance said, and he strode off at a peppy pace in his painful new pointy-toed boots. He hoped he could get a good view of the park from the trail.

He could be like an Indian scout—sorta like Tonto to Butch's Lone Ranger. The thought pleased him.

He walked across the road and entered a juniper and piñon pine forest. The trail led into a narrow canyon. Sundance enjoyed getting some exercise after so much time in the car. And he needed a break. It wasn't easy being around a guy like Butch 24/7. He had a bad temper.

***

Butch was bored outta his gourd. He checked his cell phone. Of course there was no service in this particular hellhole.

Sundance continued walking uphill along the narrow trail. He hadn't taken any water with him and, although it wasn't very warm yet, the dry desert air was making him thirsty. All he'd had to drink was coffee.

After about twenty minutes he reached the top. He was pleased to discover that he could see a fair portion of the park from the lookout.

While he was enjoying the view and the beautiful colors of the rock, the rising temperatures were roasting Butch. He couldn't take it anymore, so he got out of the car and went to sit at a nearby picnic table. From there he'd be able to see any vehicles that came by.

Meanwhile back in Tropic the tour group was ready to return to Bryce for a hike through the world famous landscape.

"You can actually see Bryce Canyon from where we are," said Alex, and he pointed to the red rock formations peeking out from behind the forest above the town of Tropic.

"If we wanted to, we could hike from here to the rim in a few hours."

They discussed that option but decided to drive back to the park and take a shorter walk among the flamboyant spires.

Steve drove them to Sunset Point. "This'll be a two or three hour hike," Alex said. "Be sure to bring plenty of water and some snacks."

Steve would meet them at Bryce Point and afterwards they'd have a picnic.

"I will stay and read this time," said Frida. "If that is allowed."

"Of course," said Steve.

She'd gotten to a great part of the first Longmire book, Chapter 12 of *A Cold Dish*. The sheriff, Walt, was trying to save a badly injured friend during a terrible snowstorm. He was having a riveting mystical or hallucinatory experience and she wanted to see how it turned out.

The group headed down the zigzagging Navajo Trail, taking photos as they went. "Don't forget to enjoy *the real thing* while taking all those pictures," Alex reminded them.

They hiked through a slot canyon and scrambled around some huge rocks. "These particular rocks fell into the canyon just a few years ago," said Alex. "It took almost two years to clear them enough to reopen the trail after they shifted."

The fact that a huge rockfall like they were hiking through could happen again at any time, especially after a severe winter, was a disturbing piece of information. Alex could tell it had set the group on edge, but he thought it was important to tell it like it was.

"In national parks people sometimes think they're in Disneyland," he said. "But this is not Imagineering. It's not under anyone's control. It's a wilderness.

"Everything here is still moving and changing. A rock could tumble and alter the appearance of this canyon at any moment. If you're lucky you won't be in the way, but if you're having a bad day in a place like this you might die."

"We're like ants here," said Gerd.

After the warning the guests glanced up nervously every few steps, checking if the rocks above them looked stable. They were clearly relieved when they got to a more open area.

***

The beauty of Bryce gradually worked its magic on the little group. It made them forget their everyday worries and soothed the trauma of the previous hours. Around every corner they found new fairy chimneys that looked like sculptures created by madmen.

They hiked through a dry wash and then started uphill along the Peekaboo Trail. Halfway up the first incline they had to move to one side of the path to let people riding mules go by.

"That looks uncomfortable," said Elisabeth. "Tonight they will be sore and sorry they did not walk."

Alex didn't agree. He knew many people enjoyed trying a bit of riding while on a western trip, but he didn't say anything. It would've been wasted breath.

Chapter 14

Butch awoke when Sundance called his name. He lurched into a sitting position, surprised to find Sundance looming over him. He'd apparently gone from sitting at the picnic table to lying on it and then fallen asleep.

"I'm climbin' a mountain to see if I can get a look at the roads and you're down here havin' a siesta? What's wrong witcha?"

"I'da woken up if anybody'd come by."

Sundance wasn't sure that was true, but he decided to let it go.

It was now noon. The two discussed the situation. They were forced to assume the group must've skipped this part of the tour. They decided to drive farther down Highway 12 and see if they could spot them.

They hardly slowed as they breezed through the microscopic towns of Cannonville and Henrieville. "Why do these places even waste money on a sign?" Butch asked as they went through yet another hamlet.

Sundance had no answer. He'd wondered the same thing himself. Why bother? The town was over before you realized you were there.

When the two mafiosos left Vegas they hadn't anticipated a road trip. Nevertheless, despite all the discomforts and inconveniences, and the failure to accomplish their mission, they couldn't avoid being charmed by the scenery. Even Butch was starting to notice it.

"You know this nature stuff," Sundance said, "after a while it starts to get to ya."

Butch nodded, and then shrugged, as if to apologize for agreeing.

***

The group finally made it up to the rim at Bryce Point, some of them were more tired than others, but all were glad to have done the hike. Steve was waiting patiently for them at the trail's end. He led them to the van where Frida had enjoyed some quiet time alone, reading, and they went back to Sunset Point to have their lunch.

Alex, Steve, and several of the guests were sitting at a picnic table when Gerd and Georg came toward them chugging from open beer cans. "Guys, guys," Steve said, "In Utah it's illegal to have open containers of alcohol in the parks."

The two men looked at him in surprise.

"Yeah," Alex said, "In more than half the states it's illegal to have open containers of alcohol in a public place. In almost all the states it's illegal to have open containers of alcohol inside a vehicle, even if you're a passenger."

Alex knew how important a beer could be to German hikers, especially to those from southern Germany where it was common to have a beer for lunch, even if you were going back to work afterwards.

"Get rid of the cans," he said. "Pour the beer into a water bottle."

The two men were surprised, but they did as he suggested.

***

Butch and Sundance made a quick trip to the Escalante Petrified Forest parking lot to hunt for the van, but it wasn't there, so they kept going. "How could they just disappear?" Butch said. "How could that even happen? There's not a lotta roads out here. It duddn't make any sense."

"Yeah, who knew nature was such a big place," said Sundance. He'd flown over it from Las Vegas to New Jersey and back, but usually on a red eye, and he'd never paid much attention.

They continued to the next point of interest on the group's itinerary. It was Devil's Backbone.

When they arrived at yet another tiny town—Boulder, Utah, population 180—they drove to the Hills & Hollows Market, a gas station up on a rise overlooking Highway 12.

"Get us some water and somethin' to eat," said Butch, as he started filling the gas tank. "I'll watch the road."

Sundance got out of the car and headed for the store.

"And bring me a bag of Chex," he called out. "The savory kind. I gotta have some salt."

***

The tour group finished their lunch and boarded the van to continue to their next stop—the Bristlecone Trail near Rainbow Point. The route went through a dense forest up to a ridge where they could see some of the world's oldest trees.

"The Bristlecone Pines here at Bryce are about 1,800 years old," said Alex. "The ones in the White Mountains of California are over 4,000 years old. And they're still alive!"

The guests examined the bristlecones with simultaneous awe and disappointment. The trees looked every bit of their great age. The trunks were gnarled and the limbs were pitifully misshapen and scraggly.

"If you had not pointed these out, I would have passed them by without a second thought," said Peter.

It was the longest utterance any of them had ever heard him make. He had a beautiful, resonant baritone voice. Tina gave him a double-take, then a triple-take. She wondered if maybe she'd missed some potential there.

***

Butch and Sundance decided to linger and eat a late lunch at the gas station. Locals and tourists walked in and out of the store while the two men sat outside on a couple of chairs underneath an overhanging roof.

They stayed until five o'clock and still didn't see the van.

They consulted Google Maps again and drove farther along Highway 12 until they found a pullout where they could wait beside the road up on Boulder Mountain.

The itinerary on the tour company's website didn't give any clues as to where the group would be staying, but there weren't many towns with lodging before the next day's main attraction, Capitol Reef National Park.

As the sun was setting they decided to drive down to the next town which happened to be the last one before Capitol Reef. Butch was letting Sundance drive and he enjoyed navigating the many switchbacks. The Mustang was designed for just that kind of workout.

Then, just as he rounded a turn, a mule deer leaped out of a ditch and onto the road. It was being chased by a coyote. Sundance slammed on the brakes and swerved. Both deer and coyote made it across, but the Mustang wasn't as lucky. The right front edge clipped a tree.

When they came to a stop, Butch mumbled, "Take a look, will ya?"

Sundance got out to inspect the damage. "Headlight cover's broke," he said, gesturing at the passenger side. He squatted down to look closer. "The bulb, too."

He got back in the car. "Was that a wolf?" Sundance said. "Do ya think he did that on purpose? It looked like he was tryin' to get us to whack that deer for 'im. Save 'im some work."

"No idea," Butch said. "That'd be the smart move, though."

They resumed their search. Nothing was said for the next few minutes. Sundance was grateful that Butch was in no position to lecture him about damaging the car.

It was no fun to drive after dark with only one headlight in such a sparsely populated area. Sundance was forced to slow down. At the reduced speed they could see how much wildlife movement there was on and near the roads at twilight.

When they got to yet another of the 200-person towns, this one Torrey, Utah, they looked for the van at the handful of hotels, but again, nada. They were starving by this point, so they decided to grab a bite and ended up at a deli inside the general store at Austin's Chuck Wagon Motel.

***

At the same time the Wild West Adventure Tour group was having a pleasant dinner and spending their second night comfortably ensconced in their individual cabins in Tropic, Butch and Sundance were cruising aimlessly, totally baffled.

There were only a few parks, each had a limited number of parking lots, and the towns were tiny. This wasn't Vegas—the food and lodging options were severely limited.

"I don't get it," said Sundance. "From the surveillance video, we know the driver and the other guy don't even know they got the thingamajig! So it's not like they're tryin' to run off with it. They're just doin' their thing.

"They got no idea we're after 'em, so they're not tryin' to hide from us."

Butch nodded.

"It don't make no sense," Sundance said. "How can we not be catchin' up with a bunch of tourists who aren't even runnin' from us?"

"Maybe we got this figured all wrong," said Butch. "Maybe one of 'em does know what they got. Maybe one a tha people signed up for the trip ain't really a tourist."

"Maybe it would help if we knew what we're after," said Sundance. "Maybe we should ask the Capo."

"I ain't askin' the Capo nothin'," Butch said. "Does it matter what kinda info the thing's got on it?"

"I dunno! 'Cause I got no idea what kinda files we're talkin'" said Sundance. "I mean is it drugs? Is it porn? Is it blackmail stuff? Is it somethin' like, you know, scientific?"

There was no scenario they could comprehend where they wouldn't have crossed paths with the tour group at least once. Butch would've liked to set up a roadblock. Turning a car sideways in the middle of a highway wasn't beyond the realm of possibility for a guy like him, but he didn't know where to do it.

He was seriously afraid of what the Capo was going to do to him if he let him down.

The men had no idea that the problem was as simple as that they were ahead of the target instead of behind it. They consulted a map again and made a plan for the next day.

They decided that the only places that would've made sense for the group to have spent the night were Boulder, Torrey, Teasdale, or Bicknel. All of those towns were near Highway 12, which became Highway 24 west of Torrey.

All of those towns were west of Capitol Reef.

"We're lucky there's not that many roads out here," Sundance said. "Once we get away from the towns there's nowhere for 'em to go."

"You're right," said Butch.

There were a couple of dirt roads into Capitol Reef. The henchmen assumed the tour group would've taken Highway 12 which was the only paved road through the park. That meant they would leave the park heading west toward Hanksville.

All other options would've meant a detour that involved several additional hours of driving. They decided to wait for the group just before Hanksville and then follow them north to Goblin Valley and confront them when they stopped.

The two slept at Austin's Chuck Wagon Motel. The next morning they scarfed down a hearty breakfast in the motel deli and left town at nine.

They drove for nearly an hour and made it almost to Hanksville when Sundance urgently needed a restroom break. Butch pulled the Mustang to a stop on a dirt road just off Highway 24 near another of the typical desert dry washes.

Once they were stopped they realized that this was as good a spot as any to wait for the group. They'd be able to conceal the car behind some rocks and take turns watching the road from a nearby hill. The one who wasn't watching would be able to wait in the shade of some scrubby vegetation.

This job was turning out to be one long rolling stakeout. It was making them crazy—and not just them. The Boss was bound to be furious. They didn't dare drop the ball on this. Their profession wasn't known for its forgiveness of mistakes.

Chapter 15

The tour group reached Kodachrome Basin State Park at nine in the morning and Alex took them on a hike along the Panorama Trail. For an hour they immersed themselves in the strange products of eons of erosion, particularly the tall white sandstone columns, called sand pipes, found nowhere else on earth.

The weird beauty of Kodachrome was followed by a stop at the Escalante Petrified Forest where the landscape was even more eerie.

"It's illegal to take rocks out of this park," Alex said. "But there's another reason you shouldn't remove any rocks from here as souvenirs. There's quite a bit of historical evidence that there's a curse on anyone who takes a rock from here when they leave. So, for both reasons, don't do it."

They stopped to take a close look at a large petrified tree lying near a parking lot. "The wood was buried by natural processes," Alex said, "and over a period of thousands of years of lying in a stream or a river, minerals were washed into the wood, gradually replacing it with agate and quartz.

"When it's dry it doesn't look very colorful. It's easier to see how pretty the stone is when it's wet or polished. Let's hike up to the plateau. There are some nice views from there and along the way you can see a lot more petrified wood."

Steve loved to hike and this time the logistics allowed him to join the group. It was still early and not particularly hot yet, but on the way up everyone was sweating and out of breath.

"Can you imagine how hot it gets here in the summer?" Alex said. "This is May!"

He pointed out an array of smallish round black stones lying around where they stood. The average size was from a marble to a ping pong ball. "They've recently discovered similar looking stones on Mars. They call them *Martian Blueberries*.

"They have a hard shell of oxidized iron ore, hematite, wrapped around a sandstone core. They're sometimes called *Moqui Marbles*. *Moqui* or *Moki* means *dead* in the Hopi language. It's a slang name for the Hopi people. We don't know the origin of the word, but we should probably stop using it."

When they reached the top of the plateau they rested. Some of the group sat on the ancient petrified logs.

"There's a good hike from here," Alex said, "but we don't want to take it unless all of you think you'll be able to manage a steep trail with an uneven surface.

"If you're up for it, I promise you'll see the best petrified logs in the park," he said. "Because the slope is so steep, a lot of ground cover is washed away during the wet seasons. So the logs there get exposed by erosion."

Only Gerd, Georg, and Elisabeth wanted to join Alex on the hike, so Steve said he'd take the rest of the group back to the picnic area and wait. They'd meet up there later to go have lunch beside the Wide Hollow reservoir.

As they were preparing to split up, Alex got a call from the tour company owner, Ellen. She had great news.

"I'll drive to Moab tomorrow and drop off a new van," she said. "And I'll pick up the church van and return it to Cedar City. A driver will pick me up in Cedar City."

Alex was glad they'd been stopped atop the mesa where there was cell service. He relayed the good news.

***

Butch and Sundance took turns standing as lookouts while the other rested in the shade. The brutal midday sun hammered down. Not being familiar with outdoor activities, especially not ones that involved prolonged daytime work, it hadn't occurred to either of them to buy sunscreen.

They'd made several big mistakes. Another of them became clear by one o'clock when they ran out of water.

***

A leisurely picnic in the shade beside the reservoir refreshed the tour group. They were ready to continue through the town of Escalante. Alex revived the post-lunch sleepiness by stopping off at the Kiva Coffee House.

The café was poised on the rim of a cliff overlooking a canyon carved by the Escalante River. It was the perfect place at the perfect time for a shot of caffeine.

Afterwards they drove down into the canyon and took another hike along the river. They saw some bighorn sheep in the distance, but it became unpleasantly hot during the long walk. Finally, they reached Calf Creek Falls, a pretty waterfall behind some trees that provided some welcome shade.

***

It was 3:30 and Butch and Sundance were still spelling each other as they kept watch on the road. Both men were horribly sunburned and dizzy from dehydration.

The situation was intolerable. They hadn't anticipated their needs and taken measures to meet them because they'd never had to work in wilderness.

One thing was clear. They couldn't go much longer without water. They were desperate to go get some, but they dreaded getting into the car. The black beast had been parked in full sun. The interior would be broiling.

When Sundance opened the passenger door a wave of heat forced him backwards. Butch waited for a few seconds, then sat sideways on the blistering seat just long enough to start the car. He got up immediately and stood as he pressed the switches to roll the windows down.

Neither of them was in any shape to drive, and they hated to abandon their post, but they couldn't take it anymore. Butch reached for the pair of gloves all career criminals kept in the glovebox and stoically took the wheel as soon as it had cooled enough for him to be able to keep hold of it.

The irony of the elegant name for the storage area now being accurate mostly for thugs never occurred to him.

He had a hard time keeping the car on the road. When they crossed the muddy Fremont River they resisted the urge to stop and take a dip, and even a sip, but they knew Hanksville was nearby, so they pressed on. It was an unpleasant drive. They were so dehydrated they were dizzy, not to mention headachy, exhausted, and barely able to focus.

They made it to the town and to the Bull Mountain Market. They went inside, grabbed an eight-pack of water from the fridge, tossed some bills onto the counter, and chugged an entire bottle each. Then they went outside where they each emptied another bottle over their heads.

They got back into the car and started the engine so they could run the air conditioning. They sat there drinking another two bottles apiece, trying to recover, neither saying a word.

***

After the long, hot walk the hikers made it back to their van. Elisabeth's constant whining was getting on everyone's nerves. Georg, her husband, seemed like a nice guy and he tried to head off her endless litany of grievances, but was only marginally successful.

Frida extracted a small cookie from her bag and offered it to Elisabeth.

The old bat grabbed it and ate it without thanking her.

The group cooled down and snacked and rested as they drove on. Up on Boulder Mountain they made two more brief stops to take in the view. There was certainly nothing to compare to it at home in Berlin, Paris, or Vienna. Spain had Europe's only desert, but it was a lot smaller and long way from Barcelona.

Butch's temper was fraying. "You're not payin' attention," said Butch. "I bet you were sleepin' on the job!"

"*You're* the one who was sleepin' on the job," Sundance reminded him.

The argument was a sign that they were recovering from their harsh encounter with Mother Nature. They eventually got themselves together enough to go back into the store and stock up on bottled water, fruit juice, energy drinks, and snacks that wouldn't melt.

They agreed to relocate their surveillance to Goblin Valley. That was the last stop for the day on the group's itinerary. They encountered some warnings of road construction on the main highway north. *Single Lane*, the sign warned, *Expect Delays.*

They turned west to check the Goblin Valley parking lot, but the van wasn't there. They waited, but the group didn't show up.

They saw a sign that touted a road as an alternate route to I-70. It was a dirt road. They glanced at each other, Sundance shrugged, so Butch took the alternate.

***

As the tour group stood atop Boulder Mountain taking in the view, Alex said, "Here's a nice bit of trivia for you." He pointed into the distance, and said, "Those are the Henry Mountains. That was the last mountain range in the U.S. to get an official name."

Steve glanced at the mountains, but then noticed the sky north of where Alex was pointing. He studied the dark clouds with an expert eye.

"Wow," he said. "You wouldn't wanna be in Goblin Valley or the San Rafael Swell right now. They're gonna have some serious flooding over there."

There was a flash of lightning in the clouds, followed several seconds later by a loud boom and rolling thunder. "We're extremely lucky we had to change our schedule," Steve said, "If we hadn't, that's where we'd be now!"

That eased Steve's conscience. The delay and rescheduling had protected them from a serious problem. *You never know what's gonna happen next*, he thought to himself.

He was more right about that than he knew.

***

Butch and Sundance made their way along the poorly-maintained dirt road. They passed an empty campground and the road got even worse. Parts of it were washed out from the previous rainy season and it looked like no repairs had been done.

They were making terrible time. The low clearance of the Mustang meant they had to go slow. And because they were fixated on the road, they didn't realize a storm was approaching.

The car bottomed out for a moment. There was a bang, followed by the screech of twisting metal, and the engine noise changed from a deep growl to the ear-splitting roar of a monster truck.

Butch didn't dare stop until he'd cleared the high center. When he was able to glance in the rear view mirror he could see the car's muffler lying in the middle of the dirt track.

He stopped and they got out, shouting at each other about the damage. There was nothing either of them could do to fix it, but that didn't stop them from arguing.

Only the first splats of rain put an end to their squabbling.

Within seconds the downpour was being driven so hard by the wind that the drops were painful. They jumped back into the Mustang and resumed their journey across the harsh terrain assaulted by the torrential rain from above and the racket of five hundred unmuffled horses from below.

There was no way to escape either problem. Wild West indeed.

Water was running in rivulets along the desert floor. The pools that were created made it hard to evaluate the depth of the many potholes. The ride was bone-jarring. The stiff sports car suspension and lightly padded racing seats did not make for a comfy ride.

They came to a wash where the runoff was flooding across the road. It was obviously too deep for them to drive through. They decided to turn around and head back to Highway 24.

That would've been a good idea, but they'd waited too long to make it. Before they could reach the road to Goblin Valley they encountered another flash flood that had washed away parts of the road.

Now they understood why it was called a *wash*.

They were well and truly trapped. So much water had dropped from the sky there was no way to make it through these insta-rivers.

The duo sat in the car on a patch of slightly higher ground and watched the water rise. Butch beat his head against the steering wheel, saying, "I… hate… this… place!"

Chapter 16

While the tour group enjoyed a pleasant dinner in Torrey, Butch and Sundance were preparing to spend another night in their car out in the middle of nowhere, this time with a very real fear of being drowned during the night. It was difficult to gauge the depth and velocity of the water in the dark and they had no way to predict how deep it might get as the hours wore on.

The best they could do to gain some altitude was to climb on top of the car, and they did that, but it was too uncomfortable in such a deluge, so they got back inside and sat there, wet, miserable, afraid to go to sleep, and too tired to stay awake.

It was hot and muggy inside and their breath fogged the windows completely. It was like being in a submarine.

The harsh reality of the desert—the darkness in the canyons, the absolute solitude—was freaking them out. They hadn't actually read the story and they didn't know many particulars, but they were Italian, so they were aware that one of their own, a guy named Dante, had written a story about a trip like this.

Neither of them could remember how it turned out.

***

Butch and Sundance passed a rough night.

The temperature dropped to 47° F. They put on the fancy sheepskin coats. They'd gotten soft in Vegas and weren't used to the cold.

"How is it possible for a vacation place to be this awful?" Butch said. "Shake, bake, soak, and freeze—all in one day!"

They kept the windows up on account of the rain. Their situation became more oppressive as the hours dragged by.

They turned the engine on and ran the heater, but they were afraid to use much gas because they knew they'd need it to get out of the desert. And without a muffler the racket from the engine was so loud it wasn't even worth it.

"I'd rather freeze to death!" shouted Sundance.

Butch agreed.

The rain clouds finally moved off so they could open the windows, but the water level in the wash remained high.

"Why's there this much water when it stopped rainin' hours ago?" Sundance mused.

Butch was too depressed to formulate a response.

The only bright spot in the otherwise unmitigated disaster was the amazing night sky after the rain moved out. "Look at that," Sundance said.

"What?" Butch mumbled, hoping it was the tour group so he could end this torture.

"The stars!" Sundance said. "Look at 'em. I never knew there was that many of 'em."

Butch glanced up with a disinterested frown that instantly turned into an expression of wonder. Sundance was right—the stars were incredible. Even transcendent. He crossed himself and gawked at the sparkling glory of the Milky Way.

Sundance reached around to wipe off the windshield on his side and then sat transfixed.

Sundance pondered this polar opposite of the Las Vegas Strip. It was a heavenly Strip. The Un-Vegas. Natural light that pierced the night and put Caesars Palace to shame.

Hours later the sun rose from behind the weird formations and painted the landscape a flaming red. That, too, was amazing to see. The color vibrated across the sand and rocks and made them seem alive.

After such a surreal and stressful night, Butch wouldn't have been surprised if some of the formations had started walking around like that superhero made of rock in the comic books he'd read as a kid.

Now that the sun was out, the temperatures began to increase, but it would take a while for it to warm up enough to be comfortable. The wash still looked impassable and for all they knew the situation wasn't likely to change in the next few hours, if ever.

They decided to turn around again and see what the story was at the other wash. The road was really muddy in a few places and several times they almost got stuck on account of having only two-wheel drive. The low slung car bottomed out a couple more times, too.

They dreaded what the Capo was gonna say when he saw what they'd done to the pricey vehicle, but at the moment they had more pressing concerns. Right now they just wanted to make it out of the desert alive.

When they reached the other wash they saw that it was still impassable, too, but the water level at this one wasn't as high as the other one. They decided to wait there.

Butch leaned his seat back and tried to take a nap.

At nine in the morning Alex and Steve loaded the guests' luggage before leaving for Capitol Reef National Park. They checked the weather forecast as usual. There'd been a hard rain during the night and a flash flood warning had been issued for the area.

The rain had cleared, but the flooding hadn't peaked yet. They'd have to be cautious about where they tried to go. Plenty of hikers had been killed in flash floods in the canyons, even experienced ones.

They paused at Chimney Rock for photos then entered the Reef. They asked about driving conditions at the visitor center and learned that the park roads had been hit hard during the night.

Usually on this tour they'd hike the Grand Wash. Steve asked about it and the ranger echoed his concern that it would be dangerous, if not impassable. So they chose to drop off the trailer and drive along the scenic road to Fuita.

When the group reached a wash that Alex and Steve knew from experience was dry during most of the year—and saw that it was flooded—they knew they'd made the right decision by not attempting to hike through the Grand Wash.

Water was running across the paved road, smearing mud everywhere. They'd be able to make it across the short, shallow sections of the scenic drive, but they wouldn't be able to make it much farther, especially not across the stretch where the paving ended and the road was just dirt. That dusty track would be a mud flat now with rivers running through it at intervals.

They decided to drive back to the historic town of Fruita. There they could have a second breakfast or an early lunch at the Gifford Homestead, a historic farmhouse where you could get fresh pie.

It had warmed up and become a beautiful day by the time Steve and Alex were taking the coolers out of the van and setting up a meal on a picnic table in front of the farmhouse while the group shopped in the small store.

***

The water level was dropping in the wash. Butch and Sundance fumed as they waited. Their anger, laced with fear and frustration, was near homicidal. But they couldn't do anything about it.

Suddenly a small pickup truck with government license plates drove up. Two women in their early twenties got out and approached the Mustang. One was blonde and the other was brunette.

"You fellas stuck?" said the brunette.

"Sure looks like it," said the blonde.

"What are you lovely ladies doin' out here in the middle of nowhere?" Sundance asked, in typical Vegas goombah glib style.

"We could ask you the same thing, especially in this!" said the brunette, gesturing at the Mustang. She bent down to look underneath the low slung car.

The blonde answered his question, "We're working."

"Oh *really*," Sundance said, smiling. "On what exactly are you workin'?"

"A science project in the San Rafael Swell," she said.

"Well, that sounds swell," Sundance joked, but neither of the women appeared to notice his quip.

"The storm that hit last night caused a flash flood that destroyed our camp," said the blonde. "We were lucky we'd seen the weather report and were prepared to get to higher ground. We sheltered at one of the old Oyler uranium mines."

"No wonder you ladies are glowing," Sundance said. "You're simply radiant."

The brunette snorted at that. Sundance's technique was not going to work with either of them.

"Getting outta here will take a couple more hours, if you can make it at all," said the blonde.

Sundance looked at her with a worried frown, suddenly serious. "What if we don't make it?" he asked.

"All we can do is wait," she said. "We filed our research plan with the main office, so if we don't show up BLM law enforcement or a ranger will come looking for us, eventually!"

She turned around and went back to the pickup truck.

The fact that they were now trapped with the two attractive women was an unexpected development. The guys were bored outta their minds in the Godforsaken place. At least now they had some company.

But in consideration of their limited food and drinking water supplies the men were still worried. Butch jumped out of the Mustang and walked toward the blonde, who was opening the door of the truck.

"Wait a minute!" he called out, "What do you mean *eventually*? How long could it take 'til they come find us?" he asked.

"Well, this isn't a very heavily trafficked road," she said, "especially when flash flooding has been predicted. People will be avoiding these muddy places.

"The closest cattle ranch is about twenty miles north," she said, "so, right now, nobody has a reason to come down here."

"Don'tcha have a radio or somethin'?" Butch asked.

"We did. At our camp," she said.

She seemed to enjoy Butch's increasing frustration.

"But no worries," she said, "We'll make it outta here somehow."

She got in the truck, closed the door, and resumed conversation with her co-worker. Butch couldn't hear what they were saying, but he heard the laughter. Dismayed, he went back to the Mustang.

"Howzit lookin'?" Sundance asked.

Butch stared at the roiling water in the wash, and said, "Not great."

Chapter 17

The tour group finished their brunch and boarded the van. They picked up the trailer they'd left at the visitor center lot and continued through the park.

On their way along Highway 24 near the Fremont River they passed through the historic orchards of Fruita. They stopped at the old Fruita Schoolhouse to take a peek into the small building, and later they viewed some of the petroglyphs in the valley.

When they crossed the Grand Wash where they'd originally intended to hike, they saw the running water. They'd made the right decision. Today they'd need waders to make it through.

The Fremont River looked like a liquid version of the Reef. It was running high and fast with brown, red, and beige water. They made a final stop in the park at the Behunin Cabin, an old one-room stone cabin built in 1883 to house Mr. and Mrs. Behunin and eleven of their thirteen children. The two older kids had slept in small caves nearby.

The group stared at the tiny one-room building, unable to imagine how difficult life must have been there in the old days. "What happened to them?" Peter asked.

"They had to abandon the cabin and move on because of the recurring flooding that destroyed their crops. This valley has flooded so deep that livestock have been washed down-river."

By the time they got to Deep Creek it looked like a lake.

***

Butch and Sundance fell asleep. It had been another rough night. They were physically, mentally, and emotionally exhausted.

When Sundance woke up he saw the women were out of the truck and talking. They went toward the wash. It still had water running through it, but it was obvious, even to him, that it was significantly shallower now.

Both women were carrying shovels and using them to test how deep the water was. The blonde called out, "You guys wanna help us?"

"Sure!" Sundance said, without having a clue about what needed to be done. Then he woke Butch up.

A lot of the road had been washed away, but because the water level had receded they could see that the water wasn't the biggest problem anymore. It was the mud. If they tried to cross the lowest area they'd get stuck.

The women explained what they needed to do to fix the road so it would be drivable. "We'll have to dig small channels to drain the worst places," the brunette said, and started digging.

When the guys offered to do the heavy labor, she said, "No worries. There'll be plenty of work to go 'round,"

When the women finished digging the first two channels, the blonde said, "Okay, now you guys can move the mud into the drains."

"How?" Sundance asked.

"Use your hands and feet," she said.

The guys took off their boots and socks and walked barefoot into the cold mud, while the girls waded around in their water sandals. This experience was really bringing home the fact that life in a wilderness was different from life in a city. Nobody should come out to places like this unless they knew what they were doing and were prepared for contingencies.

Butch and Sundance clawed and kicked at the mud to try to move it into the stream of running water so it would be carried away. Soon all four of them were hard at work with hands and feet.

***

The tour group made a brief stop for snacks and a restroom in the tiny community of Hanksville. They were amazed by the Hollow Mountain Gas

Station, a famous landmark, now a convenience store, it operated out of a cave that had been carved into the orangey-red rock face.

After that they entered the surreal landscape of Goblin Valley.

They stopped to roam around amid the mushroom-shaped sandstone formations. "Southern Utah is packed with bizarre weather-worn places," said Alex. "There are lots of different names for the odd shapes, not just *hoodoos*, but also *fairy chimneys*, or *goblins.*

"This place was used as a filming location for *Galaxy Quest.*"

The guests agreed that it looked like an alien planet.

It took about an hour for the four of them to shift enough of the top layer of mud to expose the harder, drier ground beneath. "Alright, let's collect some rocks and brush, so we can use it to level the road a bit," said Sheila.

Sundance was proud to have finally gotten the blonde's name. They dispersed to forage for what was needed. The guys took instructions from the girls as to where and how to position the rocks and brush.

After another hour of hard labor it looked as though they might possibly be able to get the Mustang across the worst of it. Butch and Sundance looked like Mudmen of New Guinea, but they didn't care.

The girls said they'd go first. Then, if the Mustang got stuck, they had a tow rope they could use to help.

The truck made it across the mire with a minimum of fishtailing.

Then it was the guys' turn.

Sheila walked back across the wash to the Mustang. "It's still pretty slick," she said. "I wish we had something more to use for traction.

"How 'bout floor mats?" Sundance offered.

She took them and positioned them. "Got anything else?" she asked?

Butch shook his head.

"How about those coats," she said.

Butch and Sundance exchanged pained looks, then Butch reluctantly handed them over.

"Geez," Sundance mumbled.

When everything was in place, Sheila said, "Your best shot to make it all the way across is to not let up on the accelerator, no matter what."

Butch was at the wheel and he was nervous. He was a good driver, but he'd never driven in these conditions. And so far, their experience had been mostly bad. Decades spent in the canyons of Manhattan hadn't prepared him for even a single day in the canyons of Utah.

Of course he felt the additional pressure that any guy would feel when trying to not look like an idiot in front of a couple of cute girls. The situation was intense.

"Once you're in the mud," Sheila said, "don't try to wrestle with the steering wheel, keep up a steady pace, and don't even *think* about braking."

"Gotcha," Butch said, gritting his teeth. He didn't like getting survival advice from a young woman, even if he was in desperate need of it.

***

The tour group was heading out of Goblin Valley when they found themselves sitting in a long line of vehicles on the road leading to Highway 24.

Alex got out and trotted up to where a flagman was standing to see what the story was. When he returned to the van he had some bad news.

"He says it'll take about thirty minutes until they can re-open the road. A truck unloaded some heavy equipment in the wrong place. They're reloading the machines now."

As they crept forward Steve noticed a sign showing an alternate route to I-70. He pointed at it, and said, "Think it's dry enough yet?"

Alex shook his head. "It's not much fun when the conditions are good, but after that rain yesterday I'd say it's still an impassable muddy mess."

"Then we wait," Steve said.

***

It didn't look perfect, but it looked good enough to try.

Butch took a deep breath and pressed the accelerator. He entered the wash, splashed around wildly in the mud, got through it, and came out the other side.

But just as he cleared the worst patch the front spoiler scraped against the dry ground and made a loud cracking sound. The car bounced hard when the back wheels hit the same spot and damaged the exhaust system even more. But they made it across.

The men tried to hide how relieved they were to have escaped. Although they'd never admit it, neither of them could remember ever being so happy in their lives.

They waved to say *thank you* to the girls. The girls waved back and zoomed away.

Only now did the men realize the women would've been able to make it across the wash in their 4x4 high ground clearance truck without doing any road work at all. In fact, they didn't even need to go out that way.

But they'd stayed behind to help the two city slickers build a road that the Mustang could handle.

It was part of wise guy culture to both love and hate wise women. As mafia men they weren't programmed to handle role reversals well.

They were both profoundly humiliated by what had happened, and by the young female nature of the persons who'd rescued them from their own folly, but they were so relieved to get out of that cursed place, they let it pass without comment.

In the wilderness—you do whatcha gotta do.

The Mustang's unmuffled engine made so much racket they wouldn't have been surprised if their ears bled. It prevented any conversation between the car's occupants.

The road wasn't what you could call *good*, but they managed to make it to I-70 without any further problems.

Both of them were thrilled as they drove up the interstate ramp.

"What a relief to get out of that freakin' mudhole," Sundance said, but Butch couldn't hear him over the sound of the engine.

Chapter 18

It took a while for the tour group to make it through the construction zone to I-70. Because they were behind schedule and tired, they voted to skip the Thompson ghost town and Sego Canyon. Everyone was fine with heading directly to Moab.

Some of the guests fell asleep during the ride down a boring stretch of Highway 24. When they were on I-70 a tremendous racket drew everyone's attention, even the ones who'd been sleeping. "Was ist das für ein Lärm?" Elisabeth screeched, trying to be heard over the tremendous din.

Georg pointed at a slower moving vehicle that they were about to pass. It was a filthy, beat-up black Mustang. Steve was a conservative driver, almost never going over sixty-five, but he floored the van to get away from the ear-splitting sounds.

When they'd left it behind they were able to communicate again.

"I've seen that car before," Klaus said, "during breakfast in Tropic. I remember that license plate SINCITI."

"What a noisy piece of trash," Gerd said. "Don't they have vehicle inspections in the U.S.?"

"Why would anyone do that to such a nice car?" Tina said.

***

Butch hated going so slow on the interstate but he had to keep his speed down because otherwise the noise was literally intolerable. They needed to find a garage where they could get the muffler fixed as soon as possible. It was their new top priority.

They looked for a garage in Green River, but had no success finding one that had the parts in stock. A guy in a convenience store told them not to worry, that they'd be able to find a place in Moab because this type of accident was extremely common in *The Four-Wheeling Capitol of the World.*

Unfortunately it was fifty miles to Moab. They bought earplugs in the pharmacy aisle of a grocery store. Even then, every second of that drive was gonna be brutal.

***

The tour group made it to Moab and stopped at the Inca Inn on the north side of town. Ellen, Alex and Steve's boss, was already there and a replacement van was parked in front of Room 7.

Alex suggested they all have dinner at the Broken Oar, a block away on the other side of the road. The group agreed to meet outside the hotel at eight to walk over together.

As soon as the guests received their keys, most of them disappeared into their rooms to get ready for dinner. Only Tina, Klaus, and Gerd stayed outside on the porch to have a beer.

Steve and Alex went to Room 7 and knocked on the door. Ellen opened it and stood on the threshold smiling. She was clearly happy to see her employees in one piece.

"That must've been quite an adventure," she said. "I'm so happy we could solve the problem. The guests can…"

Her remarks were interrupted by a thunderous noise. They turned to look and saw the Mustang coming into town.

Klaus shouted to Gerd and Tina, "There's that car again!"

Further speech was pointless until it passed and got out of earshot.

When they were able to resume their chat, Ellen said she'd join the group for dinner. Then, after dinner, the guests could transfer their belongings to the new van. She'd be leaving early the next morning to drop the church van off in Cedar City. Then she'd be picked up by Daniel, one of the tour company's other drivers, and taken back to Oregon.

"We'll be making an early start, too," Alex said. "We'll have to do Arches and Canyonlands in one day, and then hustle to make it to the hotel in Durango. But then we'll be back on schedule for the rest of the trip."

Alex, Steve, and Ellen made a five-minute drive over to the City Market to buy sandwiches and other items for the group, so they could have a sunrise breakfast at Island in the Sky in Canyonlands.

The guests were going to hate having to get up at 4:30 to make it there before sunrise at six, but they'd love their reward. Mesa Arch was one of the most amazing places in the world to watch the sun come up.

***

Butch and Sundance were reduced to lip reading by the time they got to Moab. They were too hoarse to continue shouting and so deaf, they couldn't hear each other anyway. But they were able to find a Ford repair shop that agreed to work on the car.

"It'll be late afternoon tomorrow before the car's fixed!" the mechanic shouted so they could hear him.

Butch shrugged and nodded his acceptance. He was getting good at pantomime.

The men needed a place to crash in the interim, so they got a room at the Big Horn Lodge which was almost next door. But before they went to their room they crossed Main Street and walked a block to get some beer at the City Market.

They were disappointed to discover that the beer in Utah grocery stores was watered down to 3.2% alcohol—and said so to the clerk. "I hear ya," the guy said. "The Moab Brewery has the real deal, though, and it's just a coupla blocks down Main," he said, pointing in the same direction as their hotel.

They missed the details of the clerk's suggestion, but got the gist of it. This was welcome news indeed.

When Butch and Sundance left the City Market, Alex and Steve were still waiting at the deli counter for the group's breakfast sandwiches to be prepared.

Since they had to walk right by their hotel on the way to the Brewery, the guys checked in on the way and dropped off their gear. They'd have liked to get cleaned up, but they needed to get some food into them before they crashed for the night.

They enjoyed what seemed like the best dinner *ever* at the Brewery, stuffing themselves with food and ice cold beer. They deserved it after what they'd been through.

***

The tour group was in a particularly buoyant mood during dinner and afterwards Gerd suggested they try some of the local beer at the Brewery.

It sounded like a great idea until Alex said, "We have something special planned for tomorrow. At sunrise we'll be having breakfast at a great place inside Canyonlands National Park. That means we'll need to get up 4:30 to be there on time."

Once they heard that they all decided to go back to their rooms and hit the sack. Steve asked for the checks and Alex used the stranger's credit card again.

The waiter returned with their checks and called out the names on each of the cards. Alex panicked. How could he possibly finesse *this*?

After the waiter had successfully distributed several of the checks he called out *Jason*.

Nobody reacted.

"Jason?" he said again, eyebrows raised, scanning the faces around the table. Nobody answered, but Alex was staring at him with wide eyes.

"Jason?" the waiter asked again, looking at Alex with a question on his face.

"He must be at another table," Alex suggested.

The waiter shook his head. "Nope, I took all your credit cards to the cashier and carried them back here myself."

The others were involved in conversation and not paying any attention to the waiter except for Alex and Klaus. A young man who was sitting by himself at a table nearby, however, was very closely observing the confusion.

"There's no Jason at this table," Klaus said.

The waiter looked at the check, then looked at Alex, and asked, "Didn't you have the brisket and the two lagers?"

Alex stood up, and said, "Yes, I did. Let's see what's happened here."

He half led, half shoved, the waiter away from the table. "Please," he whispered. "So sorry for the confusion. Let's keep this between us. I'm a bit of a celebrity in Europe where I go by a stage name. But Jason James Stanfield is my legal name. I use it when I travel because I don't want anyone to recognize me. Here, give me the check. I'll sign it."

No one in the restaurant made any note of the conversation, except for Klaus and the guy with the curly blonde mop at another table.

"Is everything alright?" Klaus asked, when Alex came back to the table.

Alex nodded. He was still worried, although the waiter seemed to have bought his incognito celebrity story. As the group finished their drinks, Alex noticed that the waitresses, were giggling and casting glances his way.

He had no idea what they were saying, but it couldn't be good. He pushed the group to finish, using the early start as an excuse.

He was holding the door open for the guests to leave when one of the waitresses shouted, "Excuse me!" and rushed toward him. Another waitress came running behind her.

Alex couldn't get out the door because the group was still blocking it, chattering amongst themselves in German. His heart started beating like a drum.

When the first waitress reached him she held out a napkin and a pen, and said, "Could I have an autograph, please?"

The other waitress said, "Me, too?"

Alex quickly signed the first name that popped into his head, handed the napkins back to the girls, and rushed out the door.

"What was that?" Steve asked.

"I have no idea," Alex replied.

Behind him he heard the two girls squealing, "Michael Fassbender! Oh! My! God!"

Neither Alex, nor anyone else realized that the young man with curly blond hair who'd been sitting alone nearby, watching them, was now following them through the darkness.

***

Butch's cell phone was vibrating like crazy, he assumed it was ringing too, but so were his ears. He and Sundance were staggering into their room, both intoxicated from consuming a great deal of alcohol after many hours of stress, dehydration, sleeplessness, and hunger.

Butch looked at his phone. "It's the Capo," he said, staring at the instrument in horror.

The Boss was predictably furious when he heard that they still hadn't found the van. "How hard can it be for a coupla pros to find a van on the only road through the middle of nowhere?" he screamed.

Butch had no answer for him, so he remained silent.

"Do you need me to come out there and take care of this myself?"

"No, Caporegime," Butch assured him, sobered by the call and especially by the threat of him showing up in person.

Butch knew it might be the last straw if the Boss found out they'd damaged the special Mustang, so he didn't mention it.

The boss shouted a few more choice words, then hung up on him.

Butch was in shock.

He took a deep breath, and said, "We gotta get back on the road tomorrow. He'll rip our heads off if he finds out we were sittin' on our asses all day waitin' for the car to be repaired, and doin' nothin' to find that gadget."

Neither man slept well that night.

Chapter 19

Alex and Steve packed the luggage into the trailer, but didn't hook it to the van. Later in the day, on the way to Durango, they'd go right by here again. They'd pick it up then. For now they left it in the motel parking lot.

"This is our third van," joked Frida.

"So far," added Elisabeth.

They were ready to go at 4:45 a.m. and waved goodbye to the church van as they drove off into the dark, heading north.

They reached the trailhead of Mesa Arch at 5:40. There were no other vehicles in the parking lot. That was extremely unusual.

Steve reminded everyone that on the first night of the trip they'd been given a small flashlight which they'd now need during the hike, at least until they got a bit of pre-dawn light.

"We're in an area with cryptobiotic crusts, also called *desert glue*," Alex said. "It has a type of blue-green algae, a cyanobacteria, and it can also include things like moss, algae, and lichens, that help stabilize the ground so it won't blow away. And it traps nutrients and water.

"So, stay on the trails and walk single file in areas where you can see lumpy black bumps on the ground."

It was an easy ten minute to walk to the rim of the canyon. Alex had the guests sit in a place that was slightly uphill from the world famous arch, in a position to get a fantastic view of the canyon through the arch, with the La Sal Mountains as a backdrop.

"I've never gotten to see Mesa Arch when there weren't any other people around," said Alex. "This is a real treat."

When Frida sat down she opened the dwindling bag of chocolate cookies she carried with her everywhere. She seemed to be in some pain.

Alex sat next to her, and leaned over to ask in a low voice, "Are you okay?"

"Yes," she said. "I'm fine. But thanks for asking."

The sun rose and gradually revealed their amazing surroundings. The tableau was stunning. It was worth getting up in the wee hours to get to see it. They took photos and explored the area near the arch, then Alex handed out the breakfast snacks and drinks he and Steve had carried in.

On the way back Alex was surprised to note that Frida led the pack, matching Steve step for step.

Next, they drove to the parking lot at the end of Grand View Point Road where they made a twenty minute hike along the edge of a cliff where they enjoyed views of the La Sals and Abajo Mountains, the Needles and the Maze areas of the park, and the Green River peeking out of a canyon in the distance.

Butch and Sundance sat in their hotel room, massively hungover, in a depressed silence eating a breakfast of expensive supposedly healthy breakfast bars that tasted like dirt, washed down with black coffee.

They wouldn't be able to retrieve their car until the garage opened at eight. They shared the bottle of aspirin and the antacids they'd bought at the same convenience store where they'd bought the energy bars and coffee.

A mechanic arrived to open the garage a few minutes before eight and the two goombah cowboys were there waiting. They followed him into the office.

"We need the car now," Sundance said.

"I'm sorry, sir, but the repairs aren't finished yet," the guy said. "The work you need takes time."

"My friend Benjamin will help you," Sundance said, slapping a hundred dollar bill onto the counter.

"Guys, I hear ya, I'll be as quick as I can, but it's still gonna take a couple of hours."

"We gotta have transportation now," Sundance said. "It's an emergency."

"You can rent a Jeep across the street," the mechanic said, pointing. "They're open."

Butch and Sundance traded a look and decided they liked that idea.

The mechanic tried to give them back the hundred dollars, but Butch said, "Consider it an incentive to do your fastest possible work."

The men jogged over to the Moab Adventure Center to check the availability of their vehicles. They were lucky and got one of the last two Jeep Wranglers.

The online itinerary said the group would be exploring the Island in the Sky area of Canyonlands that day, so Butch asked for the shortest route there. The girl at the front desk suggested Shafer Trail and highlighted it on the map of the Moab area they gave to all their renters.

The men jumped into the Wrangler and took off. Butch let Sundance drive.

The intentionally low air pressure in the Jeep's off-road tires made the vehicle handle strangely. It wobbled in a way that made it unpleasant and unsafe to drive on paved roads, but once they turned onto the dirt track near the Potash area it was obvious that it was configured perfectly for 4-wheeling.

Sundance had a blast driving it.

Butch wondered if the trail they were taking was slowing them down, but the ride was so much fun he decided he didn't care.

***

The tour group finished hiking the Grand View Trail and Alex suggested they make a stop at the Shafer Trail Overlook. From there they could see tire tracks where vehicles had been driven up a steep road that barely managed to cling to the side of the mountain. It had a series of hairpin switchbacks and the entire way was lined with sheer drop-offs and no guard rails. It would be a terrifying journey.

"That road looks impossible," said Frida. "I can't imagine anyone driving on it."

"This area wasn't always as barren as it is now," said Alex. "They used to pasture sheep out here and the Shafer Trail was used to drive sheep from the grazing areas into town.

"Then later, in the 1950s, it was used by trucks to haul uranium ore from the mines."

"They must have had some daring drivers to use such a road with the brakes they had in the '50s!" Gerd said. "Seeing it with modern eyes, it looks unbelievable."

"For sure," Alex agreed. "These days it's the 4x4 enthusiasts who drive it. Look!" he said, pointing. "There's a Wrangler making its way up now."

They watched the Jeep negotiate the incline for a couple of minutes. They hoped it would make it to the top safely, but didn't want to wait around to see.

They were ready to continue to their next stop—Dead Horse Point—but first they wanted a restroom break at the Canyonlands Visitor Center.

Butch was afraid of heights, deathly afraid of them. The reality of the road hadn't been apparent from the bottom of the mountain, but as they gained altitude on the steep track he flipped out. The drop-offs from the cliff edges grew higher and higher until he couldn't take it anymore.

"Stop! Stop! Stop!" he shouted.

Sundance stopped.

Butch leaped out and stood between the Jeep and the side of the mountain, hunched over with his hands on his thighs, hyperventilating. He faced toward the raw dirt and turned his back the view.

"This isn't a *road*—it's suicide!" Butch said. "I'm not gettin' back in!"

Sundance didn't share his fear, but he could understand it. He remained calm, and said, "This is the route on the map from the four-wheeling place. They woulda said somethin' if it waddn't safe."

"I'm not gettin' back in," Butch said, "I can't." He was shaking his head, still bent over and nauseous. "It freaks me out."

"You want me to take you back down?" Sundance asked.

"No," Butch said. "You can't turn around here. And you might not even be able to turn around when you get up top."

Sundance looked up. Butch had a point. The road was extremely narrow. From where they were you couldn't see any place wide enough to turn around. He assumed there'd be a turnaround up there somewhere, but he couldn't be sure.

"I'm walkin' the rest of the way," Butch said.

"What? You really wanna walk all the way up to the top of this thing?"

"Yeah," Butch said.

"Are you sure?"

"Absolutely!" Butch replied.

"Well, in that case, here's some water," Sundance said, handing him two bottles. He was learning from their previous mistakes. "I'll go on ahead and wait for you when I get to a place where the road levels out."

Sundance resumed his slow drive up the dusty incline. He glanced back at Butch in the rearview mirror. He was following the Jeep with long strides.

Sundance relished the challenging drive. He stopped a couple of times along the way to check on Butch's progress and to enjoy the views.

***

The guests finished their break at the Canyonlands Visitor Center and were ready to hit the road again. Frida came back to the van with a couple of popular fictional mysteries set in the area, both by Tony Hillerman, as well as guides to local wildlife and medicinal plants.

***

Sundance reached the top of the mesa and parked. He was treated to a grand view across a vast expanse of desert. He put the Jeep in park, set the brake, and turned off the engine.

He noticed some cars out of the corner of his eye, then glanced up and saw the van with the company logo go by. He recognized it immediately.

For a second he wondered if he'd had a hallucination. Heat waves were radiating from the top of the mesa. Could it have been a mirage, or the after-effect of drinking combined with stress?

It made no sense, but he knew what he'd seen. He'd been searching for that logo for days. He checked the map the rental place had given him and saw he was at the intersection of the Shafer Trail and the highway.

He turned the key to restart the engine and give chase, but then realized he couldn't abandon Butch in this heat with no transportation, so he waited.

At least he'd seen the van now and he knew what direction they were headed in. They wouldn't be able to get far. As soon as Butch arrived he planned to run the Jeep right up their tailpipe.

It was more than an hour later when Butch finally reached the crest, breathless, red-faced, and soaked with sweat. When Sundance saw him coming, he hopped out of the Jeep and jogged over to greet him and to give him the good news.

"I saw the van!" he said, "We found 'em! Now we can go get 'em!"

"What?" Butch said, still trying to catch his breath.

"I saw the van," Sundance said. "It went right by here on the paved road just over there. Look. There's the highway."

Butch took a couple of steps closer to Sundance, then slapped him on the side of the head, shouting, "And you let 'em go? You didn't follow 'em?"

Sundance held his arms up to block the blows as Butch continued to slap at him. "You goofball! You actually let 'em get away?" Butch ranted. "I can't believe it!"

"What was I supposed to do?" Sundance shouted. "I didn't wanna leave you alone on foot in the middle of nowhere!"

Butch stopped raining blows down on his partner. Sundance was right. What would he have done all alone on the top of the mesa with no water, food, transportation, or protection from the brutal elements?

He sighed, but was in no mood to apologize. Instead he walked to the Jeep, opened the passenger door, and said, "Let's go."

They turned onto the highway in the direction Sundance had seen the van travelling. It would be a wobbly ride on the off-road tires, and they'd have to limit their speed because of it, but at this point, those were the least of their concerns.

Chapter 20

The group spent a few minutes enjoying the glorious view from the high lookout known as Dead Horse Point, where the Colorado River curved back on itself. Looking down on the green water snaking through the red rock surroundings to form a U, you could understand why it was one of the most photographed vistas on earth.

When they'd looked their fill Steve drove them to the coffee shop at the visitor center for a boost before they left the park.

***

"They're probably at Dead Horse Point by now," Butch said, "at least that's what the itinerary says. Then they'll be heading southeast to Durango, Colorado."

They checked the two parking lots at Dead Horse Point, but didn't find the van, so they decided to go back to Moab and check on the Mustang. If the repairs were complete they could head for Durango with the pedal to the metal.

What the Las Vegas cowpokes didn't anticipate was that instead of going straight to Colorado, the group would be spending the afternoon at Arches National Park. The stop would've normally been part of the itinerary for yesterday, but the sequence had gotten scrambled on account of the trouble with the van, and they were still juggling things, trying to make up for lost time.

When Butch and Sundance were at Dead Horse Point, the group was thirty miles away, entering Arches.

***

The group's first stop in Arches was at The Windows where eons of blowing sand had carved striking formations. Steve let the guests off in a convenient spot for a short hike. Then he'd hunt for a parking place.

"I not feel vell," Tina said. "Is okay if I stay?"

"Of course," Steve said.

"Sit in front? Is more comfortable."

Steve stuttered, "Uh, … s-s-s-sure!" His face turned a deep shade of red.

Alex was at the open back hatch, handing out trek poles. "See ya in forty-five minutes!" he called out. "When we get some altitude, we'll look for ya!"

Then he set off guiding the group up the hill. Tina flashed Steve a predatory look, and said, "Forty-five minutes *plenty* time…"

Steve was sweating as he drove around looking for a parking space. He rejected one possibility after another. He knew his logic was faulty, but he felt safer in a moving vehicle. No matter how fast the van went, he'd never be able to outrun a person sitting beside him in the passenger seat.

Tina had married an old man and was predictably bored after a few years of squandering his money. Klaus had made a fortune as a real estate agent selling fincas in Mallorca after he'd retired from a government job. He could afford a young wife, so he didn't limit her spending, but she had other interests besides money.

She opened the top two buttons of her shirt. "Is hot," she said, twisting just enough in her seat to offer him a view which he declined by keeping his eyes forward.

Steve flipped some switches to turn up the air conditioning, but kept driving. He passed several more empty parking spots and continued to circle the lot. He dreaded what would happen when he stopped. She'd already tried to feel him up during the night in the trailer, but he'd used an extra jacket to block her advances.

He pulled into an area where there were several people milling around, and mumbled, "I need to use the restroom," then he jumped out and quickly walked away, struggling not to break into a run.

The group visited several different arch formations and then took the well-named, sparsely-maintained, and poorly-marked Primitive Trail back to the parking lot.

Steve stayed in the restroom as long as he could stand it. Then he reluctantly made his way back to the van, but he didn't get in. Instead he pretended to be busy rearranging gear in the small cargo area behind the last row of seats.

He got a spray bottle of window cleaner and began swabbing the windows with paper towels, although they were nearly spotless because he'd cleaned them that morning as part of his usual routine. Then he swept the carpet.

Each time Tina tried to start a conversation, he panicked and returned to the cargo area. He was so relieved when he saw the group returning, he thought he might faint.

Klaus made it to the van first and opened the front passenger door. "How are you feeling, my dear?" he asked, as the others went around to the back to have Steve stow the trek poles and refill their water bottles.

"Better!" Tina said.

"All aboard!" Alex called out. He was anxious to get moving toward their next hike at Devil's Garden.

***

Butch and Sundance made it back to the garage in Moab.

The mechanics had hurried the repairs to the Mustang and were nearly finished. They'd replaced the muffler and the missing or damaged connective parts. They'd replaced the broken headlight cover and bulb and smoothed out the various dents as well as they could in the time allotted.

While Butch settled up the bill, Sundance returned the rented Jeep and gushed to the guy at the desk about how much he enjoyed four-wheeling the Shafer Trail. Then he and Butch went to the City Market to grab an iced coffee and a quick nosh while they waited for the finishing touches to be made to the car.

***

The tour group reached Landscape Arch.

"If anyone would like a climb, we can see Navajo Arch, Partition Arch, and Double O Arch. It's not far, but I have to warn you, it's a steep trail and it's on slick rock. It's a fairly dangerous hike."

It looked like there would be no takers, which was typical for these tours, but Alex always liked to make the offer, just in case.

Then Tina said, "I go," giving Alex a wolfish smile.

"Honey, are you sure you can do it?" Klaus said, with concern.

"Ja klar," she said, and started toward the incline ahead of Alex.

During the steepest part of the incline Tina bent forward to use her hands to help her climb. Alex was following close behind her. She was wearing a pair of extremely short shorts. He struggled to keep his eyes on the trail.

As they hiked she frequently reached out for his hand, as if for support, although she'd already managed the most difficult parts by herself. Several times she let herself stumble against him, and he was forced to grab her so they'd both stay upright.

She was really trying to make it hard for him to remain professional. Alex thought her flirting was amusing, but he wasn't interested. When they'd seen all the arches that he'd planned to show his guests they started the climb back down.

He played it cool and pretended not to notice her games. Unfortunately, it was a no-win situation. The cooler he acted, the more Tina tried to get his attention.

In the meantime Steve had taken the rest of the group to Pine Tree Arch and Tunnel Arch as an alternate activity. When Alex and Tina arrived back at the parking lot they found the group having a snack at the picnic tables.

Tina sat down beside Klaus and cuddled against him, but at the same time she sent seductive glances toward both Steve and Alex. The woman was trouble.

"We usually make a hike to watch the sunset at Delicate Arch," Alex said, "but because of the changes in our schedule we'll have to head southeast to Durango now. It's a three and a half hour drive from here when you take into account the stops we'll be making."

"I've had enough hiking for now," said Elisabeth, and just this once everyone agreed with her.

They boarded the van and drove back to Moab. When they pulled into the parking lot of the Inca Inn they discovered that the lock on the trailer door had been broken open.

Steve did a quick check inside, but it looked just as he'd left it. Nothing appeared to be missing. He asked everyone to make sure their belongings were intact, and they did.

Nothing had been taken.

"That's crazy," Alex said, in disbelief. "This is the first time anything like this has ever happened on one of my tours."

Steve agreed. "Why break into a trailer in broad daylight and not steal anything?" he asked.

When they told the clerk at the reception desk he said he'd noticed four or five guys walking around on the property, but they'd left without saying anything.

"I'm so sorry about this," the clerk said. "Would you like to report it to the police?"

Alex and Steve agreed that it didn't seem necessary and would only slow them down.

"Well, at least let us buy you a new lock," the clerk said.

"Thanks," Steve said, "But I always bring a spare, so we've got it covered."

Alex smiled. Steve was such a Boy Scout. Always prepared. He was lucky to have the guy as a partner on a long trip like this.

***

Butch and Sundance left the City Market and were standing on a street corner waiting for the light to change so they could cross the road when the van they'd been chasing stopped at the light. The signal began to beep indicating that pedestrians could cross.

"Look!" Sundance said, pointing to the far lane, "There they are!"

Both men stared wide-eyed and open-mouthed at the object of their long, exhausting, humiliating search. The van was sitting right there in front of them. But before they could get anywhere near it the light turned green and Steve drove on, blissfully oblivious to another near miss.

Butch and Sundance ran toward the garage. Butch burst into the little office, breathless, calling out, "Is it ready?"

The man behind the counter said, "Yep." He rummaged through the pile of grease-stained papers on the counter, "Let me find your invoice," he said.

Butch threw a wad of hundreds onto the counter, saying, "Keep the change," grabbed the key, and asked, "Where's it parked?"

"Out front, to the right," the mechanic said, and then quickly started counting the money.

Butch and Sundance raced out the door, jumped into the Mustang, and took off in hot pursuit. They caught up with the van shortly after they passed Hole 'n The Rock.

Once they had it in sight, they forced themselves to calm down and stay at least three cars back.

In Monticello, Steve stopped at a gas station so he could top up the tank. Butch and Sundance stopped at a different set of pumps to fill up at the same time.

The guests climbed out of the van and went into the store. While Steve and Sundance pumped gas, Butch approached the van. That was when he noticed the license plate was different. He hadn't been able to see it from behind because the trailer was blocking his view, but now he could.

Other small things he couldn't put his finger on told him this wasn't the van they'd been chasing for days. *What the …. ?*

He started to panic, but then he saw that the side door was standing wide open. Gerd's camera bag was sitting on the floor in plain sight. It was within easy reach of the door.

Butch moved closer, keeping an eye on Steve through the window. When he was within inches of the van, he heard Alex call out, "Do you need anything?"

"Nope!" Steve shouted back.

Then a police car pulled up and parked in front of the store. Butch turned away immediately and grabbed a handful of towels from the pillar next to the pump, as if that was what he'd been after.

Gerd and Klaus returned to the van and Butch went back to the Mustang. "If that cop waddn't here, I'd take it," Butch muttered to Sundance.

Klaus noticed the exotic sports car parked at the pump. It was in better shape than the last time he'd seen it. He went over to Sundance and Butch, and said, "Nice car!"

"Thanks!" they answered at the same time, as they got back into the Mustang. Sundance pulled out onto the highway and drove off, but he didn't go far. He went only as far as the San Juan Fair Grounds and then did his best to hide behind a sign, so they could wait and keep watch without being noticed.

He'd chosen his spot well. A few minutes later the tour group went by. Sundance resumed following them, staying well back. Unfortunately the stretch of road was flat and not much travelled. In some spots you could see for miles.

Sundance had to work to leave enough distance so as not to be noticed, but stay close enough to keep the van in sight. He cursed the car again, this time for being so easily recognizable.

***

It was getting late, so Alex turned around in his seat and said, "Would you guys like to stop for dinner in Cortez, or would you rather continue to our hotel in Durango?"

The consensus was that they preferred to check into the hotel first and eat afterwards. They'd bought snacks at the gas station and they'd been passing them around inside the van during the drive.

It was almost nine when they reached the Durango Lodge.

Sundance watched the van make the turn into a hotel parking lot and he pulled the Mustang over to the side of the street to wait. He and Butch watched the driver and guide unload the luggage.

"Anyone who wants to go for dinner, meet back here in fifteen minutes and we'll grab a bite together," Alex called out as the group started lugging their luggage up the typical flight of metal and concrete outdoor stairs that had been popular decades earlier. Each of them had to pass through a security door at the top of the stairs to access their room.

Butch and Sundance watched Gerd until he disappeared down a hallway taking his camera bag with him. This made things a lot easier for the henchmen. They'd seen the bag. They knew what building it was in and what floor it was on. Now all they needed was a room number.

They waited for the group to come back outside.

Chapter 21

When they'd dropped off their luggage and freshened up, one after another of the guests came back down the flight of exterior stairs. The Germans were all on time.

Only the Swiss couple, Elisabeth and Georg, were two minutes late.

Elisabeth led the way down the stairs, harping, "From your behavior one would never believe that it was the Swiss who perfected timepieces."

The restaurant Alex recommended was not far away, so they walked.

Butch and Sundance waited a few moments before they made their move. Gerd wasn't carrying his camera bag, but they decided to follow him. They had to get his room number somehow. Maybe they could catch him by himself and take his key. Otherwise they'd have to jump him before he made it through the security door. They decided to play it by ear.

The historic train station of the Durango & Silverton Narrow Gauge Railway station was close to the Durango Lodge. When the train blasted its antique steam whistle, everyone in the area heard it.

A party train had just returned from Silverton. You could still hear the Dixieland music coming from one of the train cars. As the tour group walked past the station, passengers were getting off the train. A lot of happy, obviously intoxicated people poured out onto the street.

Butch and Sundance tried to hurry through the crowd, but they were surrounded by young people who were inviting everyone to join the party. By the time the two managed to shove their way out of the throng, the tour group had vanished. They looked down the street, but couldn't see them anywhere.

Alex led the group into the Diamond Belle Saloon at the historic Strater Hotel. The décor of the saloon was Old West. There was live entertainment— a singer in a cowboy costume singing Johnny Cash favorites. The interior layout of the saloon was like a typical bar in a western movie where painted ladies worked in rooms upstairs.

The young waitresses wore feathers in their hair and were squeezed into skimpy corseted costumes that showed a lot of skin. The hostess apologized that they didn't have a big enough table for the group on the main floor. She offered them two tables next to each other on the balcony overlooking the bar.

They agreed and she led them upstairs where Tina maneuvered Klaus into a corner and herself next to Peter. Elisabeth saw Georg's eyes follow the waitress as she walked away and she kicked him under the table. He smiled at her and shrugged in response.

Butch and Sundance walked down the street looking into each place of business, scanning for the group, but couldn't find them. This was because they were seated on the mezzanine level and were far enough back from the railing that they weren't visible from the entrance.

When the waitress came back to take their orders, Georg didn't dare take his eyes off his menu, but he was still smiling to himself. Tina attempted to draw Peter's attention by putting her hand on his knee.

She was not particularly successful at getting his attention, so her hand kept sliding higher up his leg until he brushed it away under the table without making eye contact or saying a word. He made himself perfectly clear without speaking, or even looking her way.

The country singer was belting out *Ring of Fire*. Georg leaned toward Alex, and said, "That's what happens when I eat too much chili."

Elisabeth gave him an elbow to the ribs for his joke. Alex wanted to laugh, but he was afraid to for fear of running afoul of Elisabeth. He didn't want to make an enemy of such a shrew, or anyone else, but especially not someone like her.

Butch and Sundance continued to search up and down Main Avenue to no avail. Eventually they realized they'd better find a place to stay for the night, so they went to the front desk at the Strater to ask for a room.

Klaus was searching for the men's room. He found it at the rear of the lobby on the main floor. The restrooms were shared amongst the hotel, the restaurant, and the Strater's two bars.

He saw the two men in cowboy costumes checking in and recognized them. He thought to himself, *What a small world!* He found it amazing that even out here in the middle of vast empty spaces, tourists tend to move along the Grand Circle in herds or packs. Like sheep or wolves.

He didn't know how right he was, especially about sheep being followed by wolves.

Meanwhile back at the dinner tables upstairs, Alex was explaining the situation with legalized marijuana in the state. "Colorado was the first state in the U.S. to legalize recreational marijuana use," he said. "The state shares a large percentage of the tax revenue from the sale of weed with the school system, so every time a person buys marijuana they're contributing to children's education. The more the citizens smoke, the better their schools will be!"

That got a laugh and everyone started cracking jokes about it. Frida was particularly interested and pressed for more specifics. "How does the system work here?" she asked. "Where do they sell the marijuana? What products do they offer?"

Alex told her what he knew.

"I tried it once when I was still at school in Frankfurt," said Tina. "One of my friends offered it to me at a party. I had never smoked a cigarette before, so it gave me a coughing fit. When I finally stopped coughing I felt so tired I fell asleep. I don't understand what people get from it. To me, it is boring."

Klaus looked at her in shock, and said, "You never told me that you used illegal drugs!"

"It was nothing, just the one time," she said. Then she turned toward the group and said, "Klaus used to work for a government agency back in the old days. From what he has told me the government did not allow the people to have any fun back then."

"I would be willing to try marijuana, just out of curiosity," Gerd admitted.

"I grew up in East Germany," he said. "That stuff did not make it across the border back then."

***

When they'd finished their meals Gerd bought each of the men a bourbon and ordered a bottle of champagne for the women.

Alex was relieved when Klaus offered to pay for his and Steve's meal. After almost being outed for using a stolen credit card last night he needed to find a different way to pay for his food.

Alex, Gerd, Klaus, and Tina had a couple of drinks, but they weren't quite ready for the night to end, so they decided to check out a few more bars.

Steve escorted the others back to the hotel.

Once Butch and Sundance were checked in at the Strater and had their key cards, Sundance went to retrieve the Mustang and bring it to the Strater parking lot. It was still parked across from the Durango Lodge.

When Sundance was returning with the car he saw Steve and some of the tour group walking back toward the Lodge. At first he didn't realize that it was only part of the group, not all of it. But when he went back to park in the same spot he'd just vacated, he noticed that Gerd was missing.

He got out of the car anyway hoping to eavesdrop on their group's conversation. He heard Steve say, "Alex will meet you for the train ride in the hotel lobby at eight in the morning. The train leaves at 8:30. We'll need to pick up our tickets well before that, and you'll need to be aboard by 8:15."

They wished each other a good night while climbing the outdoor stairs. Steve used his key card to open the glass outer door and held it for the guests. He let the door fall closed and it automatically locked behind them.

Sundance went up the stairs, intending to follow them. He tried the door, hoping it would be ajar or the lock would be broken, but it performed its function. He'd have to have a key card if he wanted to get access to the hallway.

He jogged down to the ground floor and walked to the back of the building and tried a door there as well, but it was also locked. He decided to look for another door, but saw Frida coming down the stairs and stepped back out of sight.

There was something about her movements that made it look like she was trying to be stealthy. She kept looking around like she was trying to avoid being seen. Sundance wondered why the old lady was going out on her own, late at night, in a strange town. He followed her to find out.

She went down Main Avenue then took a right onto East College Drive. The old girl was headed for the Durango Rec Room. The fact that the place was a marijuana dispensary was made obvious by the glowing green cross over the door. Sundance couldn't believe his eyes.

She stood outside, reading something posted on the door. The place was apparently closed for the night, so she turned around and walked back to Main Avenue where she saw a group of college students.

"Pardon!" she said, walking faster to catch up to them.

The five young men and two young ladies stopped and turned around. "Pardon," she said in heavily-accented, but pretty good English. "Do you know of open dispensary?"

The young people gaped at her with astonishment and amusement.

"Do you understand what I speak?" she said. "Where I go to buy?"

That provoked laughter. "You mean a store where you can buy weed?" one of the girls asked.

Frida never heard the slang term, and answered, "Not weeds. I wanting marijuana. Hashish. You understand?"

She said it loud enough that passersby glanced her way and did a double take when they saw who was asking the question. Even Sundance had heard her clearly, and he was several yards away. He couldn't help but smile at the situation.

"Ma'am," one of the boys said, "I'm afraid every place you could buy marijuana is closed now."

Another of the young guys reached into his pocket and pulled out a small plastic bag and handed it to Frida. "And here are papers," he said, handing her a small packet.

"How much?" she asked rummaging around in her bag.

"Oh, no, no, no. You don't owe me anything, ma'am. Please take it," the young man said, holding up his hand to ward off her attempt to pay him.

"Danke!" Frida said, then turned around and walked back toward the motel.

The young people stood there watching her walk down the street, then burst into laughter again.

Sundance had seen a lot of shady business being conducted in his line of work, but one thing he'd never seen before was a granny openly trying to score dope late at night on a well-lighted street. He was amused by the old lady, but he was shocked to see anybody giving drugs away for free. That was no way to do business.

Sundance wasn't the hardened criminal he was supposed to be. He made every effort to fit in to the world he'd been born into, but, at heart, it wasn't who he really was. He brought the car to the Strater Hotel and parked it, then went into the lobby where Butch was waiting.

"What took ya so long?" Butch asked.

"I saw some of the tour group and followed 'em inta the hotel, but no dice. Our guy waddn't with 'em anyway. Then I got distracted watchin' a grandma tryin' to buy pot," he said, laughing, but not explaining any further.

Butch shook his head, then they went up the stairs to their room.

Chapter 22

Butch and Sundance planned to intercept the group the next day as they boarded the train. In many ways it was an ideal scenario to put an end to this nightmare job.

Both men were exhausted from the stress of the chase, the hardships and humiliations they'd been forced to endure, and the poor nutrition provided by gas station convenience stores, but they went to sleep confident that the guy with the camera bag would be on that train in the morning, with his camera gear.

There was no way he could get away from them on a moving train.

***

Alex, Gerd, Klaus, and Tina were bar hopping their way through downtown Durango. They'd started out with beer, then moved on to cocktails. Now they were doing shots.

Alex knew better than to drink like this, but his secret new life of crime was weighing on him. He felt guilty and lonely. He was so ashamed, he couldn't even tell his wife what he was doing. She'd be angry and disappointed in him.

Klaus was ready to stop and he tried to convince Tina to accompany him back to the motel. She resisted. "I'll join you soon," she said, slurring her words.

"You've had enough," Klaus said firmly. "Come with me."

She ignored him.

Gerd got up, draped his arm around Klaus's shoulder, and said, "I'll walk back with you."

It was obvious that both men had already had too many drinks. They were swaying as they stood there holding on to each other.

"Alex'll take good care of me," Tina said, "Right Alex?"

Alex nodded, too drunk to realize that Klaus was in a bad mood and now, after successfully evading Tina's advances for days, he was about to be alone with her.

"I'll bring her home in half an hour," Alex said, staring longingly at the lavish display of bottles behind the bar.

That's the problem with these young ladies," Gerd said, as he pulled Klaus out the door. "We're too old to keep up with them."

Klaus was angry, and Gerd's comment stung, but didn't want to make a scene, so he remained silent and walked back to the motel with him.

It took much longer than half an hour before Alex and Tina decided to call it a night. They finally staggered out of the last bar at one in the morning. Tina was so heavily intoxicated that she was talking gibberish. She threw an arm around Alex and he tried his best to steer her in the right direction.

They managed to make it back to the Lodge and up the stairs, but then Alex had a problem locating his keycard to open the security door.

"We can use mine," Tina said, but she couldn't find hers either.

Alex eventually located his card, opened the door, and guided Tina inside.

"What's your room number?" he asked.

"What's *your* room number?" Tina replied.

Alex laughed, and asked again, "Come on. What's your room number?"

"Twenty-six," she said.

Alex supported her as she stumbled down the hall and they stopped in front of the door to her room.

"Where's your key?" he asked.

She rummaged through her purse again, this time for what seemed like forever, but finally found it. It took Alex several tries to get the door open, inserting the keycard into the lock and pulling it back out again half a dozen times.

"You're so kind," Tina mumbled. She decided to kiss him goodnight, but he was facing the door and didn't realize her intention. He was still fumbling with her keycard and dropped it.

Just as he bent down to get it, Tina lunged toward him, lost her balance, and fell across his back. He was startled and bolted upright suddenly, throwing her off his back and into the floor. She landed on her face.

By this time their drunken antics had woken Klaus and he suddenly appeared in the doorway. He was not happy when he saw Alex standing in front of him and Tina lying on the hall floor, face down, with her arms and legs splayed out.

He went down onto his knees next to his wife's inert body and shook her by the shoulder, trying to rouse her, but she'd passed out.

He looked up at Alex, and asked, "What is going on here?"

Alex bent down to help, but Klaus was attempting to stand up at the same moment, with Tina in his arms. The top of his head caught Alex under the chin in a full force uppercut. Alex's neck whipped back, his eyes rolled up, and he went down hard.

Klaus had unintentionally hit him in just the right spot for a knockout. When he saw what he'd done he wasn't the least bit sorry. *He's younger, but he's got a glass jaw*, he thought, grimacing in satisfaction.

All this chaotic action generated enough noise to wake nearby sleepers. Doors were opening up and down the hall and guests were being treated to the sight of Klaus standing in the hall holding a dead or unconscious woman in his arms while Alex lay inert in the floor.

Gerd came out of his room, shouting, "Stop!"

He feared Klaus was in the process of killing one or both of them in a jealous rage. At this, everyone swarmed out into the hallway, asking questions, giving advice, rendering first aid, or complaining about being woken up.

In the middle of the confused debate Alex gradually regained a bit of drunken consciousness and mumbled that Gerd should leave Klaus alone. Steve gently, but firmly, pulled Gerd away from Klaus and then steered Klaus away from Alex.

It took several minutes before everyone understood, roughly, what had happened. When a semblance of calm had been restored Steve suggested that they all try to go back to sleep.

They needed to be rested for an early start in the morning.

***

Steve had a hard time falling back to sleep after the spectacle in the hall.

Alex didn't share in his insomnia. He'd staggered into the room, half carried by Steve, then fallen crosswise on his bed, fully dressed, and immediately began snoring like he was cutting down the forests of the Pacific Northwest and Canada.

Steve was able to drift off only intermittently. He was wide awake when his alarm went off at seven. Alex, still sideways across his bed, hadn't moved.

Steve got out of bed and into a hot shower. He heard someone banging on the bathroom door and trying to open it, but he stayed in the shower. He wasn't in the mood to deal with any more of his roommate's escapades until he'd completed his morning ablutions and was ready to face the world.

Alex was shouting about something but Steve couldn't understand what he was saying over the rush of the water. In addition he didn't care what his coworker wanted.

The shouting and banging abruptly stopped. *Good*, he thought.

Steve rinsed well, turned off the water, and dried himself. When he'd finish shaving and brushing his teeth, he opened the bathroom door and was met with a terrible odor.

Alex was no longer snoring. He was lying sideways across his bed, face down, but now he was turned in the opposite direction. "I had to vomit," he mumbled. "You wouldn't open the door so I grabbed the trash can."

Alex heaved himself into a standing position, shuffled over to the trash can, picked it up, and disappeared into the bathroom with it. Steve heard the toilet flush, then the shower come on briefly, and a few moments later Alex walked out of the bathroom with a clean trash can.

He put it back into its place beside the desk and dropped back onto the bed. "I feel awful!" he groaned. "What happened last night?"

Before Steve could respond, Alex said, "I'm never gonna drink again. Oh, my head. It's exploding! And my face hurts. Why does my face hurt?"

He looked at himself in the mirror and mumbled, "How'd I get this bruise on my chin?"

Steve didn't want to get involved in a discussion about the incident, so he said nothing. Alex reached into the backpack next to his bed, brought out a bottle of aspirin, and dry swallowed several of them.

"I made some coffee," Steve said, speaking softly. "Would you like some?"

"You're an angel," Alex whispered.

After Alex had taken a couple of sips of the hot liquid, he asked, "Do you mind walking them over to the train? I'm afraid I need a few more minutes to recover, but I'm sure I'll feel better shortly."

"Of course," Steve said. "No problem."

He was relieved to escape from the sour smelling room and the excuse of guiding the group to the train station was as good as any.

Steve jogged down the outdoor stairs and headed toward the lobby. He caught the smell of something sweet and noticed Frida standing in the parking lot. He smiled, and said, "Gute Morgen."

She smiled back and nodded, but didn't say anything. It looked like she was holding her breath. Why would she be doing that? Maybe she had the hiccups.

He went to the lobby to grab an apple and what he hoped would be a better tasting cup of coffee. Then he went out front to meet the guests who'd signed up for the excursion to Silverton.

The Swiss couple had chosen not to book the ride on the antique train, so he didn't expect them, but Tina was missing. "We do not need to wait for Tina," her husband said. "She will not be joining us."

Steve diplomatically refrained from further inquiry and walked the group over to the station where he bought their tickets and distributed them.

When it was time to board, Gerd said, "Could you do me a favor? I will only need a couple of lenses during the trip up to Silverton. Would you mind taking my camera bag with you in the van? It weighs a ton. I will get it back when we rendezvous up on the mountain."

"No problem," Steve said, taking the bag and sliding the strap over his shoulder. "The bag and I will be waiting for you when you get there."

***

Alex meanwhile knew he better get a move on, so he took a quick, brutally cold, shower. That was the German cure for everything and it worked pretty well.

He felt like death warmed over, but in light of the crazy incident yesterday, which he still had only the vaguest memories of, he needed to make a respectable impression when he went down to meet the guests who'd opted out of riding the historic train up the mountain.

He adjusted the shower temperature to as cold as he could stand it. After three minutes under the icy Rocky Mountain downpour he felt better, but his head was still killing him.

Chapter 23

Butch and Sundance were jolted awake by the unmistakable blasts from a train's steam whistle. Sundance glanced over at the clock on the nightstand. "Awww geez, I forgot to set the alarm!" he said, frantic, "It's 8:25!"

Both men dressed in a flash, jammed their feet into boots, grabbed jackets, and ran out of the room. On their way downstairs they heard a few more warning toots of the train whistle.

By the time they reached the street, they realized the sounds from the train were no longer coming from the train station but were now emanating from behind their hotel, so they reversed course and ran down toward the railroad tracks.

The train was chugging languidly through town as it gradually gained momentum. It had been built in the 1800s when anything speedier than an ox cart was considered a fast mode of transportation. Even when travelling full out, its top speed was only eighteen miles an hour.

Butch and Sundance felt sure they'd be able to run it down before it got out of town. They were oblivious to the scene they were creating—two men dressed like cowboys, chasing a train on foot. The scene looked like something out of a movie.

They'd almost caught up to the last car when it began to accelerate enough to pull away from them. A couple of passengers who were standing at the back of the train thought the two guys chasing them were actors staging a show and they started cheering the men on, urging them to run faster.

The disheveled cowboys managed to catch up and grab onto the rails of the small balcony at the back of the last car. They heaved themselves up with the help of the tourists, and clambered over the ornamental railing.

The breathless duo accepted praise for their efforts from the passengers, but didn't want to draw any further attention, so they neatened their attire, waited for their breathing to slow, and then made their way toward the front of the train, scanning each car carefully as they strolled the aisle.

They found the group in the fourth car and dropped into a couple of seats three rows behind them. They exchanged exultant glances and it was all they could do to keep from slapping a high five.

A one-way trip to cover the forty-five miles from Durango to Silverton took three-and-a-half hours. They decided to make their move when they were close enough to Silverton to be able to get away clean, do a grab and run, and hop off the train in the reverse of what they'd done to get on. Until then, while the train chugged through the remote mountain terrain, they might as well relax.

***

Klaus and Peter went to the dining car, Frida went to find a restroom, and Gerd headed to the open air car to take pictures. Sundance casually bent over in his seat and was able to scan the floor throughout the car, Butch walked the aisle and looked at the contents of every seat, but neither of them saw Gerd's camera bag anywhere.

They searched the entire car twice, but the bag simply wasn't there. They went back to their seats to strategize. They agreed to split up and walk the entire length of the train, but again, they found nothing. This was extremely unwelcome news.

As the coal-fired steam train chugged up the mountain, Sundance observed the group members, none of them was carrying the bag. The faux cowboys were frustrated at being trapped on the train for the long ride, but there was no way off unless they wanted to throw themselves into a rocky gorge. Butch was almost ready to do it.

***

"Look at the two guys," Klaus whispered.

"Who?" Gerd asked.

"Those cowboy guys," whispered Klaus. "They are the ones from the black Mustang."

"Are you sure?" Gerd asked.

"Yes. We keep crossing paths with them," Klaus said. "If I did not know our route was a big circle that all the tourists take, I would be worried, but…it is probably just a coincidence."

***

Alex came down to the lobby to grab another coffee.

He didn't dare eat anything yet, but he took an apple and some Danishes for later when the odds were better that he'd be able to keep it down.

When Georg and Elisabeth came into the lobby, he put his sunglasses on to conceal his bloodshot eyes.

"Hey, Alex," Georg said. "How are you this morning?"

"Good! Doing well!" Alex replied.

Elisabeth looked at him with a skeptical expression.

She never drank more than two glasses of wine at a sitting and she felt no sympathy whatsoever for those who overindulged. They deserved what they got.

It was a strange scene she'd observed in the hallway last night, very unprofessional. She'd already had an argument with Georg about it this morning. She'd said Alex's behavior was unforgiveable.

He secretly agreed that a drunken brawl in their hotel in the middle of the night wasn't very smooth on Alex's part, but Georg understood the lad pretty well, especially considering how attractive Tina was.

He would've done the same thing if he hadn't met Elisabeth when he was only twenty-one. He often wished he'd stayed single longer and had been able to have that kind of fun, instead of living most of his life with a dragon.

***

Steve was at the van doing his morning checks. The plan was to leave for Silverton at ten, so they still had twenty minutes until departure.

Alex asked if he had an update from Tina as to whether or not she'd be joining them for the drive up the mountain.

"Nope," Steve said.

Alex decided reluctantly to go up to her room to check on her. After a couple of light taps Tina opened the door wearing only her bathrobe and showing an excessive amount of skin.

Rather than looking down at her face, he kept his gaze high and over her left shoulder. "Will you be joining us for the van ride to Silverton?" he asked.

"Well, since you asked so nicely," she said, "I will go. I need a few more minutes though. Come in while I get dressed."

"N-n-n-no," Alex stuttered. "I'll wait for you down by the van."

He turned and walked away quickly. The woman was a menace, a man eater, a femme fatale. He desperately wished he was at home with this wife and daughters, but he had to work for a couple more weeks before he could do that. He vowed to himself to stay out of trouble for the rest of the tour.

The group was waiting together at the van when Tina arrived, five minutes late. It was obvious that Elisabeth was not amused. She jumped into the van and said, "Come on! Let's go! We don't have all day!"

Georg rolled his eyes and followed.

Tina got in last.

***

On the scenic drive up to Silverton on Highway 550, nicknamed *The Million Dollar Highway*, they made a stop at the Pinkerton Hot Springs.

"If you enjoy seeing this hot spring, you'll love our Wild West Yellowstone Tour," Alex said. "On that route we get to see many different types of thermal features—hot springs, steam vents, bubbling mud pots, and geysers. Two-thirds of the world's thermal features are in Yellowstone—more than 500 geysers."

They made their way across the Coal Bank Pass and stopped at Molas Pass to take in the scenery from the overlook. It was cold at the 10,910 foot elevation, but the panorama of the surrounding snow-capped mountains was fantastic.

Soon afterwards the van, three guests, one driver, and one camera bag arrived in Silverton. It was a terrific town for tourists, filled with quaint Old West style buildings. It looked like a place where cowboys would ride by at any moment.

They drove down the main street, the only paved road in the town, and parked in front of the Grand Imperial Hotel. That put them right in the center of things. During the heyday of the area when silver and gold mining was booming, the Grand Imperial had been one of the finest establishments west of the Mississippi.

The altitude at Silverton was over nine thousand feet. Alex suggested they go for a walk around the town to get some fresh air. He'd have preferred to go into the Avalanche Brewery to drink a *counter beer*, German slang for the first beer of the day to offset a hangover, but he knew that after last night it wouldn't do to lead the group to another watering hole at eleven in the morning.

He planned to take them on a 4x4 tour into the mountains later and he'd be one of the drivers, so he needed to be sharp.

They walked along Greene Street to the town museum, which was located in an old jailhouse, then they turned east and strolled down Empire Street until they reached the train station. The train hadn't arrived yet, so they decided to walk around for a few more minutes.

They headed toward the residential area on the other side of Greene Street. There were few people around. The little town was busy only when a train was arriving or departing.

When they returned to the Grand Imperial Hotel they saw a slender man with a wild mane of curly blond hair using his hands to shield the sides of his eyes, bent toward the tinted windows of their van, obviously trying to see inside. Alex called out from across the street, "Can I help you?"

The man immediately turned and walked away without looking back. "Hey!" Alex shouted, but the guy just increased his walking speed.

They watched him stride down Greene Street and then duck into an alley two blocks away. "That was strange," Alex said. "Did anyone leave anything of value inside?"

"Gerd's camera bag," Steve said. "He asked me to bring it up for him. I'd better get it out and keep it with me."

Steve unlocked the van, climbed into the passenger area, and came out with the bag. It seemed strange to have to worry about theft in such an isolated little town. In the late 1800s Silverton had been a rowdy place for sure, but these days crime was rare.

Chapter 24

The steam train was approaching Silverton. Klaus was keeping an eye on Butch and Sundance, wondering what the two characters were really up to. Were they simply on vacation? They made an odd couple.

Nothing about them blended in. Everything they did, wore, and drove drew attention. His intuition told him there was something strange going on there, but he didn't know what it was. Yet.

***

Frida ate another of the cookies she'd been rationing, then turned to Peter and asked, "Would you watch my things. I need to find a restroom."

He glanced at her possessions and nodded to indicate his willingness. When she left the car he glanced back at her things and couldn't help but notice the bag of cookies.

Normally he'd never steal anything, but an irresistible urge to have one of the cookies came over him. He had a terrible sweet tooth. Twice she'd shared one with that harridan Elisabeth, but had hurt him when she wouldn't trade him one, even in exchange for one of his fancy Italian almond cookies, Lazzaroni Amaretti Di Saronnos.

Oh well, he thought, *people could be strange*. He, a lifelong bachelor, knew from personal experience that singletons could get eccentric and set in their ways.

But he was trapped on the train for three and a half hours and he had nothing to snack on. He snatched one of the cookies and wolfed it down before she could catch him at it.

It was tasty, but nothing special. He'd compromised his morals for nothing.

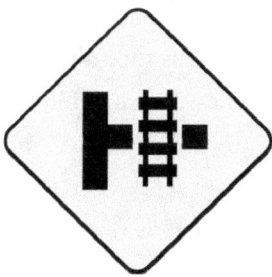

Alex and his group heard the blasts from the approaching train whistle. "It's here," he said. "Let's go."

They crossed Greene Street and walked toward the station. After a couple more whistle toots, the train chugged into view. The steel tracks were set into the road like an urban tram so the route could be used by both wheeled vehicles and the train.

The whistle drew a crowd of interested onlookers at the same time it was disgorging the passengers who'd ridden up the mountain to Silverton. When the locomotive came to a complete stop, tourists hopped down from the open doors and streamed out into the town.

A couple of men dressed in cowboy costumes jumped off, too. Alex guessed they were actors who would reenact a shootout in the street. That was a common public entertainment in the western tourist towns.

He took a few moments to locate his guests in the milling crowd. Peter, who so far had been nearly silent, strode toward his companions, gushing about how great the train ride was. He chattered excitedly and at length about the ride, surprising everyone with his new volubility.

Klaus tried to see where the two men from the Mustang were going, but he couldn't find them amid the swirling crowd. Steve handed Gerd his camera bag and Alex led the group down the street to the Eureka Station for some Cornish pasties—small pies filled with potatoes, turnips, onions, and beef.

It was one of the traditional dishes the miners had eaten for lunch. They had to eat to keep up their strength, but needed something portable that could be eaten cold. Cornishes filled their requirements very well.

The group agreed that the pasties were delicious. Peter ate three of them in rapid succession and they teased him about his appetite. After they'd finished eating and settled their bills they all headed over to the van.

When they got closer they saw the same blond guy they'd seen earlier, and he was still trying to look into the van. Alex shouted, "Hey! Mister! Can I help you?"

The man walked away again. This time Alex took off after him, but the guy broke into a run and turned down a side street. By the time Alex made it to the corner, the guy was gone, so he broke off his chase.

When Steve caught up with Alex, he said, "What was that?"

"That was the second time today I've caught that guy trying to look into the van."

"What's he looking for?" Steve asked.

"I have no idea," Alex said. "There's nothing of value in it."

Steve decided to re-park the van in a less obvious area, just in case.

Alex had reserved a couple of Off-Highway Vehicles, OHVs, for a trip into the mountains that afternoon. While Steve moved the van, Alex led the group down the street to Rock Pirates, a rental place, owned by Erick Loyer.

Alex had rented from him many times over the years and they'd become friends.

***

Despite their best efforts, Butch and Sundance lost track of the group in the surging crowd at the train station. Now they were roaming the streets of Silverton looking for them. In such a small place they should've been easy to find.

The men checked every store, every restaurant, and every bar. They even checked the two marijuana dispensaries, but couldn't find any of them. Just when they were about to give up and grab some lunch, they spotted them in the distance boarding a couple of OHVs.

They watched as Gerd set his camera bag onto the luggage rack on the back of a vehicle, wrap it in a tarp, and lash it down with bungee cords. Butch took off at a trot to intercept them, but before he could get close, the two vehicles pulled out and drove right past them down Greene Street.

Butch pulled out his chrome Smith & Wesson .357 and pointed it at Alex, shouting, "Stop!"

Alex smiled, waved, and kept going, thinking it was a reenactment scenario. The tour group and spectators on the street laughed and clapped at the show.

Sundance called out to him, "Butch! Not here!"

Butch wanted to put some lead in back of Alex's head, but Sundance was right, they had an audience. So he didn't.

The men were mortified at being ignored and then laughed at. They immediately headed to Rock Pirates to rent a chase vehicle.

"Hey guys!" Erick said, as the cowboys came through the door. "How are ya?"

"Doin' great!" Butch said. "We'd like to rent somethin'."

"Sure! What are you looking for? One vehicle or two?"

"One," Butch said. "Like the ones that just left here."

"Have you ever driven an OHV before?"

"Nah," Butch replied. "How hard can it be?"

"Well, you're right, it's pretty easy, almost the same as a car," Erick said. "We need to do a little paperwork first, then you'll be good to go."

While filling out the rental agreement and initialing the damage waivers, Sundance asked, "So where do people usually go in these things?"

"There are hundreds of options," Erick said. "We're on the Alpine Loop. So you've got sixty-three miles of scenic byways to choose from. All the routes are on low maintenance roads suitable only for high ground clearance 4x4s, but no worries. These OHVs will handle almost anything."

"What are the best places to go, like, for instance, those guys who just left," Butch asked. "Where are they headed?"

"Well, that's a friend of mine who comes through here at least four times a year. He always likes to go to Animas Forks. That's a ghost town. And he usually goes to Engineer Pass. That's a 12,800 foot pass leading to Lake City.

"And sometimes he goes to Stony Pass—that one's at 12,600 feet and it's one of the original passes into Silverton. There might be a lot of snow up there right now, though. We had a big storm a few days ago."

After Butch made their payment Erick walked the two men over to one of the machines and explained how it worked. "This is a nice new Polaris," he said.

"Are you guys sure you're dressed warm enough?" Erick asked. "It can get chilly up there."

"We're good," Butch said, and he and Sundance got into the OHV.

"Here's an important thing to remember," Erick said. "All of our machines are equipped with a GPS. If you get lost, or stuck, or anything goes wrong with the vehicle, you push this button," he said, indicating the switch.

"When you press this, we'll see the signal and come get you as soon as possible. But if you have a serious emergency, I mean life threatening emergency, you can push this other button," he said, pointing to another switch.

"This second switch calls the rescue services. They'll come with helicopters and all that stuff, so whatever you do, don't push this button unless it's a major emergency!"

The two guys nodded.

"Okay, now go have fun!" Erick said, as he slapped the roof of the Polaris. Butch gunned the engine and off they went.

They hadn't even made it to the end of Greene Street before Sheriff Daniels stopped them for speeding. The limit in the town was fifteen miles an hour and they were going almost twice that.

As he wrote the citation, the sheriff explained that there were a lot of people in town who were opposed to allowing OHVs because of drivers who went speeding through town. "If I catch you again," he said, "you're going to jail."

Butch paid the fine on the spot and promised to obey the law in the future.

***

"That was the wrong kind of gun," said Peter, "It looked too new and shiny."

The others agreed. The group's consensus was that the action and the costumes were okay, and the thwarted shootout had been fun, but the modern gun made the reenactment seem too fake.

Alex took the group to the Silverton Mountain Ski Area. It was one of the toughest ski areas in the world. The owners were passionate freeskiers and snowboarders who leased a local mountain and created a ski area for dedicated athletes.

It was a spartan setting with only a tent and an old chairlift they'd bought used from Mammoth Lakes in California. The lift took skiers to a ridge from where they could hike to what Alex described as, "The craziest freeride terrain ever created inbounds of a skiing area, with unmaintained runs through avalanche chutes and trees.

"They also have some steep, narrow runs between rocks, that are extremely dangerous and difficult to ski."

Alex was a freeskier himself and he was excited when he described the place. "I got into a small avalanche when heliskiing there. I managed to stay on top of the avalanche and didn't get hurt—it was only a small slide—but it taught me respect for the location."

After taking a look at the ski area they rode the OHVs to the end of the road to check out a mine that had reopened a few years ago.

"The new mining technology has made it economically viable to reopen some of the old mines and also to try some new areas," Alex said. "Prospectors are still finding silver, gold, and other valuable minerals in the Rockies. Some of the companies are even scavenging through the debris left by the old mines."

The guests took a few photos then the group turned around and headed back the way they'd come.

When Butch and Sundance left Silverton they decided to drive to the place Erick suggested, Animas Forks, the ghost town with a mine, a mill, and a cluster of other abandoned buildings.

The mafiosos figured it would be the most likely place to take a bunch of tourists because of the scenery and the historic interest. They hadn't discussed it, but there was tacit agreement that the time for stealth and subtlety was over.

The road was rough, but their vehicle handled the bumps extremely well. They learned that the faster they went, the smoother the ride was. They even passed some tourists in Jeep Wranglers.

The Jeeps were tough enough to manage bad roads, but they weren't really made for higher speeds across this particular type of terrain like the OHVs were. Butch enjoyed passing them.

When they arrived at Animas Forks, Butch stopped and got out in the middle of what was left of the town. He stood there in the middle of the ghost town in his boots, jeans, and cowboy shirt looking like a gunfighter in a Western film.

The problem was that his opponent was nowhere to be found. They'd have to continue stalking their prey along the route Erick had outlined.

Unfortunately it involved traversing an unpaved track to Engineer Pass which was a shockingly steep, rugged, climb with a lot of sharp switchbacks. Butch's fear of heights made him shudder with dread just looking at it.

Sundance would have to make this part of the trip alone while Butch waited at one of the old abandoned buildings. Sundance was happy to do as Butch asked. Despite his apparent gentleness he was fully capable of doing what needed to be done if he caught up with the group.

The ride was bumpy, but Sundance relished the thrilling drive. One could hardly imagine how it had been possible to use such a terrible road to haul anything, much less heavy machinery and supplies for the mines.

But what great scenery! He could see several 14,000 foot mountain peaks from the track. When he reached the top, he was disappointed to find himself alone.

He got out to look around. It was obvious he wouldn't be able to go any farther. There was too much snow. And there weren't any tracks in it, so he knew for certain that nobody else had attempted to go beyond this point.

The group may or may not have made it this far, but they hadn't gone past where his vehicle sat. He turned around and headed back down the mountain, but not without stopping a few times to enjoy the splendid view. He wished he'd brought a camera. Maybe he'd buy one.

Chapter 25

Alex decided to take the guests up Stony Pass. He loved the steep, winding road that went through a forest and then through alpine tundra. It must've been terrifying in the old days to ride horse or ox drawn wagons up and down it. But in an OHV it was pure fun.

Steve struggled to keep up with Alex. He preferred to go slower and pause more often. This seemed to be a logical approach, but it wasn't always the safest way to proceed in that sort of terrain. When it came to driving on bad unpaved roads, Alex had a lot more experience.

He'd crashed his first ATV in Cabo San Lucas, Mexico, just before his sixteenth birthday. Since then he'd continued to push things, but he'd never crashed again and had rarely gotten stuck. He'd learned the hard way that one of the prime tactics in a difficult off-road driving situation was often that you might need to keep the machine rolling, *no matter what.*

It was almost always a bad idea to stop while you were in the middle of a bog. Once you stopped moving, the wheels would lose traction and bury themselves in the mud, or sand, or snow, when you tried to resume movement.

Another strategy he'd learned was to roll forward or backward to a less steep area, whichever way would give better traction, and try again. He knew from observing stuck vehicles that many people hadn't acquired those two basic insights.

Their mistakes had dug the ruts that made roads like this progressively more bumpy until the local officials were forced to send heavy equipment out to smooth them out again—after which the process started all over.

The group in Alex's 6-seater was having a great time, especially Peter, who was screaming like a kid on a roller coaster.

Steve was an excellent driver on paved surfaces, but he was less confident about his off-road skills. He worried that he wouldn't be able to get them to the top of the incline. This was not a road you could afford to be half-hearted on.

Alex made it almost to the top of the pass, but then encountered too much snow to proceed any farther and turned back to warn Steve.

When the group was together again they took some more photos and played around in the snow, enjoying the break, and frolicking about. The Germans were shocked when Alex said, "We're now at an altitude that's more than 3,000 feet higher than the highest mountain in Germany."

Neither the drivers nor guests wanted to leave, but eventually they had to head back down.

***

On his return Sundance stopped at the ghost town to pick up Butch. When he rolled into the abandoned village he saw Butch sitting alone on an old wooden porch like a kid who had no one to play cowboys and Indians with.

He reported what he'd seen and they discussed what to do next.

"What was the mountain pass the rental guy mentioned?" Sundance asked.

"Rocky Pass?" Butch suggested, as he struggled to recall.

They scanned the map Erick had given them. It showed all the scenic byways. They couldn't find a Rocky Pass.

"I think it might be this one," Sundance said. "Stony Pass."

"Yeah, yer right," Butch said.

"Alright, let's hit it!" Sundance said, turning the key to restart the engine.

***

Alex believed that you couldn't have a full OHV adventure experience without crossing at least one creek. He knew a great spot near the Animas River, just off the main road.

153

Back in the days when Rock Pirates still rented out two-wheel drive Tomcars, Alex had gotten stuck once, but those vehicles were now being used for cruising the deserts of Baja California, Mexico, where Erick had opened a new branch.

The machine Alex was using today was four-wheel drive, but he was still careful because no one wanted to get stuck in the middle of a frigid stream created by melting snow. He needed to find a place where the water level was low enough and slow enough to make the crossing safe.

They cruised off the main road, Byway 2, and alongside the Animas River. Steve left some space between Alex's lead vehicle and his. Soon they sighted a likely looking creek.

Alex pressed on the gas. Peter screamed. *Where did that quiet guy go?* Alex wondered, *and who is this new fellow?*

The OHV hit the water and made a big splash that sent fountains of cold water into the air. The windshield wipers were momentarily overwhelmed by the volume of water, so the vehicle's occupants were blinded for a few seconds. Alex kept going, though, as was his mantra, and made it across. His little group let out a cheer.

Steve, watching the wild splashing from behind, hit his brakes, and shouted, "Oh no!"

***

Butch and Sundance saw from the map that the fastest way to Stony Pass was by staying on Byway 2 and then taking a left near Silverton, so they kept to the road, not realizing that the tour group was having an aquatic adventure only a few hundred yards away.

The American West was a huge place. And, as the saying goes, a miss is as good as a mile.

***

Alex got out of his OHV and waved to Steve to indicate that he should come on across and everything would be fine, but Steve was afraid of getting stuck.

"Pedal to the metal, buddy!" Alex shouted.

Steve took a deep breath and stomped on the gas. He hit the water at speed, but he'd forgotten to turn on the windshield wipers. A wave splashed up, and they made it through, but Steve couldn't find the switch for the wipers, so the visibility was almost nil during the crossing.

It was thrilling anyway and everyone in the vehicle shouted with excitement. When he reached the other side of the creek Steve was a little late hitting the brakes and made a scary slide toward Alex and the parked OHV.

Alex leaped out of the way and Steve managed to get stopped inches behind the other vehicle. "Dude!" Alex said. "That was close!"

Steve's passengers jumped out, laughing, and marveled at the tiny gap between the two machines. They were all so full of adrenaline they laughed when Steve apologized.

"What a great adventure!" Peter said.

Gerd decided to check on his camera bag. It was still strapped to the back of the vehicle. He removed the tarp and was pleased to see that everything was dry. He decided to hold the bag on his lap for the rest of the ride, so he'd have access to different lenses.

The group was laughing and talking much more than they had before. This pleased Alex and Steve. They liked to see their guests having a good time.

The next destination would be Animas Forks and after that Alex wanted to try to get all the way up Engineer Pass. On the way he planned to point out Eureka, a former boom town, and stop at some of the old mines and mills for a look around.

The group's dumb luck was still holding. Without even trying, they were evading pursuers they'd barely noticed. The innocent changes in their schedule were wreaking havoc on the Vegas mob. Mob guys had anger management issues. They didn't care if the havoc was being caused on purpose or not. *Somebody* would have to pay for all this extra effort.

***

When Butch and Sundance arrived at an extremely steep section of the road up Stony Pass Butch's heart began to pound and he could feel himself hyperventilating.

He was quiet while Sundance drove the first few switchbacks, but then he suddenly shouted, "Stop this thing! I gotta get out!"

Sundance stopped immediately.

"I'm gonna wait here," Butch said, climbing out of the OHV.

"Are you serious?" Sundance asked.

"Totally!" Butch answered.

"Okay. I'll go up and take a look," Sundance said. "I'll be back as quick as I can." Then he drove away.

For a few minutes Butch stayed near where he'd been dropped off, then he decided to walk downhill to find a more comfortable place to wait. He found a fallen log and sat on it.

Meanwhile Sundance did a good job driving up the steep incline. He was getting used to the extreme roads and was enjoying himself. Parts of the trip had been rough. The long chase was maddening for sure, and he was terrified of the Boss, but the journey had also given rise to some wonderful experiences.

He knew he'd remember the challenging roads and the grand mountaintop panoramas for the rest of his life. Of course, the way things were going, that might mean only a couple more days.

***

As Peter's buzz wore off he realized that the cookie he stole from Frida had been drugged. Probably with cannabis.

This was why she hadn't shared the cookies with anyone else but Elisabeth, and then only when the dragon needed to be sedated.

So he'd accidentally drugged himself and displayed a baffling intoxication to the group. That was embarrassing, but a totally deserved punishment.

The tour group reached the highest point of Engineer Pass and made a photo stop. The view was awe-inspiring.

"This is the best part of the trip so far," said Frida. "I like it even better than Bryce Canyon."

Steve agreed with her, but he also took note of some dark clouds rolling in from the southwest. He turned to Alex and said, "We'd better head back to Silverton. It looks like there's a storm coming."

***

Sundance was getting into progressively deeper snow at Stony Pass, but he was seeing fresh tracks ahead so he followed them to see if they'd been made by the people he was looking for.

He suspected they'd gone on ahead, but Butch had the map, so he couldn't check to be sure where the road led. He continued to the point where the other tracks ended. There were no vehicles there, so he had no choice but to go back the way he'd come.

He was an inexperienced driver in off-road snowy conditions, though, and he gave the vehicle too much gas as he tried to make a three-point turn. He buried the rear tires in the snow. After that, despite several tries, he couldn't get the OHV free.

He panicked when he realized he was stuck. He couldn't remember which lever to pull. He didn't dare guess wrong and call the authorities. If he made that mistake the press would get hold of it for sure. It was imperative that he and Butch stay totally under the radar.

Walking back to Silverton would take all night. He dreaded Butch's reaction to the screwup and the utterly miserable night that lay ahead of them both, not least because by the end of it the trail would've gone cold, no pun intended.

***

Butch sat on the log waiting until he couldn't take it anymore. He needed to relieve himself. He could've done it right where he was, but something about being on foot in the wilderness made him feel too exposed, so he stepped off the path and walked a little way into the woods.

He found a spot that suited him but he heard a branch snap and glanced up to find himself looking into the eyes of a bull moose a few yards away. The creature didn't appear pleased to see a city slicker in his territory.

Butch froze. The moose was taller than he was and it was making strange wheezing and grunting sounds. He was paralyzed by the sight of the massive animal.

He stood like a statue for what seemed like forever until he heard a couple of dirt bikes coming around the corner behind him. They were making an insane amount of racket.

The moose heard the noise, too, and he didn't like it either. He turned around and walked away slowly. Butch watched the huge beast disappear in the woods.

When it was out of sight he calmed down enough to notice that he'd emptied his bladder inside his pants. *Geez*, he thought. *I hate this place. I hate this job. I wanna go home where the bathrooms are indoors.*

***

When Sundance calmed down he remembered which button would call Erick and he pushed it. He was as relieved as Butch, but he didn't need a fresh pair of trousers.

Chapter 26

The tour group made it back to the Rock Pirates shop in good time. Alex was standing at the counter chatting with Erick when an alarm came in.

"Oh dude! No way!" Erick said. "I had these really strange guys in here earlier today. They seemed like city people—no clue what the outdoors is about. They hardly listened to anything I said. I've been worried that they'd get themselves into trouble. Now it looks like they have."

"Uh oh," said Alex.

"It's been great seeing you again, Alex, but I've gotta get onto this pronto and see what's happened."

Erick grabbed some raingear from wall hooks, saying, "There's a storm coming. It's gonna get nasty soon."

Then he went outside, got into an OHV, and roared away.

As the group made their way back to the van the first raindrops began to fall. Moments after they were all aboard it started to pour.

***

The rain brought cold air with it.

Well before the rain reached Butch he was already freezing and totally miserable on account of standing out in the open at high altitudes without proper clothing. The wet pants added an additional element of torture.

When the full force of the rain hit him he was even more uncomfortable, but at least the situation with his pants was no longer discernable. For a guy like him, saving face was worth almost anything.

He'd seen no further sign of the moose, so he decided to take a chance and take whatever shelter he could find in the edge of the woods. He squatted down underneath the trunk of a huge fallen tree.

He got dirty and felt like a caveman, but it provided a nice amount of shelter from the wind and rain.

***

Erick had studied the day's forecast and knew he needed to hurry. He speeded along the track and buzzed right past Butch, not even noticing a guy sheltering in and under the brush beside the trail. Butch had tried to get up and flag the guy down, but he'd had trouble crawling out from under the tree. His legs were cramped and he'd slipped in the wet debris of the forest floor.

He shouted but Erick couldn't hear him over the roar of the engine, the rain, and the wind.

Up on Stony Pass the precipitation was in the form of huge, pretty snowflakes. Erick wasn't comfortable driving on snow, especially as it was falling, but he wouldn't slow down until he'd reached the OHV emitting the distress call.

He rounded a curve and spotted the machine with Sundance sitting inside. He stopped next to it, and said, "Hey there, are you okay?"

Sundance nodded, frowning.

"What's happened?" Erick asked politely, although he could see the problem.

"I got stuck," Sundance replied.

"Okay," Erick said. "Let me see if I can get you out."

Sundance gave the man his seat. Erick started the engine, looked down, and noticed the gear shift was set to two-wheel drive. He switched it into four-wheel drive, low-ratio, and pressed gently on the gas. The vehicle crawled out of the deep ruts it had dug for itself. In a few seconds he'd freed it.

He turned the machine around, and said, "You'll be fine now." He waggled a finger at Sundance, and said, "You guys should've listened closer to my instructions."

He looked around, and said, "Where's your buddy?"

"He's waitin' down at the bottom of the trail. Didn't you see him as you came by?"

"Nope," Erick said, "Why's he down there?"

"He's scared of the steep stuff," Sundance said.

"Oh. Well, a lot of people are. Let's go get him."

Sundance followed Erick back down the mountain.

As they lost altitude the snow gradually turned to icy slush and then to rain. The freezing water poured into the open-sided vehicles. Sundance was soaked and chilled to the bone but he made the drive.

Butch wasn't where Sundance had left him. Sundance guessed he'd walked down to an even less risky area, and sure enough, as soon as they got away from the steep cliffside area Butch was easy to spot. He was out in the open, running around in circles in the cold rain, trying to stay warm.

"What took you so long?" he shouted. He was bedraggled and enraged.

"I got stuck," Sundance replied, shooting Erick a look that begged him not to say anything.

It was late by the time Erick and his wayward renters made it back to Silverton. The last train had left for the day, and the last bus as well. Butch and Sundance were stranded high in the Rockies until morning.

The two men couldn't cope with the idea of spending the night in such a tiny isolated place, or losing the group again, so they offered Erick a ridiculous amount of money to drive them back to Durango.

He agreed to take them. They bought Rock Pirates t-shirts and hoodies and changed into them so as to have something clean and warm to wear on the trip down the mountain.

The irony of hoods wearing his company's hoodies was lost on Erick because he didn't know who they were.

***

The tour group was lively on the drive back, joking and telling stories. The adventure expedition on the OHVs had produced the effect Alex always hoped for when he worked as a guide.

He'd taken many guests on similar rides. Some of them weren't enthusiastic at first, but things would gradually change as the pristine wilderness scenery and the fun of the bumpy ride got to them.

Some of the guests asked for a stop at a grocery store, so when they got to Durango Steve took them to the City Market. This reminded Alex of his monetary dilemma. He didn't need a *lot* of money, but he needed at least *some* because he was almost broke.

While a few of the guests shopped for food for their next picnic, others asked if they could get a coffee. "Of course," Alex said.

Privately he was trying to figure out the best way to scrounge a few bucks to buy some food without having to take the chance of using Stanfield's credit card. There was an ATM at the store so he decided to try to make a withdrawal.

He opened the wallet and pulled out the piece of paper with the telephone number written on it. He put his mirrored sunglasses on, raised the collar of his coat, lowered the visor of his cap, and tilted his face down so the ATM camera wouldn't get a good picture of him.

He inserted the card and typed the last four digits of the telephone number. It was the wrong PIN. Okay, so that was a failure. He took the card out of the machine and turned away from the camera. He was putting the card back into the wallet when he noticed the first four digits of the phone number were the same as the date of birth on the driver's license, but in reverse.

If the birthdate hadn't been so simple, 1-1-90, he wouldn't have recognized it backwards.

Alex knew he'd get only two or three tries, so he needed to be extremely careful. The numbers had to be exactly right. There was no margin for error.

He inserted the ATM card again, and this time he typed in the first four digits of the phone number.

It worked! He'd done it! It was a miracle. It was all he could do to keep from shouting *Yes!* and doing a fist pump.

He requested $200, the amount he thought was a safe daily maximum, and the machine dutifully doled out the bills. Alex sent up a thanks to the universe, stuffed the cash into the billfold, and left the store.

As he was walking back to the van to wait for the group, someone approached him from behind and tapped him on the shoulder. He turned around and instantly recognized the person standing before him as the same one whose picture had stared back at him from the driver's license in the wallet he was carrying.

"I think you have something that belongs to me," the man said, in a soft voice.

"Wha …whaddya mean?" Alex said.

"Come *on*. I know you've got my cards. I've been following the transactions. I get a message on my cell phone every time they're used," he said. "I know you just withdrew two hundred bucks."

"Uh, …" Alex mumbled.

"You don't have to explain," he said. "You can keep the cash. But I need you to give me something you've got in the van that belongs to me. Do it right now and be quick about it, and we'll call it even."

"I don't understand," Alex asked, baffled. "What else do you have in the van?"

"That bag," he said, pointing through the open door at Gerd's camera bag which was all the way in the back.

"That's my client's bag," Alex said.

"Give me the bag." The volume of his voice was still almost a whisper, but he was significantly more insistent.

"But…," Alex said.

The guy interrupted him, "You've been using my credit card and now you've used my ATM card. You've stolen money from me. I'm not gonna call the cops if you'll hand me that bag. If you don't, some extremely bad things are going to happen to you. Do you understand?"

Alex didn't understand any of it, but he said, "Okay, okay, I'll get it," and he climbed into the van and stooped to make his way to the back.

He squatted down and reached for the camera bag. While he was focused on getting hold of it and backing out of the van, an unmarked delivery truck rolled up next to the van and stopped.

Two men leaped out of a side door, grabbed Stanfield from behind, covered his mouth with a folded piece of cloth, and dragged him backwards into the truck. Then they sped away.

The entire procedure took only a few seconds.

Alex maneuvered himself backwards out of the van, and stepped down onto the ground, oblivious to what had just transpired.

He turned to give Stanfield the bag, but he was gone. He'd vanished.

Where'd he go? Alex wondered. He stood there with the bag in one hand and the guy's wallet in the other and turned in a 360, but couldn't see the guy anywhere. He'd disappeared.

How was that possible?

Alex saw Gerd coming back, so he returned the bag to the van and stuffed the wallet into his pocket.

Steve and the other guests soon appeared as well. Steve noticed that Alex was wearing a strained expression. "Everything alright?" he asked.

Alex looked around, shook his head slightly, and said, "Yeah! Sure, I'm good!" then climbed into the front passenger seat.

Chapter 27

Erick drove the two goons along Highway 550 in his pickup truck. They were almost to Durango when an unmarked delivery van roared out of the City Market parking lot. It veered in front of the pickup, cutting them off.

There was nothing Erick could do but stomp the brakes.

"Did you see that?" Erick shouted. "We're lucky we didn't broadside them. Geee…"

"That was *close!*" Sundance agreed, settling back into his seat.

They watched the van speed away.

Erick continued to the Strater Hotel without further incident and dropped off his two passengers. The henchmen were ecstatic at being back in civilization.

They rushed to their room arguing about who'd get to take the first hot shower. A usual, Butch won.

***

The tour group arrived back at their own more modest accommodations a few minutes later. Alex was still freaked out about what had just happened to him. He was mortified to have been caught stealing and terrified of what might happen next. This resulted in him being unusually subdued.

He had no idea what to do. He was trapped between a rock and a hard place. He had to have enough money to eat during the rest of the trip and his own funds were unavailable. He assumed Stanfield's funds were still available until such time as he decided to turn off the tap by reporting the cards stolen.

Maybe he wouldn't do it for a while yet. The cards were the only way he had to track Alex.

It was a horrible dilemma, but as the saying went, *In for a penny, in for a pound.* He'd keep using the cards, but only for necessities. He wouldn't squander the guy's money.

"Let's meet for dinner at 6:50 at the lobby," Steve said, before the guests got out of the van. "We've reserved a table at a place that's only a couple of blocks away. We can walk down together."

The group broke up and went to their rooms, all except for Frida and Peter.

"I would like to speak with you privately if you do not mind," Peter said. "I need to make a confession to you."

"Oh?"

"Yes, I stole one of your cookies and ate it."

"Oh!"

"I am sorry and must apologize. I did not realize they contained your pain medication."

Frida said nothing.

"I have a second confession. I am a palliative care physician. So, although I have never been exposed to the drug before, I believe I recognize its effects.

"My third confession is that I work in a monastery as a lay monk."

"Is that why you confess a lot?"

"Undoubtedly."

"Well, I'm not Catholic, but that's a lot of interesting information in an admirably concise format," said Frida. "I'm a writer, so I admire that sort of thing. Can I confess now?"

He nodded.

"My confession is that I write mystery novels and that, by choice, I've never married. I value my independence and peace of mind too much. I created my own order and live in a monastery for one and I love it."

He smiled.

"So the monk came to Las Vegas for a change of scene?" she said.

"Yes, noise, excessive lighting, bad art, watching strangers throwing money away for sport, and killing themselves by overindulging in every sort of unproductive activity in an enclave devoted to vice—it's the polar opposite of caring for dying monks in a small, nearly silent, enclosed world."

She laughed.

"It's been wonderfully refreshing," he said.

"If you won't be offended, I'd like to share with you that I have a lot of experience dealing with stiffness caused by prolonged stillness. We're in the praying business, of course. I've found that massage and myofascial release movements are more effective for pain relief than chemical interventions."

"I can well imagine your wish to self-medicate after prolonged sitting that writers must endure. And typing or writing. Your hips and shoulders must get painfully stiff and your hands painfully overworked."

They discussed cannabinoids, the kind that was smoked and CBD oils and creams. Peter outlined the various chemical compositions and strengths allowed in the US, Germany, and France.

"If you will allow me, I will show you some basic myofascial release stretches that you can do yourself. I am certain they will relieve your pain."

"Alright. I would like to learn. But, just to be clear, if I decide to give Elisabeth another cookie, will you object?"

"No, I will not. In fact, I will be grateful."

They parted, smiling, and Frida decided to take a stroll down Main Street. This time she bought a jar of expensive face cream and a jar of high potency CBD cream and took them back to her room and carefully switched the contents.

***

At 6:50 Alex arrived in the lobby to find everyone already there. They were chattering amongst themselves, all except for Peter. He'd resumed his usual quiet persona after the wild OHV ride.

Alex led them to the Mahogany Grille in the Strater Hotel. Their table was ready and they were seated immediately.

***

Butch and Sundance were safe, clean, warm, and dry now, but they were still feeling exhausted and traumatized by their experiences in the high altitude wilderness. They decided against eating in a sit-down restaurant. Instead, they went for carryout from a Cajun place recommended by the desk clerk.

As they walked past the Mahogany Grille, Klaus spotted them through the window. "There they are again," he said, pointing.

"Ja. They seem to be travelling a similar route," Gerd said, in a bored tone.

***

It was only six, but Butch *had* to get up. He felt sick and he had a splitting headache. During the night he'd developed a scratchy throat and now that he was awake, he began to cough and sneeze. He had a cold. Great. Just what he needed.

He was startled when Sundance came into the room carrying an armload of clothing

"Where ya been?" Butch asked.

"Doin' some laundry," he said, and tossed some clean and dry garments on the bed.

"They leave it unlocked all night?"

"Nope. I finessed the lock."

Butch tried to smile at this, but flinched instead.

"What's wrong witcha?"

"I feel awful. I think I got somethin'."

"The fun never ends," Sundance said.

Butch got up and prepared to leave. He was moving, but a lot slower than Sundance. He tried to speed up. He had no choice. They needed to grab breakfast and be at the Durango Lodge before the tour group left.

"Thanks for doin' the washin'," he said.

Sundance nodded, then made a quick dash to the City Market to get some aspirin, cough syrup, and lozenges for Butch.

***

Alex and Steve woke up at seven. Steve had a slight head start so he showered first.

Alex prepared coffee using the machine in the room and was glad for a few minutes of private time to call home. Münster was eight hours ahead of Durango, so first thing in the morning here was mid-afternoon there. This was the best time to call because he'd be working all day and by the time he was back in his hotel, his family would be asleep.

He called home via WhatsApp. His ten year old daughter, Amilia answered immediately and they had a short video chat that made him feel happy and homesick at the same time. This was the worst part of his job. He missed his wife and children.

Unfortunately for Alex, his eight year old, Vianne, was scheduled to meet a friend, so she didn't have time to talk. His wife didn't either, because she'd promised to take their child to see her friend.

They'd gotten rid of their car, so his wife would walk their daughter to her destination or ride a bike alongside her. If necessary they could make a five minute walk to a garage and use a code to unlock access to a vehicle she'd booked using a car-sharing app.

When he hung up Alex turned on the television and tuned it to a 24-hour news station. After some political reports, the driver's license photo of J.J. Stanfield popped up and filled the screen. Seconds later the name in the caption left no doubt.

Alex was shocked to the core. *Ach du Kacke! What now?* Was he becoming a global outlaw? Would he be tracked by Interpol for finding Stanfield's wallet and making a desperate choice to use his plastic for a few hundred dollars? It had only been for modest food and drink. He hadn't bought a single luxury item.

He struggled to block out the panicked voice in his head and focus on what the commentator was saying. Apparently Stanfield had been reported missing by his colleagues at the New York media behemoth where he was employed.

The anchorman said Stanfield was thought to have been working on a story about the connections between high officials of the current administration, the mob, and foreign governments. He'd missed several of the scheduled check-ins he was supposed to make with his colleagues.

That sounded ominous even to Alex, and he'd seen the guy just yesterday. Because of the sensitive nature of the story Stanfield was working on, his colleagues were worried that he was in trouble.

Alex felt himself freaking out.

When Steve came out of the bathroom, Alex went in. While showering Alex tried to strategize. The last thing he wanted was to get involved in a situation like this. He hadn't wanted to do anything wrong, but he'd made a bad decision under pressure and, after that, things had just snowballed.

He didn't understand what had happened at the City Market yesterday. Why had he been able to see the journalist during the time he was supposedly missing? The guy was alive and unharmed, so things weren't too bad.

One thing was certain, he needed to get rid of the wallet and cards as soon as possible. The authorities would doubtless be tracing transactions and even now could be heading his way.

Were the cops minutes away from breaking down the door of his hotel room? Would he be dragged away to languish in an American prison never to see his family again? Had that brief call been his last contact with them?

Alex had to steady himself against the shower walls to keep from sliding into the floor.

***

The tour group met at nine to leave for Mesa Verde. As the guests boarded the van, Butch and Sundance sat watching them. The Mustang was in the Narrow Gauge Railway parking area. From there they had a good view of the hotel lot.

For the first time in this whole enterprise the two men had malice in their hearts. Enough was enough. There was gonna be a showdown, and it would happen very soon. Their livelihoods were at stake. Maybe even their lives.

Klaus' eyes missed nothing. "There they are again," he mumbled to his wife, tilting his head toward the car. "I do not know why they are doing it, but I am absolutely certain that they are following us," he added.

"Why would anyone be following us?" Tina asked petulantly, exasperated with his obsession with the Mustang. "This group, this trip, is beyond boring.

170

There is absolutely nothing of interest here, for anyone."

Gerd overheard their exchange, and said, "I think Klaus is right. Back in the '80s in East Germany I was sometimes followed by intelligence officers. I know how it feels when someone is on your tail."

Klaus looked at Gerd in surprise, as if he'd just seen a ghost.

Steve carefully guided the van out of the parking lot and onto the street. Gerd, Tina, and Klaus swiveled their heads and watched the Mustang follow them through downtown Durango and onto Highway 550.

Chapter 28

As they made their way along Highway 160 from Durango to Mesa Verde, Gerd and Klaus had to rely on the van's side mirrors to keep an eye on the black Mustang, because the trailer blocked the back window.

"It is still there," Klaus said, glancing at Gerd.

"What are you talking about?" Peter asked.

"Nothing," Klaus answered.

As they approached the exit for Mesa Verde, Steve flipped the blinker on to signal his turn. Klaus watched in the mirror as the Mustang also indicated a turn. "They are turning, too," he said.

Gerd nodded. It would be a likely place for anyone to turn, but both Klaus and Gerd had developed an acute sensitivity for this kind of situation during the post-war decades in East Germany.

Steve parked the van in a lot adjacent to a glamorous curving stone and glass visitor center and Alex explained the agenda for the day.

They'd go into the visitor center for access to the restrooms and exhibits explaining the history of the cliff dwellers. Then they'd buy tickets for a ranger-led tour of the Balcony House—one of the park's large cliff dwellings.

There was a high demand for that particular tour and because of the complicated logistics involved in the tour itself, they'd be given tickets for a specific time later in the day, as scheduled by the National Park Service.

"It's worth the wait," Alex promised.

The ancient forty-room mansion was a favorite place for Steve and Alex. "Before you decide whether or not you want to take this tour you need to understand that there are some steep ladders to climb and at one point you'll have to crawl through a dark, narrow tunnel.

"Is everyone okay with that?" Steve asked. "Anybody claustrophobic or not comfortable on long ladders?"

They all agreed that they were able to meet the challenges and would like to go.

***

Butch and Sundance watched Gerd leave the van without his camera bag. They got out of the Mustang and nonchalantly ambled over. They glanced inside the van and tried all the doors, but found them locked.

There were too many people and too many surveillance cameras for them to break in without being noticed. No way did they want trouble with the feds.

They'd wait for someone to unlock the van, then they'd make their move. So they followed the group into the visitor center. They watched Steve and Alex stand in a ticket line while the rest of the group wandered around looking at the displays.

Sundance got close enough to Steve and Alex to hear what they were talking about while Butch pretended to study the exhibits. Sundance heard them request nine tickets for the one o'clock tour of the Balcony House.

Gerd and Klaus watched the two absurdly dressed men. At least their ridiculous cowboy attire was now mud free. Whoever they were, they had no concept of blending in. Their bizarre clothing was attracting attention, and not of a good kind.

It was obvious that the two men weren't paying attention to the displays. But every time Klaus and Gerd got close to the them they moved on to the next exhibit.

Gerd noticed this, so he repositioned himself to approach from the other side, so as to hem them in. He felt like he was in a slow motion rodeo, rounding up two skittish wild horses.

When Klaus and Gerd had closed in to stand about five feet away on either side of them, Sundance went to join the line for tickets and Butch went outside.

Gerd followed Butch and saw him sit on the low stone wall in front of the building. Butch was still feeling unwell, and he was groggy from taking more than the recommended dose of the strong cough syrup.

Gerd moseyed out and sat down a few yards away. When Butch realized Gerd was so close, he got up and went to the Mustang. He wanted to get his gun and force Gerd to open the van, but only the driver and guide had keys, so he decided to recline in the passenger seat and wait.

Meanwhile, inside the visitor center, it was Sundance's turn to buy tickets. The ranger began to explain to him about the ladders and the tunnel, but Sundance interrupted him, saying brusquely, "Yeah, yeah, yeah, we know all about that. Gimme the two tickets."

Then he added, "Smokey," in an insolent tone while staring at the ranger's iconic flat-brim Stetson. The ranger frowned, but didn't say anything. He rang up the purchase and handed over the tickets.

***

There was a special lot set aside for trailers before the road into the park became steep. Steve and Alex made a brief stop there to unhook the trailer and leave it. They'd retrieve it on the way out.

Now Gerd and Klaus could see out the back window.

When the group arrived at the first stop inside Mesa Verde National Park, they walked up a steep paved path to Park Point Overlook. From there they had a great view of the area. They could see the entire park spread out before them to the south, as well as grand vistas in every other direction.

To the east were the San Juan Mountains in Colorado, to the north were the La Sal and the Abajo Mountains in Utah, to the west was Sleeping Ute Mountain in Colorado, and more than fifty miles away to the south, in New Mexico, far beyond the park boundary was the Ship Rock monadnock, an enormous chunk of stone that jutted up from its surroundings in the manner of Ayres Rock.

It was a splendid panorama, but Klaus wasn't seeing it. Instead he was staring at Gerd's profile and a memory was coming back to him. When he'd worked for the Stasi, the *Staatssicherheitsdienst*, or East German State Security

Service, he'd been part of a formidable and feared secret intelligence and police agency.

Klaus pulled Tina aside, and whispered, "When I met Gerd in Las Vegas there was something about him that seemed familiar. I thought maybe I'd heard his name before, but I couldn't quite recall the details. Now I do."

Tina looked at him in surprise.

"There was this guy in '88 who was involved in church gatherings. He was provoking political unrest and I was put on his tail. My report cost him at least five months in jail and then we expelled him from the country."

Tina's expression changed to astonishment.

"It has taken me all this time to be sure, but now I am certain it was Gerd. When he said the Stasi had been on his tail back in the day in East Germany I started to remember him and now I realize he was the man I sent to jail."

"Are you sure?" she asked.

"Yes."

"Honey, you were young," Tina said, "and you believed in the system."

"Does that make it alright?" Klaus asked. "I do not think so. He is such a nice guy! I feel so guilty for doing that to him!"

She put an arm around him to comfort him.

Gerd came over to the couple in concern. It was obvious that something was wrong. "Hey guys, what is wrong?" he asked.

He looked at Klaus and said, "You look pale."

"I am fine," Klaus said, obviously lying. "Just feeling the altitude, I guess. And my breakfast is not agreeing with me."

Chapter 29

It was a while before the Balcony House tour, so the group got back into the van and drove further into the park where they made a couple of stops for viewing the ancient Native American pit houses and other structures.

During this time, the Mustang was nowhere to be seen. Gerd tried to start a conversation with Klaus, but Klaus was too upset to be much of a talker or a listener.

"Hey guys, it's about time to head back for our tour of the balcony house," Alex said, and rounded up the guests.

When the group arrived at the parking lot where the Balcony House tour would start from, Klaus saw the Mustang again. It was parked nearby and no one was in it.

Butch and Sundance were standing across the road in the shade of an overhanging roof pretending to listen to a ranger's interpretive lecture on ancient indigenous cultures. They watched the tour group head over to join the others who'd be on their ranger-led tour.

As he approached them, Gerd realized that Sundance and Butch were both staring fixedly at his camera bag. That was bizarre. He switched the bag to his other shoulder and watched their eyes move to follow it. What the heck?

The ranger explained various details about the tour, warning about the ladders again in case some people might not want to climb them or not be able to climb them, but neither Butch nor Sundance was paying any attention. Instead, they were trying to maneuver themselves closer to Gerd without making a scene.

The tour began and Gerd managed to work his way to the front of the group. Elbowing one's way through a crowd was a German national sport. Gerd had a great deal more experience than any American, so Butch and Sundance had no chance of being able to keep up with him.

Klaus followed closely behind the two pseudo-cowpokes. He didn't know what their game was, but he was dying to bust those two broncos. He knew they'd disregard him as a threat on account of his age. Good. He'd exploit their ignorance.

Butch was so busy keeping a watch on Gerd that he didn't realize there was a steep drop-off on one side of the trail. It took him all the way to the first ladder to realize he'd made a serious mistake.

He waited as the group's forward movement bogged down and watched from behind as the people in the front started to climb up a thirty-two foot ladder. *What the ...?* He started to panic.

"You wanna turn around?" Sundance asked. It was obvious that Butch was freaking out.

Butch shook his head, and said, "We can't afford to mess this up again."

They held back and let all but the stragglers in the group go ahead of them, then Sundance said, "You first."

"Uh...," Butch mumbled.

"I'll be right behind ya. I won't let ya fall. Just rememba, don't look down. You got this."

Butch didn't move.

"Are ya okay?" Sundance asked.

Butch didn't speak, but he shuffled closer to the ladder and took hold of it. He climbed the first three rungs and felt his legs turn to rubber. He was also hyperventilating.

An old lady shouted in a southern accent, "Hey there, you young fellers! Are y'all okay?"

At first they thought the woman was concerned about them. They tried to mutter assurances to set her mind at ease, but maybe she was making fun of them. They weren't sure. Hillbilly types could be hard for outsiders to read, but whatever it was, it helped galvanize Butch.

Gathering every shred of Italian macho and mob bravado he possessed, he somehow managed to force himself to the top, with arms and legs that were visibly shaking. But then, when he made it to the top, he realized he'd have to let go of the ladder with both hands and crawl off of it and onto the bare dirt of a high ledge.

He froze. He literally could not make himself move. He looked at his hands and seemed unable to exert any influence over them. They were not letting go of the ladder.

Sundance shoved from below and the man who'd been in front of Butch turned to give him a hand, and encourage him. Together they heaved and wrestled Butch off the ladder and onto the ledge.

Sundance followed him.

There were a lot of people on this tour, so Butch and Sundance had their work cut out for them trying to get close to Gerd's camera bag. Each time they seemed to be gaining on the guy, he'd execute an impressive German crowd cutting maneuver to take a different photo.

Klaus kept an eye on Butch and Sundance as they remained fixated on Gerd.

The ranger leading the tour was a funny guy. He educated and entertained the crowd with his descriptions of the native people who'd built and lived in what was now a ruin.

Then the crowd arrived at a place where each tourist had to crawl through a twelve-foot-long, eighteen-inch-wide tunnel. It would accommodate only one person at a time. The old lady from the south who'd made comments to Butch and Sundance was ahead of them and she started in.

Then it was Sundance's turn. *Uh oh*, he thought. Now he was the one who was in trouble—he was seriously claustrophobic. He let every person in the group pass him. He couldn't bear the idea of being in that place with people in front of him and behind him, too.

He waited until he could go in last. Butch went through ahead of him and, when he came out the other end, he remained on his knees, looking back into the tunnel, to encourage his partner.

Sundance was deeply frightened. For him, this was by far the worst moment of the whole trip. Even the freezing night in the desert was nothing compared to this. He was sweating and shaking.

"Keep your eyes on me, buddy," Butch said. "I'm right here. You can do it."

Sundance didn't move.

"Okay," Butch said, "try closing your eyes and coming toward my voice."

Sundance closed his eyes and crawled toward his co-worker who was softly singing Sinatra and he somehow managed to make the hellish trip through the tunnel and come out the other side without vomiting, fainting, or having a heart attack.

The ranger was giving a short talk about the newer area of the historic site which neither man had the slightest interest in, but it gave them time for a breather before whatever hideous ordeal awaited them next.

Butch was standing right in front of his worst nightmare, but hadn't noticed it until the group began the ascent. He would to have to climb up sixty feet on ladders and stone steps cut into a sheer rock face, secured by thin metal fences and chains.

Butch stared in disbelief, totally stupefied. He was trapped. This time there was no way out. Or, at least, no way he could cope with.

He toyed with the idea of going back the way they'd come, but he knew Sundance would never be able to manage the tunnel a second time and, on the way back there was a ladder. Climbing up it had been terrifying, but climbing *down* would be so much worse.

Overdosing himself with flu medicine that morning hadn't made the situation any easier. He was so dizzy he thought he might faint. So this was what panic attacks were like. Nothing in his upbringing or mafia experience had prepared him for this.

He decided his only hope of getting out of this place and retaining his sanity was the last bit of coke in the stash he'd brought from Vegas. He moved to an outer edge of the crowd of milling tourists and turned his back to them. He reached into a jacket pocket and removed a tiny bottle. He screwed the cap off and snorted everything in it.

The powder took only seconds to kick in.

Stacking flu medicine and coke didn't give him a perfect result, but it was good enough. He was still a bit dizzy, but he felt strong and brave. The coke gave him a sense of invincibility.

Now when he thought about the ladder he found himself looking forward to the climb as a way to work off the excess energy flooding his system.

He snorted like a bull on his way up the side of the mesa. When he reached the top he threw his arms into the air like Rocky. He felt like he'd just climbed Mount Everest. The other tourists looked at him askance.

It would take Butch and Sundance a while to realize it, but during the stress of dealing with the ladders and the tunnel they'd totally forgotten about Gerd and his camera bag.

Chapter 30

Butch and Sundance made it back to the parking lot alive, one of them shell-shocked, and the other buzzed out of his mind. They stood on the paved, level ground without speaking, both needing time to recover.

Unfortunately they didn't have any time. The tour company van drove slowly past them, headed toward the exit. Suddenly they recalled what they were there for and broke into a run.

They leaped into the Mustang, with Butch taking the driver's seat. When he started the engine Sundance suddenly realized that it might not be wise for Butch to be driving with an unpredictable drug cocktail fueling his system.

"You're high," Sundance said, with unusual force. "Better let me drive."

His request penetrated the fog in Butch's brain and they each jumped out of the car, intending to run around it to switch seats. But Butch had already shifted into reverse before they decided to change sides, and he'd failed to put the car back into park before getting out.

Just as they were about to pass each other behind the vehicle they noticed it was moving backwards, toward them, and also toward the edge of a cliff. They tried to stop the backward motion by shoving against the trunk, but of course that didn't work, even with Butch all coked up.

Butch continued to shove uselessly against the trunk as Sundance sprinted for the driver's seat and jumped in. Before he could get a foot on the brake, the car hopped the curb and continued toward the wooden railing that prevented pedestrians from walking too close to the rim of the canyon.

Butch sprang out of the way before the car crashed into the fence and

Sundance managed to get the Mustang stopped before it went completely through the barrier and off the cliff.

He immediately pulled the car forward, crossing the curb again to get back onto the paved area. Tourists who witnessed the accident were shocked. It was an appalling brush with catastrophe.

Butch glanced at the damage inflicted by the fence. They were gradually destroying the beautiful car. "We better get outta here before somebody calls the cops or the rangers or whatever they got," Sundance said.

So they did. Or at least they tried to. They made it across the parking lot, but before they could get out, their exit was blocked by three buses from a local Cortez middle school that stopped to let students off for an educational excursion to the ruins.

It took several minutes before the kids were all offloaded and the buses moved out of the way. Sundance steered the Mustang toward the exit and was itching to floor the car when he realized that a National Park Service SUV was just ahead of them.

"Uh oh," Sundance said. "What if that guy gets a call about us?"

Butch checked his phone to be sure, then said, "I got no bars, so nobody coulda called to report anything."

The men meekly followed along behind the ranger.

The tour group was retrieving their trailer. Steve and Alex were hooking it up to the van in the special lot right next to the main road. Lucky for them, Butch and Sundance were so traumatized by the tour, which seemed like one long near death experience, and so unnerved by the Park Service vehicle in front of them. They didn't even notice the van.

Once Butch and Sundance reached the park boundary and the ranger got out of their way they sped off toward the highway to Cortez.

They made a brief stop at a gas station with a repair shop. They spent another hundred for a few quick and well-placed strikes of a hammer that repaired the trunk lid well enough to open and shut properly. Then they whizzed on through the little town of Cortez.

***

Steve drove south on Highway 491 and then took the so-called *G route* west toward White Mesa which would take them by Ute Mountain.

Traveling north would've been quicker, but Alex asked Steve to take the southern route because the guests had already seen the northern part when they came down from Moab.

Alex hated to backtrack during a trip.

Steve drove at a leisurely pace and they stopped a couple more times for photos. As the afternoon wore on the guests got quiet as usual and many of them took naps.

Alex popped a cowboy music CD into the dashboard player. Iconic western songs from Roy Rogers, Gene Autry, and Frankie Lane sang their hits to the van full of stone-faced or sleeping foreigners.

It was a strange experience for Steve, as the only American. He'd grown up with this music as a small child and knew all the songs. He couldn't imagine what Europeans made of it.

When that CD was finished, Alex put in another. This one was Ennio Morricone music from spaghetti westerns. It was beautiful, haunting background and music from films like *The Good, The Bad, and The Ugly* and *For a Few Dollars More*.

That put everyone else to sleep. Even Alex dropped off. Steve smiled as he chauffeured a load of sleeping tourists through the barren, but beautiful landscape.

When Butch and Sundance got to the intersection in Cortez their GPS sent them on the shorter northern route on Highway 491. Sundance increased his speed to catch up with the van. It took them less than an hour to cover the eighty-mile stretch to Blanding, Utah.

When they hit town, they checked all the hotels, but the van wasn't there. Butch was truly suffering at this point on account of his cold and because the drug cocktail was wearing off. He'd felt bad this morning, but now he felt a lot worse.

"We can run 'em down tomorrow," he said. "Let's stop for now. I need a bed."

They checked in at the Four Corners Motel. Soon Butch was tucked in and sleeping like the dead.

***

They made it to Blanding about an hour and a half behind Butch and Sundance and checked into the Stone Lizard Lodge. The group agreed to have dinner together at a steak house a block away, next door to the Four Corners Motel.

Alex held the door for everyone as they filed into the restaurant. Gerd, Klaus, and Tina went in last. Just before he went inside the restaurant Klaus glimpsed the Mustang.

"Look at that!" he said. "There is that same car *again!*"

"Are you sure it is the same one?" Gerd asked. "I do not remember that big dent in the rear bumper."

"I am sure," Klaus said. "It has got the same license plates."

"Yes, you are right," Gerd said. "What are they doing to that car? They must be the worst drivers in the world."

***

Sundance was starving.

He tried to rouse Butch for dinner, but it was a no go, "Lemme sleep," Butch mumbled, "Gotta get some rest."

Sundance was forced to venture out alone in search of a place to grab a bite. Fortunately he didn't have to go far. The first building he came to was a steak house right next door to the motel.

184

A steak would be great, but he wasn't keen on sitting in a restaurant like that by himself. And the place looked packed. There weren't a lot of dining options in Blanding and a coach tour had just arrived at the Four Corners Motel to disgorge its passengers.

He decided to walk over to the gas station and see what they had in the way of food. He figured Butch would wake up sooner or later and be hungry, so he decided to bring something back for him to eat, too.

Sundance was desperate for a beer, but his craving was not to be satisfied. The station attendant explained that Blanding was a dry town. After the day he'd had, it was hard to accept more bad news without flying off into a rage, but he restrained himself.

He fantasized about what he would do when he got back to Vegas. But first he needed to get the thingamajig. He glanced at his watch and did a mental calculation—he should have it in about ten hours from now.

Yeah, tomorrow he'd get the gadget. Then he could go home.

Sundance was walking back from the gas station carrying bags of snacks and bottled drinks when Klaus happened to glance out the window of the steak house. "That is one of the men from the Mustang," he whispered to Gerd.

"Yeah, you are right," Gerd said. "It is weird that they are always wearing the same thing. Who goes on vacation without a change of clothes?"

"Maybe the airlines lost their luggage," said Klaus, but he didn't believe it for a minute.

Chapter 31

Butch awoke to the sound of his cell phone ringing.

He answered it in a groggy haze, but when he realized it was the Boss calling, he instantly snapped fully awake.

"Where are you?" the Boss asked.

"We're in Blanding," Butch replied.

"And where might that be?"

"Utah."

"Utah? Have you accomplished your objective?"

"We're gettin' closer."

"Whaddya mean *gettin' closer*?" he shouted. "Are you kiddin' me? You been chasin' 'em for over a week! What the frack is goin' on?"

Butch stuttered, "We … we …. tried…."

"*Tried*? Did you say *tried*? Whaddya think this is, elementary school? You wanna A for effort? You get me that freakin' thing *now*!" he screamed.

There was absolute silence for a few horrible seconds, then he said, in an ominously soft voice, "Or do you need *me* to take care of it? If you don't wrap this up quick I'm gonna send a freakin' army down there and you'll see how *I* deal with it. And you'll see how I deal with *you*."

"Boss…Utah is…I can't explain it …."

"Shut the freak up! Utah! Utah! What's so special about Utah? You guys partyin' with them freakin' polygamists? Party's over boys. You better hurry up and bring me that gadget, or you're both *done*! You hear me?"

He slammed the phone down.

Butch sat up in bed holding the phone to the side of his head for a long time before he could make his arm move to lower it.

"What'd he say?" Sundance mumbled, still in bed.

"If we don't wrap this up pronto," Butch whispered, "he's gonna kill us."

***

The tour group was enjoying a hearty breakfast in the garden of the Stone Lizard Lodge. It was Alex and Steve's favorite hotel of the whole tour. "I love these homemade biscuits," Alex said.

He'd gotten up early so he'd be finished with breakfast well before the scheduled departure time. That way he'd have time to speak with his family again via WhatsApp.

In Germany his kids were already back from school and he was delighted to get to see them both and catch up by video chat. He showed them his room and the view outside. They always liked to see the places he stayed.

They had a nice talk, then he rang off and his heart sank. He sat for a few moments in silent sadness, then recovered himself and was ready to go to work.

***

After breakfast the group headed down to Bluff, Utah where their first photo stop was at a strange double pinnacle named Twin Rocks near the entrance to the tiny town.

Then they drove on to the Bluff Fort and stopped at the museum dedicated to the first Mormon settlers in the area. They'd been part of the Hole-in-the-Rock party, a famous wagon train that had to somehow move people, wagons, and animals down what was probably the steepest manmade wagon trail in history.

When the group walked into the stone building that housed the museum and a store they were greeted by volunteers dressed in cowboy attire. Alex told the man that they'd like to watch the short film explaining about the Hole-in-the-Rock expedition.

"A group just went into the theater and the movie's already running," said the docent. "Would your people like to see it in German? You can do that over in the old schoolhouse building, and that way you won't have to wait."

"Sounds great," said Alex. "Thank you."

Everyone but Klaus walked over to the schoolhouse.

"I need to make a call to Germany," he said to the docent. "May I use your Wi-Fi?"

"Our connection is really slow, but there's a public library with decent speed just across the street. You can sit on the bench in front of the library and you'll be able to get a good connection from there. It's open access, so you don't need a password."

***

When Butch and Sundance reached the museum they saw the van parked out front. *Finally* they'd caught up to the freakin' bag. Just in the nick of time, too.

They parked the Mustang right next to the van. They didn't bother with stealth this time. They got out and peered through the van's tinted windows to see if the camera bag was inside. Neither of them saw it, so they walked toward the museum.

"Do Mormons still have more than one wife?" Butch asked.

"Dunno," said Sundance. "Why're ya askin'?"

"The Boss says he thinks we're partyin' with polygamists."

"Ha!" barked Sundance, as he opened the door of the museum.

Klaus, sitting on the other side of the street, saw the men go inside.

"I have to hang up now," he said, and ended his call. Then he took off toward the schoolhouse.

Inside the museum the friendly volunteer in the cowboy costume greeted Butch and Sundance. "Welcome to Bluff Fort!" he said.

Butch and Sundance were so focused on the task at hand, they were startled by his greeting.

"Have you been here before?" the docent asked.

"Nah," Butch said, looking everywhere but at the docent.

"Well, welcome! I'm happy you found us!" he said. "This museum will teach you the story of the first settlers who came into this area, members of the Church of Jesus Christ of Latter-day Saints, also known as Mormons, or LDS for short."

"Were they polygamists?" Butch asked.

Sundance shot him a quizzical look. This was not the time for chats about religious or cultural history.

"That's a good question. Polygamy was never something most Mormons practiced. There were various offshoots where it existed, but the U.S. government made it real tough on all the Mormons on account of some of them having multiple wives.

"So the church elders ordered it to be stopped. That was in 1890. Of course, it took a while for it to die out. And there are still some people who practice it, but they're not bona fide members of the Church."

Sundance casually moved toward the other side of the museum store as the volunteer put a hand on Butch's shoulder and turned him to face a picture hanging on the wall.

"This is a picture of Hole-in-the-Rock," he said, "a steep road the early travelers built down to the Colorado River. It was the only place where the pioneers could get across the rugged landscape. You've timed it right to see a short film that explains it all!"

As he spoke, he steered Butch toward the theater door.

"But we…," Sundance said.

"It's only about fifteen minutes long and it's free!"

Butch and Sundance exchanged a look and Butch shrugged. The people they were following, and the camera bag, would be inside, so why not go in and scope out the bag's location?

The docent gently shoved them through the theater door and they stepped inside the room where the documentary was playing. Coming from the outside, it would take a couple of minutes for their eyes to adjust to the darkness. They waited in the back of the room.

***

Meanwhile Alex's group was finished with the German version of movie at the schoolhouse. Klaus was concerned about the proximity of the men in the

Mustang. "I am bored by this place," he said to Alex. "We should leave."

He was trying to get the group out of the area before the two cowboys came out and saw them. He didn't know what they were after, but he knew they were trouble, and he knew they were following someone on this tour.

Bluff Fort was actually interesting. Alex thought it was great, but he could tell Klaus was agitated. Before he could say anything to change Klaus' mind, the guests agreed to leave. They were an easy going bunch.

Alex was disappointed, but went along with the suggestion.

***

It was dark inside the theatre. At first Butch and Sundance were unable to make out anything but the pale flicker of vintage sepia images.

They strategized in whispers. They'd stay by the door and grab the camera bag as the guy was leaving. They separated to stand on either side of the exit.

The little film wasn't bad. *The stunts those pioneers did with the big oxes and wagons to get to a freakin' desert was crazy*, thought Butch.

Sundance thought they were awesome.

The men waited until the lights came back on. Only when everyone was standing, had gathered their belongings, and turned to face the exit did the men realize that none of the people looked familiar and the camera bag was nowhere to be seen.

People on their way out were blocking the door asking the volunteer questions about the local history. Butch and Sundance had to muscle through the crowd.

The museum was next to several log cabins that used to house the families who lived in the fort. The place was filled with a milling crowd of visitors. A large bus load had been discharged since the men had gone into the museum. They split up and ran through the fort area, checking the cabins, to see if they could find their target.

When they'd run the full length of the fort they knew for sure that the man, the bag, and the van were long gone. They jumped into the Mustang and raced toward Mexican Hat.

Chapter 32

Klaus, Tina, and Gerd sat together in the back row of the van, whispering.

"This is not a coincidence," said Klaus.

Tina and Gerd reluctantly agreed.

"What could they possibly be after?" said Tina.

None of them could come up with anything. It made no sense.

"One of us has something that is meriting an extremely persistent pursuit."

"Gerd, this sounds crazy," said Klaus, "but at Mesa Verde they seemed to be interested in your camera bag."

"I noticed that too. My equipment is not fancy," Gerd said. "And it is old. It is not worth very much."

"Then maybe they are not interested in your equipment," Klaus said. "Maybe they are interested in a picture you have taken."

"What kind of picture?"

"I do not know," Klaus said. "Maybe you have photographed something they did not want to be photographed."

At that moment the van arrived at the Valley of the Gods.

They parked, and Klaus murmured, "Let us talk more about this later."

Alex and Steve looked at the dirt road ahead and saw a huge muddy mire about fifty yards away.

"Normally we'd take this route to get through the Valley of Gods," Alex said, "but the road looks impassable right now. We'd need a four-wheel drive vehicle to even attempt it. There's a huge mudhole here in front of us, and I know from experience that the road beyond here will be even worse.

"There's another place where we can get a nice view of the valley and the surrounding area, but we've gotta get turned around. Hang on."

Steve and Alex jumped out, unhooked the trailer, and turned it around. Then Steve got back in and made a three-point turn to reverse the van on the narrow dirt road, hopped out again, and helped Alex reconnect the trailer.

They were experienced with the maneuver, so it took less than five minutes and they were ready to get out of there. They backtracked to Highway 163 to reach a paved surface and headed south.

A few minutes after they'd disappeared from view Butch and Sundance arrived at the turnoff. Sundance was driving significantly above the speed limit and the turnoff to Valley of the Gods was on a long curve.

He saw the sign at the last moment and took the turn onto the dirt road at speed. By the time he noticed the huge muddy mess inside the valley wash, it was too late.

He slammed on the brakes and sent the Mustang sliding sideways toward the mud patch. Both men shouted, "Noooooooo!"

The Mustang made it to a stop just as the spoiler and the front wheels encountered the mudhole.

"Are you insane?" Butch shouted, "Haven't we had enough trouble already? Let *me* drive!"

He jumped out of the passenger door, ran around the car, jerked the driver's door open, and hauled Sundance out by the collar. "But you...."

Sundance tried to defend himself, but Butch got into the driver's seat and slammed the door with a bang before he could finish his sentence.

Obviously he had no say in the matter, so Sundance walked around the back of the car to get to the passenger side. Butch pressed the gas and the back wheels began to spin. Sundance had to jump out of the way or he'd have been run over.

If the Mustang hadn't had rear-wheel drive, they'd have been stuck in the mud again. But this time they got lucky. Unfortunately not everything looked rosy. A glance at the gas gauge revealed that they were nearly out of fuel.

This, too, made Butch furious. "Any idiot knows ya gotta keep the tank topped up when you're out in a remote area!" said Butch. "It could be a hundred miles between gas stations!"

He wanted to strangle Sundance. He was so angry he forgot he was sick.

A good night's sleep, death threats from the Boss, his fury at the terrain, his partner, and that maddening tour group were working on him like a tonic.

He got the car turned around, rolled down the window, and shouted, "Get in!"

Before Sundance's rear could touch the seat, Butch took off.

"Hey, watch it!" Sundance shouted. The car's surging momentum slammed the passenger door for him. He was lucky his leg was inside when it closed.

Then, just as Butch rocketed back out onto the highway, a tractor—the tall cab that was the front half of a tractor-trailer—came roaring around the curve. It was flying without a trailer. The truck driver saw the Mustang too late and had no choice but to stand on his brakes.

He was able to get slowed down enough so as not to rear-end them, but he laid long black rubber lines to do it. If he'd been pulling a loaded trailer he'd never have been able to get stopped in time.

He gave an extra-long blast on his extra-loud horn. It was ear-splitting. And he stayed right on their rear bumper. That was downright terrifying.

The grille of the tractor filled the rear view mirror. Sundance glanced in the side mirror and saw the truck only a few feet behind them.

"Are ya tryin' to kill us?" he said.

"Shut the freak up!" Butch said, staring at the road ahead.

The trucker stayed right on the Mustang's tail, blasting his horn in long bursts over and over even though Butch was doing seventy-five on the curvy road. For long minutes the enormous grille continued to loom menacingly.

"I've seen a movie like this," Sundance shouted to be heard over the horn and the engine noise.

"You want I should slow down? You wanna talk to the guy? Reason with him?"

Sundance turned in his seat to look back at the grille filling the rear window, and said, "Nah."

"Then shuddup."

The Mustang's power was more than enough to leave the tractor in the dust if they'd been on a straightaway, but the road was curvy and the truck driver obviously had a serious anger management problem.

They couldn't shake him.

"I'll put two in his hat," Sundance said, pulling a pistol out from under his seat. That was Mafia-speak for two bullets to the head. It was a signature move for when they wanted to make a statement about who did the job.

Sundance rolled down his window and prepared to sit on the sill so he could face backwards for a clear shot.

"Better not," Butch said, concentrating on the road, and doing an excellent job driving in trying circumstances. "This ain't our territory. We'd need to clear it first and that's not gonna be possible given our current situation."

"Right," Sundance said, but he kept hold of the pistol just in case. "How 'bout a tire. That'd do the job at this speed. Nobody'd be the wiser."

"I wish. But a lotta trucks got cameras on 'em now. He could be filmin' us."

Sundance wanted to at least show his pistol to the maniac, but he resisted the impulse for fear of ending up on YouTube.

***

Steve turned left onto a dirt road at Mexican Hat Rock for a photo stop at a famous, precariously-shaped formation of a wide, flat, roughly sombero-shaped stone perched awkwardly atop a sandstone outcropping. The rock looked capable of toppling off its base at any second.

The guests were all out of the van taking pictures of it when they heard the loud continuous blaring of a tractor-trailer horn in the distance. It was coming their way.

When they turned around to see what it was, they saw the black Mustang flash past with a truck cab hovering incredibly close on its tail. In seconds the two vehicles had disappeared down the road.

Butch and Sundance couldn't help but notice the group standing next to the van. "There they are!" shouted Sundance.

Butch screamed something unintelligible, but dared not slow down.

"Wow!" Klaus said, "Did you see that?"

"Something is wrong with those men," said Gerd.

***

The high-speed chase continued through the little town of Mexican Hat and down a steep road. When the two vehicles reached a curve at the San Juan River, the truck had a tough time making the turn. If it couldn't stay in the road it would face-plant into the side of the San Juan Inn.

The driver managed to negotiate the curve and the bridge. The race was still on, but now both cars were on lands owned by the Navajo Nation.

On this straighter road Butch was able to give the Mustang its head and the truck gradually fell back. There was a steep incline that enabled Butch to leave the big rig so far behind it finally went out of view.

Chapter 33

"What's wrong with that guy?" Butch said, once the truck was no longer visible.

"Who knows?" Sundance said, stretching his shoulders in an effort to relax now that it was all over. "Prob'ly too much of that 5-hour energy stuff."

Butch laughed.

It took a lot to unnerve a couple of mafiosos, but that guy had done it.

Soon the road led through a stretch of desert and they could once again see the truck in the distance. It wasn't close by any means, but it was still coming their way.

Butch had more experience than he wanted in dealing with men in homicidal rages, though, so he pressed a little harder on the accelerator. The open range cattle they saw standing near the road were all that kept him from going over a hundred.

You wouldn't want to collide with a cow going that fast.

They came to an intersection and decided to leave Highway 163. They took a right onto Highway 261 hoping to get away from the maniac.

They kept going until they came to a shocking dead end. The road appeared to end at the base of a mesa.

"What's that?" Butch said.

"Does the road just stop?" Sundance asked.

"There weren't any signs," Butch said.

They slowed to a crawl as they approached, to see if the road continued somehow through a tunnel or up an unimaginably steep rise.

"Whaddya wanna do?" Sundance said.

Butch shrugged, and said, "I don't wanna see that guy again."

Sundance agreed, so they forged ahead, driving the car at walking speed.

"What the frack?" Butch muttered, steering into the first curve.

He had to slow down even more, because it was a narrow switchback. He continued at less than five miles an hour until he saw where the road was taking them. He hit the brakes hard then and brought the car to a complete stop.

In front of them was a steep gravel road that hugged the side of a mesa with no guard rails to prevent vehicles from taking a nose dive off the sheer cliff walls.

It was so steep you couldn't even see where the road was going.

"I'd rather be killed by that truck than drive this!" Butch said. "The people out here are insane! Why would anyone build a road like this? It makes no sense!"

"You want I should drive?" Sundance said.

"There is no freakin' way you're drivin' me up there!" Butch said.

They sat without moving or speaking for a moment, then they heard the sound of an engine. From their vantage point they couldn't see the truck, but they could hear it. The sound of the engine was burned into their brains.

He was still following them, trapping them. No way would that guy let them out without a serious confrontation. Butch would've enjoyed killing him, but he didn't dare do it until he was sure whose territory he was in.

This Utah bunch seemed scarier by the minute. He didn't want to start a war with these people. The truck was creeping toward them up the dirt road.

"He's comin' after us," Butch said.

"Yep," Sundance said.

"There's no way I'm goin' up this road," Butch said. "It's suicide. At least this guy, I can whack. I don't care anymore. He's way ova tha line."

Butch leaned down to pull his pistol out from under his seat.

Sundance got out of the car, went around and opened the driver's door.

"Get out," he said.

When Butch refused to budge, Sundance punched him hard in the face, twice. That put him out for the count.

"This is for your own good," he said, as he hauled his bleeding, unconscious partner in crime out of the driver's seat, dragged him to the rear of the Mustang, opened the trunk, and heaved him inside.

He slammed the lid, got back into the driver's seat, and set off up the incredibly steep track, carefully navigating the switchbacks in a car this time. He was glad he'd gotten practice in the OHV. When he reached the broad, flat top of the mesa he stopped and got out to take a look.

His first view out over the jaw-dropping vista startled him so severely, he forgot about the truck for a few moments, but then he heard something. He scanned the steep zigzagging dirt track, but he couldn't see the big rig. Had the guy finally given up?

It was unlikely, but Sundance couldn't spot the guy anywhere—and from this lookout he could see for miles. And miles and miles.

He decided to stay up top for a while, just in case.

Gradually he began to relax and enjoy the extraordinary view. It was truly spectacular. Bright blue sky, a few white puffy clouds, every shade of red and brown spreading out before him as far as the eye could see. He'd never been in a place where he could see that far.

From where he was, a place Google Maps identified as the top of the Moki Dugway, he could see the Colorado Rockies in the distance. He was so diverted by the panorama and his geographic research that he was momentarily confused when he heard banging, and shouting coming from the trunk of the car.

Butch had regained consciousness. Sundance could hear him punching and kicking the trunk lid from inside.

"Lemme outta here!" he shouted.

"Calm down!" Sundance called out. "I'm comin' ta getcha."

"I'm gonna kill ya!" Butch screamed.

"Not a smart thing to say to a guy you're askin' to let ya loose," Sundance said.

Butch continued to bang, curse, kick, and threaten, so Sundance said, "I'll let ya out, but ya gotta calm down first!"

Butch got the message and after a few more minutes his profane threats changed to apologies and pleas for mercy.

In the meantime Sundance checked more maps on his cell phone and discovered that there was a back way off the mesa. The detour would allow them to avoid having to drive back down the Moki Dugway and encounter the crazed truck driver on a cliffside road with no guardrails, but it looked like it would add ninety minutes to the drive, if not more.

They'd lost a lot of time already. Another hour and half would allow the trail grow cold and they might lose the van altogether.

If that happened again they'd lose their lives.

So the choice was between facing the truck driver or the Boss. No question, Sundance chose the truck driver.

He waited up top for nearly an hour, then decided the guy would've turned around by then. Who'd be suicidal enough to try to drive a tall ungainly tractor cab up this horrible road? Surely even nut jobs wanted to stay alive.

Even the worst sociopaths had a strong instinct for self-preservation. Sundance's parole officer had shared that bit of wisdom with him and the insight had helped him more than once when dealing with a tough customer.

Sundance went to free Butch, then realized it wouldn't be smart to let him out before he got the car back down off the mesa. He didn't need any distractions as he zigzagged back down the dirt track. And he didn't want to have to wait for Butch to walk.

Sundance wasn't a mean guy. He tried to explain to Butch what he was doing and why. "I'm doin' ya a favor, Butch" he said. "I'm doin' us *both* a favor."

Then he added, "This hurts me more than it does you, buddy."

But Butch remained silent, so Sundance knew he was thinking murderous thoughts.

Sundance started down the mesa and Butch resumed his banging with a vengeance, as well as screaming curses and death threats.

He could feel the switchbacks from inside the trunk and he knew they were on that nightmarish road again. The only thing worse than being on the road was being on it locked in a trunk.

He was going to kill Sundance.

Sundance guided the Mustang down without stopping until he was safely at the bottom of the mesa. When he made the last switchback he saw the truck again. It was sitting where the road leveled out at the bottom.

Sundance was gonna need help. He stopped the Mustang about seventy-five yards from the truck, jumped out, and jerked the trunk open. He leaned over to help Butch get out and was instantly met by his partner's fist.

With a single savage punch to the nose Butch managed to knock Sundance out cold. He dropped like a sack of rocks and lay on the pavement behind the car. *Now we're gonna even the score*, thought Butch.

He awkwardly scrambled out of the trunk, intending to toss Sundance in for revenge, until he saw the reason his partner had stopped.

The door to the truck cab opened and the driver climbed out. He was a huge guy wearing mirrored sunglasses and a leather vest without a shirt.

It wasn't a good look. There was too much body hair, too much body fat, and too many badly-designed tattoos. Heavy metal music poured out of the open door of the cab.

The man approached Butch slowly with a crowbar in one hand.

"You idiots! I'm fed up with your stupid tourist crap. You act like you're the only people on earth! You come out here from Minnesota or some other freakin' hole, rent a fancy sports car, and think you're the king of the road! You almost killed me back there!"

Butch put his hands in the air with an apologetic gesture, and said, "Sorry! Didn't see ya. I swear."

The trucker didn't seem to care about the apology or the explanation. He continued walking toward the Mustang. When he got close enough, he smashed one of the headlights with the crowbar.

"Stop that!" Butch screamed as he ran toward the guy. He grabbed at the sweaty, hairy arm holding the crowbar, but didn't manage to get control of it before the trucker bashed the Mustang's grille.

Sundance appeared out of nowhere. The lower half of his face was covered with blood streaming from his nose. He was standing behind the trucker with his pistol against the man's ear.

"Drop the crowbar," he said, calmly.

The trucker didn't drop the crowbar, but he raised both hands.

"Okay, okay," the trucker said. "Easy buddy."

Then he slashed backwards with the crowbar.

Sundance got his face out of the way in time, but the gun was knocked out of his hand. When it hit the ground the impact discharged the chambered round.

The stray bullet struck Butch and he fell. "You shot me!" Butch shouted, looking at Sundance accusingly. "I can't believe you shot me!"

The trucker turned around and walked back toward his truck, laughing. "Idiots," he muttered. "Go ahead. Kill each other. Save me the trouble."

He got back into his rig and drove away.

Butch was lying on the ground whimpering. Sundance went to render aid, but couldn't see any blood. He helped him sit up.

"Where'd he getcha?" Sundance asked.

"My foot," Butch said.

He tugged at his partner's boot to evaluate the severity of the wound. Butch screamed.

When Sundance managed to pry the boot off, Butch turned his face away from the carnage, and asked, "How bad is it?"

Sundance examined his partner's foot, but couldn't locate a wound. He pulled Butch's sock off and still failed to find any evidence of an injury.

Butch lay back on the ground with his eyes tightly shut. "Am I losin' a lotta blood?" he asked, his voice noticeably weakening.

Sundance sat down in the road beside his partner, exhausted, elated, and coming down off a very long, very high, adrenaline rush.

"The boot's totaled, but your foot's fine," Sundance said, laughing.

"I think I'm goin' inta shock…," Butch said, his voice so weak Sundance could hardly hear it.

"The bullet didn't even make a hole in your sock!" Sundance said. "It tore the heel off your boot, but we can find that and put it back on.

"You swear?"

"I swear!"

This gave Butch the courage to open his eyes and take a look for himself. When he confirmed that Sundance was right, he put his sock back on, then his boot, and stood up, embarrassed.

Sundance picked up his gun.

"Be careful with that thing," Butch said, limping back to the car carrying his boot heel. "Can I drive now?" he asked.

"Sure," said Sundance.

Chapter 34

Alex took the guests on a short walk from Mexican Hat Rock down to a bench beside the San Juan River. It was a beautiful place with a nice view of the river and some more of the interesting rock formations.

Steve and Alex dropped the trailer at the San Juan Inn where they'd be spending the night. They checked in and received a bundle of six room keys, but didn't remain at the hotel.

Instead, they continued to the Moki Dugway scenic area—one of Alex's favorite lookouts on the whole Grand Circle drive.

Alex loved the thrilling dirt road with its sheer cliffs and he found the view extraordinary. Usually he took his guests from there to Muley Point where there was an amazing view of Monument Valley, but he knew that after all the rain during the last couple of days the road to Muley Point would be too messy to attempt.

***

"What's next?" Butch asked, while driving back to the highway.

Sundance scanned the itinerary on the tour company's website, "It says Gooseneck State Park."

"There it is!" Butch said, pointing at the sign indicating the turnoff. He turned onto the park access road.

The van was approaching from the opposite direction. Steve drove past the road to Gooseneck State Park and continued on toward the Moki Dugway

"Look," Klaus said, pointing out the window, "There is that Mustang again!"

He'd seen the car when it turned off the main road. Now it was disappearing into the distance.

***

Butch and Sundance paid their entrance fee and went straight to the parking lot.

"Ya wanna see the Gooseneck?" asked Sundance. "It says here it's a curvy cliff in the shape of a gooseneck with the San Juan River runnin' through the bottom.

"No!" Butch snapped. "I've seen enough cliffs on this trip to last me the rest of my life, should I even live to get outta this freakin' place."

There was no way he was going anywhere near the edge of a cliff if he didn't have to. He decided to stay in the car while Sundance wandered around like a tourist. The guy was going native.

They waited at the park without any luck until they were forced to assume that the group must've come and gone already. The men were fed up with all the wandering and waiting.

This was turning out to be a nightmare job. Moments of bladder loosening terror, mind-numbing boredom, heart-stopping panoramas, accompanied by arguing, and death threats. Wash, rinse, and repeat

It reminded Butch of family vacations when he was a kid.

A few minutes later, Alex said, "See that cliff? We're gonna drive up the side of that rock."

Everyone laughed, because they thought he was joking. It was ridiculous to think that there could be a road up the side of such a sheer mesa.

"No, for real!" Alex said.

So much for Klaus, Tina, and Gerd's feeling of relief.

Steve drove them carefully up the road and made a couple of photo stops along the way. When they reached the top the guests couldn't believe the view.

"*Mein Gott!*" Elisabeth said, "All this empty land! Now I see why Americans are so foolish about overpopulation and environmental issues. From here these things do not appear to be a problem."

Georg turned to Steve with an apologetic expression, and said, "In Switzerland we do not often have views from high places like this. We live near the bottom parts of our mountains so we typically only see the sides of them in front of us."

***

"Pull over and let me see if there's any way to stop that rattle," Sundance said. Butch pulled to the side of the road. Sundance walked around the car looking for the source of the sound. "Cut the engine," he said.

Butch switched the ignition off.

Sundance dropped to the ground, rolled onto his back, and shimmied his head and shoulders underneath the Mustang. "I can't see anything without a light," he called out.

They didn't have a flashlight.

When Sundance tried to wiggle out, he found that he was stuck. "Butch? Butch? I need your help. I can't get outta here."

***

Gerd was taking photos with a zoom lens attached to his camera.

"May I borrow that for a moment?" Klaus asked.

"Of course," Gerd said, handing him the camera.

Klaus used the long lens to scan the area.

He was able to pinpoint the Mustang. It was stopped beside the road. One of the men was underneath the car with only his legs sticking out. He started to thrash around and kick with both legs.

Then, as Klaus watched, the other guy grabbed him by the ankles and pulled him out.

"Okay, everyone aboard!" Alex said, "Let's go have lunch at the Gooseneck!"

"Can we stay here for just a few more minutes?" Klaus asked, still staring through Gerd's camera. "This place is so amazing!"

"Sure," said Alex.

Klaus watched Sundance get up, dust himself off, and get back into the Mustang. Then watched as the car got back on the road and drove away. He lowered the camera, turned around, and said, "Okay, let's go!"

Alex and Steve shared a bemused look at the quick change in Klaus's requests. They loaded their guests, closed the van doors, and headed down toward Gooseneck State Park. More than one of the passengers kept their eyes closed during the hair-raising drive back down the mesa.

When they reached the Gooseneck Alex and Steve began preparing a picnic table for lunch. While the guests walked along the rim, talking and taking pictures, they set out a meal in an open pavilion near the edge of the cliff.

***

Butch and Sundance decided their next move should be to drive to Monument Valley.

Along the way Butch kept shooting worried glances at the gas gauge.

They were running very low on fuel and there was only empty desert around them as far as the eye could see. "Why didn't you fill up yesterday?" Butch said.

"We coulda got gas in Mexican Hat," Sundance said, "but *nooo*, you decided to play chicken with that crazy truck driver instead."

***

As the group was enjoying their picnic lunch a couple walked by and stopped to chat with them. They talked about how much they were enjoying the

Grand Circle tour and how beautiful the western parks were.

"You won't believe this, but just now there were two guys stopped here in a banged up Mustang," the wife said. "One of them stayed in the car *the whole time* while the other one got out and walked around.

"Can you imagine? How could anybody come this far, and be right here in this place, and not even get out to take a look at the canyon?"

"They were dressed in these garish cowboy costumes," the husband added, "and both of them had significant facial bruising, like they'd been in a brawl. It was rather bizarre."

***

"We better find a gas station," Butch said, "and *soon!*"

Less than a mile later, the Mustang sputtered briefly, and the engine died. Butch had a tough time keeping the car in the road as they went around a curve. The power steering went out, as did the power brakes.

He managed to get the car to the side of the road, but there was almost no shoulder. As it rolled to a stop, it ripped out a strip of dry scrubby bushes.

Butch banged his hands on the steering wheel while shouting, "No! No! No!"

It took several minutes for him to calm down. When he finally ran out of steam, Sundance said, "Let's see, if we can flag down a car and get a ride to a gas station."

They got out and walked a hundred yards back the way they'd come to reach a straightaway before the long curve. That way passersby would be able to see them in time to stop and pick them up.

They made quite the sight, two men in rumpled cowboy outfits, one wearing a boot with a missing heel, both sporting black eyes and faces flecked with dried blood.

Of course no one would stop for them. If anything the cars were speeding up and veering away from them as they whizzed by.

Then the van went by. And there was absolutely nothing they could do about it. "Perfect," said Butch. "Just perfect."

***

The tour group headed for Gouldings Lodge and a museum with displays about the Goulding family and the famous Western films shot in the area, many of them featuring John Wayne.

When the van drove past the two men on foot, Klaus and Gerd instantly recognized the duo. Then, a few seconds later, they rounded a curve and saw the abandoned Mustang.

"Those guys must be in trouble," Alex said. "Let's go back and see if we can help."

"No," Klaus said, "let us keep going! They looked like questionable characters."

"Alex, we can't pick up strangers," Steve said. "It's against policy. I'd have to get the company's permission first."

"We can't just leave them out here in the middle of the desert!" Alex said.

"Perhaps you could call the police," Klaus suggested. "They could take care of them."

"Yeah," Steve said, "that's a good idea."

"You guys are right," Alex said. He grabbed his phone and checked for a signal. He had no bars so he'd have to wait to dial 911.

***

Butch and Sundance were still standing beside the road, broiling in the full desert sun in their black clothing, when two officers pulled up in a Navajo Nation police cruiser. One of the cops activated the light bar atop the car.

"Aw geez," Butch mumbled.

"Is it illegal to hitchhike?" Sundance whispered.

"Dunno," Butch said, without moving his lips.

A Navajo policeman got out of the passenger side and slowly walked toward them. "Are you gentlemen having a problem?" he asked.

"Yes!" Butch said. "We ran outta gas."

"That happens a lot in this area," the policeman said. "Where's your vehicle?"

"Just around the bend in the road," Butch said, pointing.

The three men set off walking around the curve. The other policeman followed them in the cruiser with lights flashing.

"What happened to you two?" the policeman asked.

"We ran out of gas," Butch repeated, getting more nervous.

"No," he said, "I mean, what happened to your faces?"

"Uh, … oh! We had an accident," Sundance stuttered.

"Mmm hmm," the policeman said, nodding. "What kind of accident?"

"Uh, we slipped and fell," Sundance said.

"Both of you?"

"Yeah, crazy, huh?" Sundance said.

The cop wasn't buying the story, but he withheld comment.

They stood to one side as he inspected the Mustang.

He looked at the damaged rear bumper. "What happened here?" he asked.

"We backed into a tree," Sundance said. "It was an accident."

The policeman walked around to a side window and peered inside.

Butch shot Sundance at look that said, *I put my gun away. Did you put your gun away?*

Sundance gave an almost imperceptible nod to indicate that he had.

"You guys on vacation?" the policeman asked.

"Yeah," they answered at the same time.

"Where ya from?"

"Vegas," Butch said.

The policeman walked to the front of the car and inspected the damaged grille and broken headlight. "How'd this happen?"

"Vandalism," Butch said. "Last night."

"Did you report it?"

"Nope," Butch said.

"Why not?"

"Didn't wanna bother," Butch said. "The car's insured."

"Glad to hear it," the cop said, smiling. "Where'd you fellas stay last night?"

"Blanding," Sundance said.

"Let me see if I've got this right. You both slipped and landed on your faces, bruising them badly, and then someone smashed your headlight in a town like Blanding, but you didn't report it?"

Butch and Sundance gave synchronous nods.

"Have you been drinking?" the cop asked.

"No!" Sundance said.

The policeman walked closer, took off his sunglasses, and looked carefully into each man's eyes. "There's something wrong with you two and I'm gonna find out what it is."

He put his right hand on the gun in his holster, and said, "I need you both to turn around and put your hands on the roof of your car."

They did as he said.

He came closer and kicked the men's feet wider apart. "Are either of you carrying anything that could hurt me, any needles, knives?" he asked.

"No," both said at the same time.

The policeman was searching them when a bus stopped in the road, turned on its flashers, and a group of foreign tourists hopped out and began taking pictures of the scene. This was exactly the sort of thing they'd expected to see in America.

"You people get back into that bus!" the policeman shouted.

A woman translated what he'd said and the tourists were visibly disappointed, but reluctantly returned to the bus and drove away.

The policeman's search didn't reveal anything suspicious. "Do you mind if I look inside your car?" he asked.

"Yeah, I do," said Butch. "We ran outta gas. We haven't done anything wrong."

"You're driving with a broken headlight. That's an offense in this jurisdiction."

"It's broad daylight," said Butch. "I don't know how *Indians* handle this kinda situation, but in the United States you need a search warrant."

"How about I show you how indigenous people deal with folks like you?"

He got into the police cruiser and as his partner drove away, he waved, leaned out the window, and called out, "Good luck!"

Chapter 35

Butch and Sundance stayed with the car and held their thumbs out while dozens of vehicles zipped by. Not a single one would stop for them. This was not good. They were stuck in the middle of a desert with very little water and zero shade.

Meanwhile the tour group arrived at the Monument Valley Tribal Park boundary. They bought tickets at the entrance kiosk and headed for the attractive visitor center that formed a complex with a shop, restaurant, and a ritzy hotel. All the buildings had striking views of the valley.

Gerd, Tina, and Klaus went out on the viewing terrace to take in the rock formations called the *Left* and *Right Mittens*.

"Gerd, I think it's one of two things," said Klaus. "Either you have taken a picture of something those guys are interested in, or you have accidentally captured something they do not want anyone else to see. And that is why they are after your camera."

"Maybe he does not even have such a photo," said Tina, "but they fear that he might."

Klaus nodded. "Yes, it could be that also."

"But the only things I have photographed are the same things that are typical of anyone on vacation in this area."

"Perhaps it is something in the background of a photo, or the face of a person in a crowd," Klaus suggested.

"I can't imagine what it is," Gerd said.

"Shall we get together at the hotel tonight and look through your images," Klaus said, "to see if we can find anything?"

"Okay," Gerd said, "We can do that."

While Gerd took pictures from the terrace, Klaus went to the parking lot to see if the black Mustang was there. That left Gerd alone with Tina. She tried to capture his attention, but he ignored her. She was pretty, but she was obviously a tart.

There was a black Mustang at the far end of the lot. He walked toward it to get a closer look. It was cleaner and in better shape than the one he was worried about. A young couple in their mid-twenties were standing next to it speaking French.

He turned and went back to the visitor center.

The tour group met back at the van by five for the next activity.

A heavily-modified high-ground-clearance pickup truck came to meet them. It had an extended bed that contained several rows of benches and a roof to shade passengers from the relentless sun.

Alex had a quick chat with the Navajo driver to confirm the details of the custom guided tour. Then he indicated that the group could board the vehicle and buckle up for an expedition through the world famous valley.

***

Butch and Sundance were badly wilted by the sun and desert. They decided to take turns standing beside the road with a thumb in the air while the other one waited in the car. They hoped that maybe a solitary man would get more sympathy from passing vehicles than a pair.

After an endless stream of vehicles sped by for an hour and a half they decided to start walking. They knew the gas station in Mexican Hat was pretty far away, so they decided to go south, hoping the next town would be closer.

It would take a while for them to realize it, but they were wrong. Again.

***

The tour group was thrilled with their adventure ride through Monument Valley. Their Navajo guide was knowledgeable and wonderfully entertaining.

He knew all the best places to stop for perfect views of the various monuments and he was happy to provide expert assistance to each of them in getting the best photos with their camera or phone, no matter what brand or model they were using.

It was an impressive display of tech-savvy. This wasn't the sort of Native American the guests had expected to encounter, but they were pleased by the modern reality.

Each time they resumed their travel from one viewing point toward the next, Paul, the guide, shouted, "Rock 'n Roll!" making a gesture with his index finger and little finger. The guests were a bit disappointed that his name wasn't something more like *Crow Man* or *White Buffalo* or *Dances with Coyotes*, but they rolled with it.

"Was ist das?" Elisabeth asked, imitating Jimmy's hand gesture.

"It can mean several different things," Alex said. "Because he's saying *Rock n' Roll*, when he makes the gesture, it's probably mostly a reference to rock music. Many heavy metal bands use the sign.

"It can also refer to the horns of the devil—it's a sign to ward off evil in multiple religions.

"Sometimes it can be a reference to cattle horns. The *hook 'em horns* sign is common in connection with various sports teams, particularly in Texas, but it's also used by other teams.

"The U.S. contains a vast mixture of wildly varying cultures," Alex said, shrugging.

Sundance made a temporary repair of his boot heel by banging it against a rock to hammer the sharp end of the nails back into the bottom of the boot, then he and Butch walked alongside the highway for a long time. The bottles of water they'd brought with them were now empty and littering the roadside. They were scorched and parched.

People these days were wary of hitchhikers. Nobody stopped for the two grungy urban cowboys.

In one way the guys were lucky that they had no idea where they were. If they'd seen their location from the air, they'd have been suicidal. It was bad enough from ground level, staring out at the endless expanses of sand punctuated by the occasional red stone plates.

Sundance decided that the heroic and romantic image of a cowboy wasn't what it was cracked up to be. "I want outta this place, outta these clothes, outta this situation," he said.

The Vegas cowpokes were both at the end of their rope. They were actually past it, but they hadn't fallen over dead yet. No, that would've been too easy. Instead they were on an endless march through hell.

Eventually they reached a crest in the road and were suddenly treated to a view of the spot made famous by the film *Forrest Gump*. It was where Forrest finally stopped running after three years on the road. They were about to retrace his footsteps after he'd turned around and begun his long walk home.

They paused and stared. Then they exchanged a look. Neither of them said it, but both were wondering the same thing. Were they Butch and Sundance? Or were they Forrest and Bubba?

A van roared past, then pulled over and parked beside the road about a quarter of a mile away. Half a dozen blonde tourists leaped out and began reenacting the scene from the movie while a member of the group filmed each of them.

Before the two swarthy, bruised, and dusty creatures were able to limp their way down to ask the Vikings for a ride, they got back into their van and sped off.

Eventually the men came across a tiny roadside stand selling Navajo jewelry. It was manned by a Navajo lady who sat in a pick-up truck awaiting potential shoppers.

It was clear from her expression that she was not pleased to see Butch and Sundance coming. It was obvious that she would've preferred to drive away when she saw the two strangers, but she couldn't afford to leave her jewelry unattended.

Sundance held up a hand, fingers together, palm facing toward her, and said, in a husky dry-throated whisper, "How."

The lady frowned.

Then he croaked out, "We come in peace."

Butch burst out laughing, "We come in peace?" he said. "We come in peace? We're not in a freakin' Western!"

"No," said Sundance, sighing, "We're not. We're in Forrest Gump!"

That made the Navajo lady laugh.

It broke the ice enough so that she listened while Butch and Sundance explained their situation. She, like the cop, wasn't buying their story about how they got the black eyes. She had three sons and she knew better.

She agreed to help them anyway, but she still had a business to run, "I'll take you to get gas, but I gotta work. I won't pack up until six."

They nodded and mumbled their thanks. Then they went to sit on the ground in the shade of her truck.

She felt sorry for the pitiful creatures, so she gave them each a bottle of water which they chugged.

"How much do ya make sellin' your stuff?" Butch asked.

The woman had no intention of discussing finances with such a disreputable looking road rat. She gave him an annoyed look instead.

"No offense intended. I'll give ya four hundred bucks to drive us to the closest gas station," he said, showing her the money. "Now."

She took the bills out of his hand and astonished them with how quickly she packed up her gear. In minutes the three of them were sharing the bench seat in her old truck, jouncing down the highway on squeaky suspension.

The lady brought them to the gas station at Gouldings Lodge where Butch bought two plastic fuel containers and filled them. He set the cans into the back of the truck. Sundance bought an eight-pack of cold bottled water and he and Sundance drained several each as the woman drove them to their car.

They thanked her profusely and waved as she drove away.

Once the car was refueled they took off for Monument Valley doing eighty, swerving wildly around slower driving tourists, more to burn off built up vexation than to get there any faster.

Flashing lights appeared in the distance in the rear view mirror. They dropped to the speed limit, but it was too late. The cop car pulled up behind them, gave them a couple of whoops with the siren, and stayed on their bumper until they pulled off the road.

The passenger door of the police car opened and the same Navajo officer as before got out.

Chapter 36

"Another name for the Navajo people is Diné," said the Navajo guide. He took the tour group to see a hogan, the traditional dwelling of the Diné. He played a Native American drum for them in a huge open cave, and after that he took them to a community center just off the main highway for a Navajo dinner.

***

"I see you got some gas," the policeman said.

Neither Butch nor Sundance responded.

"You guys don't wanna play cowboys and injuns no more?" the policeman said. "Yeah, it's not as fun nowadays. At least not on the rez."

He showed his disappointment in their behavior by giving them a citation for driving without wearing seat belts, for having a broken headlight, for speeding, and added an enhancement for reckless driving.

It was a miracle he didn't take them to jail.

When he let them go Butch and Sundance continued to the business hub inside Monument Valley at a slower speed. They checked the parking lot for the van and weren't surprised at all when they failed to find it.

They decided to make a token pass through the rest of the valley, just in case, to see if they could get lucky. Butch would never have admitted it, even to his own mother, but this time he silently prayed to St. Jude for a miracle and to St. Anthony who would help find lost items.

They headed down the rutted dirt track toward the famous buttes and in less than a minute they realized why people paid to be driven through the area by experts in specialized vehicles. Half a mile of bone-jarring travel was enough to convince them to turn around.

They went to the viewing terrace to wait, hoping the group would come out the same way they'd come in, as most people seemed to be doing. This time they knew to check the occupants as well as the vehicles.

At least here there was food and water. They could get cleaned up in the restroom and buy clean t-shirts.

Butch didn't get the miracle he'd prayed for but he had to admit that sitting on that viewing terrace, eating two gigantic servings of butter pecan, and watching the extraordinary sunset was totally amazing. When it was full dark they decided to see if they could get a room at the hotel next door. They walked over to *The View Hotel* and it became obvious how it got its name. An entire side of the building faced the valley.

There was a vacancy, but only one. There'd been a late cancellation on a suite and they took it, but the price was eye-watering.

***

The tour group was scarfing down a tasty Navajo dinner at the community center and watching some terrific traditional dances at the same time that Butch and Sundance were getting cleaned up in their suite at The View Hotel.

The goombahs had gone shopping at the store in the visitor center.

They both snagged wide-brimmed straw cowboy hats, although it was too late to save them from the blistered faces they were confronted with in the bathroom mirror.

Talk about your red skin.

The men were ecstatic to be able to take showers and change into clean, dry clothes. And to have indoor restrooms and be able to lay in clean, comfortable beds in an air-conditioned room.

They changed into the *Hoodoo You Love* and *Take a Hike* t-shirts and the nylon khaki pants they'd bought earlier and Sundance ran everything else they had through the hotel laundry.

They were presentable enough to be able to eat in the restaurant but they were too tired, so they hit the sack. Minutes later both of them were sound asleep.

***

The tour group said goodbye to the Native Americans and rode out of the valley to the San Juan Inn Motel.

After their frank conversation and mutual disclosures Peter had been seen visiting Frida's room in the evenings. Tina and Elizabeth gossiped about it.

"Neither of them is married, as far as we know," said Tina, "but who knows the truth?"

"The age difference is unseemly," said Elisabeth.

While some of the group enjoyed a view of the river and the remainder of the evening with beer and wine on the balcony of the motel, Klaus, Tina, and Gerd met in Gerd's room to have a look at his pictures.

Gerd inserted the camera's memory card into his laptop and made copies of all the photos. Then he opened the files and all three of them sat side-by-side on the foot of his bed to review them.

They started with the photos taken in Las Vegas. There were a lot of them. Gerd had arrived a couple of days early and spent the time touring all over town.

When Tina saw that there were over two hundred images from Las Vegas alone, she knew it was going to take a long time to look through them.

"I will get us something to drink," she said, and went to their room next door. She came back with a six-pack. They sat there together looking through the pictures and drinking beer.

Occasionally they'd zoom in on something, but they couldn't find anything that they could identify as being of particular interest to anyone but Gerd. There was nothing that seemed to have the potential to reveal a secret of any sort.

Klaus was extremely professional in viewing the images. This got Gerd's attention. "You are studying these pictures like a pro," he said. "Where did you learn to do that?"

"I used to work for the government."

"Doing what?" Gerd asked.

Tina glanced at Klaus to see his reaction.

"I worked for the administration in Berlin," Klaus said.

"Oh, a *Sesselpupser*, an armchair farter," he said.

"Exactly," Klaus said, laughing. "I believe it is called a *desk jockey* in the U.S."

They all laughed.

Gerd knew that people who worked for the East German government were anything but rebels. Actually they needed to act in total conformity with the one-party system, or they were out.

Gerd didn't press for more information. Many of the people raised during the autocratic socialist era were extremely conflict-avoidant. They weren't comfortable engaging in boisterous political debate.

Although Gerd had been one of the countless victims of the old system, he'd always understood that some people were easily brainwashed. After the reunification he'd forgiven his enemies and tried to get on with his life.

He knew the former government workers had done their jobs for a cause they believed in, and he felt pity for them. They'd been weak and blind. There was nothing he wanted to say to Klaus about it.

"May I make copies of the photographs?" Klaus said.

"Ja, natürlich," Gerd agreed. "I'll back the data up to my cloud storage." After a couple of minutes they realized that the motel Wi-Fi was far too slow for such a large amount of data.

Klaus went next door to his room and returned with a flash drive and used it to copy the images.

They finished their beer and Klaus went back to his room.

"I want to see if the others are still outside," Tina said.

If they were, she intended to join at least one of them.

***

Peter demonstrated another of the myofascial release stretches and Frida imitated his movements. He had been right. She could tell this was exactly what she needed.

"What was it like for you to see Las Vegas after the cloister?" she asked.

"At first it was disorienting to be out in the wide world and away from the dying, but this trip has been good for me. It has opened my eyes."

He showed her another of the stretches.

"Do you ever wish you had married and had children?" he asked.

"No," she said. "Do you?"

"No."

They laughed.

"I think many people do not enjoy their own company."

"I think many people marry for economic, or social reasons."

"We were both lucky we did not have to do that."

***

When Tina appeared on the balcony overlooking the San Juan River, everyone but Steve had already retired for the night. Steve had hoped to have some time alone to relax and enjoy the evening outdoors, but it was not to be.

"Hello there," Tina said, in a seductive voice that sounded like Marlene Dietrich pretending to be a Nazi spy. It made him smile because it also reminded him of the seductress in the Rocky and Bullwinkle cartoons, except Natasha had a Russian accent.

"What are you doing out here all by yourself?" she asked.

Here we go again, he thought.

"N-n-n-nothing. I mean, it's a n-n-nice night," he stuttered. Then he pointed at the sky like maybe she didn't know where it was.

"It most certainly is," she purred. "It is Perfekt."

She leaned against the railing and looked down at the river. "Und you are the perfekt Begleiter."

He was racking his brain for low key weapons he could use to repel her advances. The only thing within reach was a flower pot containing a small cactus. But he was distracted by her remark. What was a Begleiter?

It sounded like it might be painful. He shot her a look of confusion.

"Companion, I think is how you say."

There was no telling what she thought the term companion entailed and he didn't want to find out.

The sky was clear and the moon was bright. They were in an area with almost no light pollution, so the Milky Way was magnificent.

"Wow, … so many stars," she said. "Wie traumhaft!"

"Mmm hmm," Steve mumbled.

"What is gate for?" Tina asked, pointing toward a fence next to the parking lot.

Uh oh, thought Steve. "There's a p-p-path d-d-down to the river," he said.

He hated that he stuttered whenever he tried to talk to a good-looking woman. He tried hard to focus, then said, "Sometimes you find w-wildlife down there, like burros and deer."

He said this to try to dissuade her from going.

"Really?" Tina said, looking down. "Will you join me to safari?"

He had no desire to do it, but out of long habit as a travel professional, he said, "Uh, … okay."

He scooted his wrought iron chair back and stumbled out of his seat awkwardly.

They walked down the hotel stairs, found the path, and Steve opened the gate. It squeaked on its hinges. They went through the gap and he closed it behind them.

As they walked down the dirt trail, Tina said, "Is dark! I hold on."

He wasn't sure where she was going to grab him, so he held out an elbow before she could get a handful of anything else. Her hanging onto him made him even more nervous.

He found Tina attractive, but she was married, and her husband was nearby. When they reached the river bank he tried to get loose, but she only tightened her grip. The woman was surprisingly strong.

"I never have seen such stars," she said.

When Steve looked up, he felt her snuggle even closer. This made him feel like he was going to explode out of his skin. It was extremely unprofessional to be in this situation with a guest's wife. It was dangerous to be in this situation with *any* man's wife.

When he turned and looked down at her to protest she grabbed a handful of his hair, pulled his face toward hers, and kissed him on the mouth.

Even though he was deeply shocked, he kissed her back just a little.

After a few seconds he realized what he was doing and jerked his head back. "We s-s-shouldn't...", but Tina grabbed two handfuls of his hair this time and used both hands to force his head down toward her again, saying, "Sei still!"

Then she laid another smooch on him.

It took Steve a little longer this time to separate his lips from hers, but he was a man and stronger than her. He removed her hands and backed away, saying, "No!"

"I gotta go," he said, and he walked quickly up the path toward the hotel, but at the last moment was too much of a gentleman to leave a woman standing down there alone in the dark.

"You shouldn't stay here by yourself," he called out.

She pouted, but reluctantly started back. He held the gate open for her. Once Tina was through, he closed the gate, and said, "Have a great night."

He wasn't stuttering anymore.

"Gute Nacht," she said, obviously angry.

Steve went back the long way, using the staircase at the far end of the building to get to his room. He didn't want her to know which one was his.

***

Alex was watching the news. The Stanfield story was getting more coverage.

"Investigative journalist J.J. Stanfield is still missing," the reporter said. "Las Vegas police are asking anyone who may have seen him recently, or been in touch with him, to contact the nearest police station."

Mein Gott, Alex thought.

"Stanfield was believed to be working on a story revealing ties between Las Vegas organized crime, the casinos, and state and local government. Mr. Stanfield's movements have been traced through Utah and into Colorado.

"He is believed to have gone missing in Durango. The police..."

When the door opened and Steve came into the room, Alex switched off the television.

"Hey there," Alex said, trying to appear relaxed, while deeply disturbed by the news.

"Hey there yourself," Steve replied, trying to appear relaxed while deeply disturbed by Tina.

Neither of them said much as they prepared for bed and neither of them noticed that the other was totally preoccupied.

Chapter 37

Neither Steve nor Alex got a decent night's sleep.

Steve was worried about what Tina might tell Klaus. He had zero experience with married women, but he was pretty sure that their husbands wouldn't be happy to hear that they were being kissed by other men.

That fact that a stunner like Tina was into him was a new experience, though. It was both exhilarating and terrifying.

Alex, on the other hand, spent the night thinking about what he'd seen on the news. He knew that one of the easiest ways for law enforcement to trace the missing journalist would be by tracking the use of his credit and ATM cards. When they did that, which they probably already had, the trail would lead them straight to him.

Of course the same was true for anyone trying to find Stanfield. Law enforcement might put Alex in jail, but other sorts of interest groups might put him in a shallow grave.

Alex decided it was too risky to continue using the man's cards. It was too risky to even *have* the man's cards.

The group's schedule called for an early start. Steve was already down by the van doing his precheck.

Alex turned on the television for one last peek at the news and the first thing he saw was a picture of himself wearing mirrored sunglasses with his hat pulled down to cover part of his face.

"…withdrew money from an ATM at a Durango grocery store. Please contact the police if you recognize this man. If you see him, do not attempt to engage him, immediately report his location to ...."

Alex switched the TV off.

He grabbed J.J. Stanfield's wallet, rifled through his suitcase for the t-shirt and sweater he'd been wearing when he'd withdrawn money from the ATM. He grabbed his hat and sunglasses, too, and shoved all of it into a white plastic bag the motel supplied for laundry.

He crammed the bundle into his backpack, then zipped his suitcase and brought both bags with him as he left the room.

The group gathered at the van and Alex and Steve loaded luggage. Steve avoided eye contact with Tina.

"Steve," Klaus said, "can I talk to you for a second?"

Steve's heart began to pound.

Klaus indicated they should step away from the group to have a private conversation. Steve's heart rate rose even more. When they were out of earshot, Klaus said, "Would you do me a favor?"

"W-w-w-what?"

"You know the location where they shot the famous scene in the film *Forest Gump*?"

Steve nodded.

"Can we stop there, so I can make a group picture?" Klaus asked.

"Oh! S-s-s-sure!" Steve said. He was so relieved that he almost burst into tears. There was something about Klaus that was intimidating, even when he wasn't trying to be.

They took Highway 163 South and Steve stopped at the spot as promised. Klaus placed his camera on a tripod in the middle of the road and asked the group to pose for a picture. Tina slipped her arm around Steve.

Klaus clicked a button and then ran over to Tina's other side. The camera flashed three times as it counted down for the delayed exposure. Just as the shutter was about to click they realized a truck was approaching.

The driver honked a long blast on a loud horn, but he didn't slow down at all.

Klaus leaped into action, running to save his camera. The rest of the group scrambled to get out of the road.

Klaus grabbed his gear and kept running to the other side of the road. He cleared the pavement seconds before the tractor roared past.

The tattooed driver held his middle finger out the window, and shouted, "Tourons!"

"Is that the same truck that was tailgating the Mustang yesterday?" Gerd shouted across the road to Klaus.

Klaus nodded in response.

"Americans are a repulsive people," said Elisabeth, "such a filthy country, too. Just look around. Dirt everywhere."

After that encounter the group was shell-shocked. They climbed back into the van, their giddy mood considerably dampened. Steve resumed their drive, going especially slow in an effort to ensure they would *not* catch up with the trucker.

***

Butch and Sundance were sure the group would use Highway 98 to get to Page, Arizona. They reluctantly left their luxurious hotel suite very early to find a spot where they'd have a clear view of the road.

***

The tour group reached Kayenta and stopped at a huge parking lot near the intersection of Highway 163 and Highway 160. They split up to get breakfast at the various places nearby. Some went to the grocery store, some to McDonald's, and others to Burger King.

Tina asked Steve if he'd like to join her and Klaus at McDonald's. "Gotta get gas," he mumbled, and drove over to a nearby station to get a safe distance away from her.

Alex looked around carefully to make sure no one was paying him any attention, then he removed the white plastic bag from his backpack. It contained his sweater, hat, sunglasses, t-shirt, and J.J. Stanfield's wallet and credit cards. He tossed the bag into a dumpster beside the grocery store, and leaned in to scatter discarded fruit and vegetables over the top of it.

From now on he'd have to use his own cash or borrow from Steve.

***

While the tour group was eating breakfast Butch and Sundance reached the intersection to Kaibeto and decided it was a good place to lie to wait for the van to drive by. The visibility was perfect.

***

The guests finished eating and were ready to head toward Page. It took them about eighty minutes to get from Kayenta to where the Mustang was parked.

Steve was a conscientious driver, always observing the speed limit even in the middle of nowhere, but today he was even slower because he was so flustered by the events with Tina during the previous evening and the deranged trucker that morning.

A line of cars built up behind the van. And that made it very easy to spot.

When Butch and Sundance saw it, they started the engine, intending to follow, but had to wait for nearly twenty cars to go by before there was a large enough gap to pull out.

Sundance drove aggressively in an effort to catch up, but the traffic was heavy on the road that connected two major tourist destinations. Each time he tried to pass a vehicle there'd be another one approaching from the opposite direction and he had to abort the maneuver.

As he neared Page they were still pretty far behind.

***

Steve glanced over at Alex and noticed him squinting in the glare of the desert sun, "Did you forget your hat and sunglasses? Do you wanna stop and get them out of your luggage?"

"I forgot them. They're in the hotel room," Alex said.

"Oh, gee. Sorry,"

"Yeah, I'm gonna call and ask housekeeping to hold my things, so I can pick them up on the next trip," Alex said. "I can get some new stuff in Page."

They arrived in Page forty-five minutes before check-in would begin for their Antelope Canyon tour, so Alex suggested they fill the time by going to a scenic overlook at Glen Canyon Dam where they'd have a great view of Lake Powell.

Butch and Sundance were held up by a stop light near the city limits of Page. They sat watching as dozens of cars went through the intersection before the light changed. They'd lost sight of the van, so they'd have to go into town and look for it.

They cruised along *Church Row* on Lake Powell Boulevard where a dozen different denominations had churches very close together. It made for an unusual sight.

Then they drove all the way down to the dam, but didn't see the van. "What's next?" Butch asked.

He had no idea what to do next. He felt a burning in his stomach and thought he might be getting an ulcer. This job should've been a snap, but it had turned into one long bad dream. He was ready to wake up.

"They're gonna go to Antelope Canyon," Sundance said, scrolling and reading from the tour company's website on his cell phone. "I shoulda just printed all this out days ago, but I keep thinkin' every day we'll wrap it up."

Butch sighed, "Me, too. Where's the Antelope place?"

Sundance pulled it up on Google Maps. "Looks like we passed it on the way into town," he said. "But it's in the middle of nowhere."

"This whole trip is in the middle of nowhere."

"No, I mean this time I don't even see a road."

He tilted his phone toward Butch and they studied the satellite image together. They could see a parking lot labeled *Antelope Canyon Navajo Tours*, so they made a U-turn, drove as close as they could, and decided to wait at a parking area near the canyon.

It was time for the Antelope Slot Canyon Tour. While Alex checked them in, the guests enjoyed watching a young Navajo man doing a traditional hoop dance. The guy was an impressive athlete.

The guests boarded an extra-long, specially-modified truck that would take them to Navajo lands.

Alex and Steve stayed behind in Page. They'd use the time to eat a leisurely meal at Subway, have a coffee, and shop at the grocery store, and Alex would spent a few precious dollars to buy a new cap and sunglasses.

***

When the Navajo truck reached the parking lot, Klaus spotted the Mustang right away and pointed it out to Gerd and Tina.

Butch and Sundance were waiting for a van. The variety of vehicles used by the many different tour companies caused them not to realize that the group they were looking for had just gone by in a truck carrying several groups together. So, while the tourists strolled through the extraordinarily narrow canyon, between whimsically eroded sandstone walls enchantingly lit by sunbeams through crevices high overhead, Butch and Sundance sat staring at the road.

When the group finished the tour of Antelope Canyon they were carried out of the sandy wash in the same high-ground-clearance Navajo truck that had brought them there.

"Those men are *still* sitting there!" Gerd said, pointing at the car when they passed it to enter the highway back to Page. "What are they *doing*? They are at this famous place and have not gotten out to look at it! That is very crazy."

"What do you expect?" said Elisabeth. "They are Americans. They have no taste, no culture. Perhaps they are touring parking lots of the Wild West."

Her comment provoked laughter among all the German speakers aboard the truck.

Chapter 38

Later, while the group was strolling around Page shopping and visiting restaurants for lunch, Butch and Sundance were still sitting at the entrance to Antelope Canyon, scanning vehicles.

"I hate this freakin' job!" Butch said. "I hate it! I'm sick of sittin' around in these hellholes waitin'. And I don't even know what for!"

"I hear ya," Sundance said.

Finally, after hours in the parking lot, they realized that the groups coming from Page were all being driven by Navajo guides in Navajo vehicles. It took a while to figure it out because there were so many different tour companies and they used a great variety of conveyances.

Too late, the guys realized they never should've been looking for the *van* in the first place. They should've been looking for the *people* instead. "Ah geez," sighed Sundance. "Not again! My brain's fried by all this sun. It's makin' me stupid. Let's get outta here."

***

The group visited the awesome overlook at Horseshoe Bend where the Colorado River curved back on itself. The curve at Dead Horse Point had been fantastic, but this was fabulous, too. Then they continued to the Wahweep Marina for an evening cruise on Lake Powell.

***

Butch and Sundance finally gave up and drove to check Horseshoe Bend, but of course the group was long gone.

The two men were crazed by this point. But there was nothing they could do about it. They had to stay the course. So they drove to the town and methodically resumed their search.

"What does the itinerary say?" Butch asked, dreading more forced tourism.

"For today it says they got Horseshoe Bend, Antelope Canyon, Lake Powell, and Page," Sundance said.

"Then they gotta be here *somewhere!*" Butch said.

The men continued to drive around town, then they went back to the parking area at Horseshoe Bend, checked the visitor center at Glen Canyon Dam, and as a last ditch measure decided to take a look at the Wahweep Marina.

By the time they got to the marina, the cruise was over. Steve was leaving at the same time Butch and Sundance were arriving through a different entrance.

The mafiosos checked the marina parking area and drove over to the beach. If they'd had any idea how many times they'd had near-misses to their quarry, they would've lost it.

Butch would've had a stroke.

"How are they doin' this?" he said. "It makes no sense that they always manage to totally disappear. I'm startin' to think that the Boss has misunderestimated these guys. I'm thinkin' they're pros. Maybe this *tourist* thing's just an act."

Sundance was too depressed to respond.

Butch steered the car back onto the highway and headed toward Page. Along the way he noticed a nice little side road leading up to a lookout, and he took it.

The road wasn't scary. When he got to the top of the rise, the road ended. He stopped the car and turned the engine off. The light was beautiful and it turned the lake a warm orange.

"Geez," Sundance said.

"Yeah," Butch agreed. "You know what? Let's hang here 'til after sunset and then we'll check every hotel in town. That's the smart move. We'll find 'em tonight."

Then the two men fell silent and sat there together, spellbound, watching the glorious sunset.

***

In previous years the tour groups had spent the night in Page, but recently they'd begun to offer an option to visit the White Pocket, a particularly striking desert landscape. That meant that instead of spending the night in Page, the group stayed at Cliff Dwellers Lodge.

It held the ruins of an old house that had been built in the middle of nowhere in the early 1900's in a place discovered accidentally by a Ziegfeld Follies dancer whose car broke down when she was taking her husband to a dry climate to help him recover from tuberculosis.

It was a good location for breaking a journey and later a motel, a restaurant, and a gas station were added.

Guests enjoyed the spartan place because there was virtually no light pollution. The night sky was absolutely breathtaking. It was quiet, the restaurant was good, and there was plenty of outside seating.

It was a fantastic experience to be there at night.

On their way to the hotel the group saw Marble Canyon, the Vermillion Cliffs, and an edge of the Grand Canyon, which was only a tiny slot at this end.

At twilight they made a stop at the striking Navajo Bridge, actually a pair of bridges—one new and one old—that straddled a tip of the Grand Canyon and the Colorado River.

From the bridge you could observe rare California condors nesting in nearby rocks. "If you're headed west, this bridge is the last place where you can cross the Colorado River for the next 280 miles," said Alex. "The next crossing is at Hoover Dam near Las Vegas."

The group reached Cliff Dwellers in the dark. They checked in and enjoyed dinner outside under the star spangled sky, blissfully unaware of Butch and Sundance's increasing desperation and fury.

The mafiosos were jarred awake by Butch's phone ringing at six the next morning. They'd slept for only a couple of hours because they'd patrolled for the van until three in the morning.

"Hello?" Butch said, warily.

"What's your status?" the Boss said.

"We lost 'em," Butch said.

"Whaddaya mean, *you lost 'em*?"

"We saw 'em yesterday mornin' and then just when we were closin' in on 'em, they disappeared," Butch said.

"You idiots! Are you freakin' kiddin' me? I'll give you *one more day*! If you don't have that flash drive by tomorrow night I'm comin' out there and I'm gonna take care of it *myself*!" He hung up on them.

"Uh oh!" Butch said. "If we don't have it by tomorrow night, he's gonna come out here!"

"What're we gonna do?"

"Dunno! But let's get outta here," Butch said, leaping out of bed and pulling on his pants.

Minutes later the two men were out of the hotel and headed south. Butch let Sundance drive because he was shaken up by the phone call. Before they made it to the Navajo Bridge the warning light for the fuel tank came on.

"Aw geez I *hate* this freakin' place! There's *no* freakin' gas stations. You can drive for miles and *nothin'*. Not even a freakin' *town*! I hope we can find somethin' soon," Sundance said.

They crossed the bridge and a few miles later they found a Chevron station at the Marble Canyon Lodge. Sundance got out of the car to fill up, but he couldn't get the pump to work.

The clerk opened the door of the station, and shouted, "Sorry guys! The pumps are down! Our electricity is out!"

"Where's the next station?" Sundance asked.

"It's a few miles down the road by Cliff Dwellers. Maybe they'll have power. Good luck!"

Sundance got back into the car and they headed for the next station. A few miles later, after driving by the Cliff Dweller ruins, they made it to a gas station on the motel property. The pumps there were working.

Sundance paid cash inside and had just put the nozzle into the tank when Butch saw the van pull out of the hotel parking lot and onto the highway.

"Hurry up!" he called out, from the passenger seat. "There they are!"

Sundance looked frantically at the pump. "The pump's slow, but we gotta have gas!" he said. When he'd pumped ten gallons he jerked the nozzle out and they hit the highway.

The clerk ran out of the building, shouting, "Hey! Wait! You forgot your change!"

They were making good time until suddenly a mirage appeared in the distance. It looked almost like a herd of cattle were in the road. Seconds later Sundance realized it was a herd of cows. They were standing around, apparently bored, totally blocking the road. The Mustang slid to a stop on squealing tires.

Neither man moved.

The cattle made a slow motion swarm that engulfed the Mustang. Sundance crept along until he made the tiniest bit of gentle contact with one of the animals. The cow didn't move out of the way, but instead gave the front bumper a swift kick.

Sundance stopped. "Your turn this time," he said.

Butch reluctantly got out of the car.

"Yippee ki yay!" Sundance mumbled.

Butch attempted to force the cows off the road by shouting and clapping and waving his arms. When that didn't work, he tried shoving one of them from behind, barely avoiding being kicked, butted, and trampled.

What he couldn't avoid was the inevitable byproduct of the herd's high fiber diet. Fresh manure was everywhere and he was stepping in it.

These animals were not used to being handled, and certainly not by one person standing on the ground. The respected experienced wranglers on horseback, but this guy, not so much.

Sundance sat in the car watching the world's worst cowboy try to herd about a hundred little doggies across the road without any equipment or knowhow. He began to softly sing the parts he could remember from *City Slickers*.

"Rollin', rollin', rollin … Rawhide! Round 'em up, ride 'em in, get 'em up, get 'em dressed, comb their hair, brush their teeth, Rawhide!"

The herd's movements bore only the most tenuous relationship to Butch's efforts, so after several minutes of attempting to wrestle with walking hamburger, Butch came back to the car, grabbed his pistol from underneath the seat and, before Sundance had any idea what was going on, he fired a shot into the air, and shouted, "Heeyah!"

That got more response than his previous tactics, but unlike in a cowboy movie, it didn't start a stampede. Instead the beasts milled around in a configuration that left enough room for Sundance to get through at a crawl.

Soon afterwards they spotted the van. It was sitting on a road that branched off the highway. A Suburban was parked nearby.

Before they could reach it, they saw several members of the tour group get into the Suburban and drive away. Steve and two others stayed behind waving. The guy they were after was in the Suburban, so Sundance followed it down a small paved road marked House Rock Road.

The Suburban was moving pretty fast until it turned off onto a dirt track. Eventually the dirt became sand and the Mustang had to break off the pursuit. They'd learned that lesson the hard way.

Sundance now had enough experience to realize if he followed the Suburban any further, he and Butch would get stuck. So he stopped. "We can't follow 'em," he said. "There's no way we can get through that."

"What're we gonna do?" Butch asked.

"Check the map and see where this road comes out," Sundance suggested.

Butch pulled out his cell phone, but there was no reception. "Let's head back to the main highway and see if we can get a signal there," he said. They turned around and soon got a good enough signal to pull up a map.

The road the Suburban was on was a dead end. It would have to come out the same way it went in. Butch and Sundance drove back to the dirt road. The Mustang was now sitting in a perfect place to intercept the group as they came out and this time there was nobody around to see anything or disrupt the plan.

They blocked the road with the car and waited.

Butch took his pistol out, checked the ammo, and chambered a round. "I'll get the camera bag," he said.

Sundance retrieved his pistol, too, and checked and readied it for action. They didn't know how long they'd have to wait, but this farce, this nightmare, would definitely be over before the day was out.

Chapter 39

Sundance watched Butch try to clean cow poop off his boot with sand, a small branch from a bush, and some fast food napkins. His effort was generally successful, but they still needed to leave the car windows open or the smell was too strong.

***

After a long drive on the sandy, rutted road the Suburban reached White Pocket. The guests hopped out and the guide, John, led the way through the sand and into the wonderland created by wind, water, sand, and sandstone.

The place was extraordinary.

The group hiked across uneven ground, and there was a bit of climbing, but they found amazing rock formations around every corner. After two hours they found a place to sit down in the shade and John unpacked sandwiches for everyone.

Gerd had experienced some stomach issues that morning, so he ate only half of his sandwich and stashed the other half in his camera bag for later.

After the lunch break they spent another two hours hiking around in and photographing the strange landscape as they made their way back to the Suburban.

Butch and Sundance heard the sound of an engine and the bouncing of a vehicle's suspension. They jumped out of the car and hid behind some juniper trees on either side of the trail, leaving the Mustang sideways, totally blocking the road.

The Suburban stopped when it got close and John got out to see what was wrong.

When he bent over to look inside the car, Butch jumped out, ran over to the open driver's door of the Suburban, and pointed his gun at the passengers, shouting, "Hands up! All of you! I wanna see your hands in the air right now!"

Even though their English wasn't great, it was perfectly clear what was happening, except the cowboy clothes made it seem a little like a staged scene. Could this be a planned bit of entertainment? Like one of the shootout reenactments they'd seen in the little towns?

John turned around to see what was happening and couldn't believe his eyes. Sundance pointed a gun at him, and said, "You, too! Hands in the air! And get over here."

Sundance walked around to the other side of the SUV, jerked the passenger door open and began pulling group members out. "Out! Out! All of you! Out! Right now!"

Butch and Sundance shouted orders and did a lot of gun pointing until they had everyone gathered together. Butch aimed at Gerd. "Where's the camera bag?" he said.

"In there," Gerd said, pointing toward the back of the Suburban.

"Get it!" Sundance said.

Gerd climbed in, reached into the back, and came out with his camera bag.

"Set the bag on the ground," said Butch.

Gerd obeyed him.

"Now empty it and lay everything out where I can see it.

Gerd looked at Butch in confusion and said, "There is nothing of value in there."

Butch stepped closer and held the gun to the side of Gerd's head and said, "Empty it now, or else."

"I swear to you, I have nothing you are wanting."

Butch made Gerd back away and gestured to Sundance that he should search the bag. Sundance moved toward it, but before he could reach it a coyote leaped out of the roadside brush and streaked between him and the SUV. The animal grabbed a mouthful of the bag between its teeth and raced off with it.

Butch shot twice at the scruffy varmint and missed both times. Then he and Sundance took off after the creature on foot, shouting and cursing.

Butch stopped running to take aim at the coyote and fired a couple more shots, but missed again. The rascal was fast.

Although the bag was heavy and the coyote had to struggle to half carry, half drag it over large rocks to make good on its escape, its four furry legs were still a lot faster than two city boys in cowboy boots.

***

When the thugs were a safe distance away Alex jumped into the Mustang.

"The key's in the ignition," he said, "John, you guys, get back in the Suburban! Let's get outta here right now!"

Alex had spoken in English, but it was the fastest Alex or John had *ever* seen a tour group get themselves loaded into a vehicle. Alex started the Mustang and John fired up the Suburban. They took off leaving a huge cloud of dust behind them.

Butch and Sundance heard the engines and realized, too late, what was happening. They turned around to chase the cars, cursing.

First they'd chased a jacked up wild dog and now they were chasing cars.

Butch shot at the vehicles until he was out of ammo. He'd succeeded in shattering the rear window of the Mustang, but the driver didn't slow or demonstrate any ill effects.

***

Alex and John flew down House Rock Road as fast as they dared. As he followed Alex, John tossed his phone to Peter, and said, "Call 911 and report an armed robbery, give a description of the two men, and their location."

To the group's surprise, Peter did just that, and in fluent English.

The two vehicles reached the intersection with the highway. Alex stopped the Mustang and John stopped the Suburban right beside him.

Alex got out of the Mustang, boarded the Suburban, and said, "Go, go, go! Let's get outta here!"

John drove the Suburban up onto the highway and took off, heading south.

***

The group had made it half way up the Kaibab Plateau when a highway patrol car zoomed past them headed in the opposite direction, lights flashing and siren blaring.

"Wow! That was fast," John said. "Usually there's not much police presence in this area. We got lucky. They must've been somewhere nearby."

Soon afterwards a local law enforcement vehicle blasted by, also with lights and sirens.

"Another one!" John said.

Everyone was chattering, wondering what the men had been talking about. Why did they want Gerd's bag? Why did they think Gerd had what something they were after? But no one had any answers.

"John, what should we do now?" Alex asked.

"I'll take you to your hotel in Kanab," he said. "I know the sheriff's deputy in Fredonia, so I'll drop you guys off and go to the station and see what's going on."

Alex twisted around in his seat, and said, "That was so weird! How did they know you had a camera bag? Why were they interested in it and not in anything else?"

241

"I have no idea," Gerd said, and he shot Klaus a look.

Just before the tour group reached Jacob Lake two black Suburbans, each with a portable flashing blue light set atop the dashboard, sat blocking the road. A man wearing a bulletproof vest and a windbreaker emblazoned with *FBI* held up a hand to indicate that John should stop.

"Good grief!" John said. "They've sent an army!"

The tour group was both terrified and thrilled. It was like the wreck with the elk. They were living another real-life Wild West adventure and this time a cavalry had ridden to their rescue.

The FBI agents ordered everyone out of the vehicle. This was the second time the guests had been made to do this in less than an hour. They were getting better at it.

The tour group was nervous and curious, but their guide was freaking out. Alex feared they were looking for the man in the photo taken by the ATM in Durango. In other words, *him*.

"We're the ones who called you," John said, as he got out with his hands in the air. "We reported the incident and the victim of the robbery is in the SUV."

The agents didn't respond to John or react at all. It was as if he hadn't even spoken. Two agents climbed into the Suburban while another one opened the back hatch.

"Don't you need a warrant for that?" John asked, but got no response. That made him angry, "Hey!" he said, "We're the good guys! The ones you're looking for are down on House Rock Road."

The agents continued to search the car without speaking. When they were done, one of them said, "Where's the bag?"

"What bag?" Alex asked.

"The *camera* bag," the agent said.

"That's why we called you!" John said. "It was stolen! Those guys took it."

The agent gave him a hard look.

"And then a coyote ran off with it," he added, in an apologetic tone.

"What did you just say?" the agent asked.

"We called you because we got robbed," John replied, speaking slowly.

"*You* called *us*?"

"We called 911 a few minutes ago because we got robbed," John said enunciating carefully, as if he was talking to people who weren't very bright.

"Where did this happen?" the agent asked.

"Don't you guys talk to each other?" John said. "As we told 911, we were accosted at House Rock Road and Pine Tree Road. Two armed guys approached us there and stole one of the guest's camera bag."

"Who were they?" the agent asked.

"Two guys!" John said. "They were robbers! I don't know their names! Do victims usually know the names of people who rob them while they're on vacation?"

The FBI agents quickly exchanged glances and then got back into their black Suburbans and raced off down the highway.

The tour group stood in the middle of the road wondering what had just happened.

"What was *that*?" John asked.

"I have no idea," Alex said, thrilled that the agents were gone and that he wasn't in handcuffs in the back of one of those black Suburbans.

"They didn't even ask for a description of the robbers or let us tell them about the car," John said.

"Or the coyote," said Frida, smiling. She was having a great time with all the chaos. It would make a great premise for her next mystery.

"I guess we're free to go. Let's get outta here."

They all loaded back into the white Suburban and left the baffling encounter in the dust.

Alex was ecstatic that none of the chaos had anything to do with his use of Stanfield's cards. For obvious reasons he kept his joy to himself.

As they rode away Gerd questioned why there was suddenly so much interest in his camera bag from such a diverse group of individuals.

"You know something else weird about this?" John said. "We didn't even mention the bag when we called 911, and yet the FBI asked about it specifically. They said they didn't know about our call, but they were after the bag, too."

"This is so exciting," said Frida. "I cannot wait to see what happens next."

Even Peter looked animated, "I called 911," he said.

Alex didn't trust himself to participate in the conversation because he was so giddy with relief, but he thought to himself, *That coyote better watch its back.*

Chapter 40

John dropped the group off at the Parry Lodge in Kanab. It was a famous old style motel where movie stars and film crews used to stay while working in the area. There was a handout at the front desk listing some of the stars who'd slept there.

It was formidable. Alex gave the guests a copy: Tyrone Power, Gregory Peck, Ronald Reagan, John Wayne, Omar Sharif, Lana Turner, Charlton Heston, Frank Sinatra, Dean Martin, Sidney Portier, James Garner, Jane Russell, and many more.

The list included some of the famous movies that were made in the area—everything from *Maverick* to *Planet of the Apes*. And beloved television shows, as well, such as *The Lone Ranger*, *Lassie*, and *Gunsmoke*.

"Stay and have dinner with us," Alex said.

"Thanks," John said, "but I gotta get goin'."

He smiled and kept his response friendly, but he'd had enough of this bunch. On the surface they seemed normal, even boring, but obviously they were not what they pretended to be. It was all he could do to keep from laying rubber as he left.

The van was parked in front of the hotel office, so Alex knew Steve, Georg, and Elisabeth had arrived earlier in the day following their alternate itinerary of a short hike at Lee's Ferry and visits to Marble Canyon, Jacob Lake, and Pipe Springs, New Mexico.

Alex opened the door of his room, and greeted Steve with, "You won't believe what happened today!"

"You won't believe what happened to us either!" Steve said.

"Let me tell you first!" Alex said.

They sat down and Alex started his narrative. When he got to the part where they were stopped by the FBI, Steve interrupted to say, "We got stopped by the FBI, too! But it was this morning!"

"This morning?" Alex said. "But the robbery wasn't until this afternoon! What did they want?"

"They asked for permission to search the van, but wouldn't give me a reason," Steve said. "We had nothing to hide, so I let 'em do it. Then they asked where the other guests were and I explained that you guys were touring a different area. They wanted me to show them which way you'd gone and I told 'em you usually stopped for restrooms at Jacob Lake and then went down through Fredonia to Kanab."

"Didn't you wonder what they wanted?" Alex asked.

"Of course I did! But it was the FBI!" Steve said. "I asked, but they wouldn't tell me anything. I was afraid you might've been kidnapped or were being held hostage by terrorists, or something. They were all tricked out in bulletproof vests and assault weapons. I assumed they were trying to rescue you."

Alex's phone rang. It was John.

"They got 'em!" John said. "I'm here at the sheriff's office with Deputy Hankins. He told me they found the two guys and the bag. He said they claimed to have taken it away from a coyote," he laughed.

"This whole thing's crazy!" Alex said, laughing. "That's an awful lot of trouble for a small reward. It doesn't make any sense."

"Agreed," said John. "Do you want to come to the sheriff's office? It's down in Fredonia, Arizona. When you cross the state line and drive into town you'll see the Cowboy Butte Steak House on the right. On the corner of Hortt Street, you'll see the police station. It's on the left," John said. "The sheriff would like to talk to you and the owner of the bag."

Alex was concerned that the sheriff might recognize him from the picture in the news, so he said, "Is it okay if Steve brings Gerd? He's had time to rest."

There was a brief muffled conversation on the other end of the line, then John said, "The deputy wants to see *you*."

"Oh, … okay," Alex said, "I'll get Gerd and we'll be right over."

Alex turned to Steve, and said, "The sheriff wants to talk to me and Gerd."

Alex didn't want to leave Gerd stranded if they arrested him, so he asked, "I'm tired. Do you mind driving us?"

"No problem," said Steve.

They got Gerd, who was happy to learn that his bag had been found. Then they drove seven miles to the state line between Utah and Arizona. The trip took less than ten minutes. As they were going into the sheriff's office they saw two black Suburbans pull away from the curb and turn onto the main road, heading south at a speed well above the posted limit.

The three of them walked into the little building where John and Deputy Hankins were waiting. The deputy looked at Alex, then said, "Aren't you…?"

Alex almost had a heart attack. He interrupted the deputy, saying, "I don't think so."

"No, you *are*!" the deputy said, "You're the guy whose Jeep we pulled out of a flash flood near Pipe Springs a while back."

Alex nearly fainted with relief. "Oh, …yeah! You're right!" he said, "That was me." Then he added, "That was years ago. You have a good memory!"

"Not really," the Deputy said, laughing, "It's just that there aren't many people who try to drive through five feet of water!"

Alex blushed and refused to make eye contact with Steve. "Two-wheel drive," he mumbled.

"Sorry to bother you fellas," the sheriff said. "I was just gonna call you with an update. The FBI was here. They just left. They said this incident is part of a federal investigation and they said the bag was evidence. They took it with them."

"When will I get it back?" Gerd asked, crestfallen.

"I guess they'll return it to you once they're finished with it," he said. "I'm sorry, but I don't know when that might be. I can take down your contact information. I suspect they'll be getting back in touch with me later."

Gerd's disappointment was obvious. "I'm sorry sir," the deputy said, "but just so you know, the bag was a mess. You were gonna have to get a new one anyway. That coyote chewed it to pieces. Apparently there was some food in there and that's what the animal was after."

Gerd nodded, "Half of my sandwich," he said.

"What about the two guys?" Alex asked.

"They were taken into custody."

Gerd left his contact information with Deputy Hankins and they drove back to Kanab, Utah. He was upset. "We're going to the Grand Canyon tomorrow," he said, "and now I don't have any of my equipment!"

***

That evening when the group met for dinner at the Rocking V Café they had a lot to talk about.

Klaus and Tina shared their confusion over the day's events.

"I don't understand Americans," Tina said. "Why would two criminals follow us for days, make such a long drive, then rob us at gunpoint, but take only a camera bag of no special value?" Tina asked.

"Why would the FBI be interested in such a small crime?" Klaus asked.

"Why did the FBI stop Steve *before* the robbery?" said Tina.

"And why did the FBI take the camera bag away from the coyote, the robbers, and Gerd?" Klaus added.

"At least this confirms that the two men in the Mustang really were following us all this time," Gerd added. "They weren't on vacation."

"But *why?*" Tina asked.

No one had an answer.

***

The next morning, after breakfast, the group was gathered at the van looking forward to a day at the North Rim of the Grand Canyon when Alex's cell phone rang.

It was John.

"Hey, Alex. Can you run by my house? One of your guests left something in the Suburban," he said.

"Sure, thanks for the call. We were just about to head out to the North Rim," Alex said. "We'll stop by on the way. See ya in a few."

***

When they got to John's house Alex hopped out of the van. John handed him a flash drive, and said, "One of your people must've dropped this yesterday. I found it on the back seat when I cleaned the car."

"Thanks!" Alex said. "What a crazy day."

"No kidding. And the camera bag thing wasn't all," John said. "Something else weird happened. I told the FBI about the Mustang that you left near the highway, but they said they didn't find it."

"Hmm," Alex said. "That's strange. Who'd stumble on a car in such an isolated area and steal it?"

"I don't know," John said, with a shrug. "The whole thing's bizarre."

"Well, thanks for this!" Alex said, clapping John on the shoulder and brandishing the flash drive. Then he went back to his group.

Steve pulled out and as they were cruising through town, Alex shared what John had told him. He, too, was baffled by the odd events.

Alex turned around, held up the black flash drive, saying, "Which one of you dropped this during all the excitement yesterday?"

Nobody reacted.

"Oops," Alex said, and dialed John's number. "Hey, it's me, Alex! That flash drive doesn't belong to any of our guests."

"Someone in your party must've lost it," John said. "I check very carefully each time I finish a tour. I'm certain there was nothing in the car from the day before. Then yesterday evening it was there."

Alex looked at the passengers again, and asked, "Are you *sure* none of you recognize this thing?"

They all shook their heads.

"Nope! It's not ours," Alex said.

"Well, you guys can keep it anyway!" John said. "You don't need to bring it back to me."

"Okay. See ya on the next go round," Alex said, then disconnected the call.

He slipped the stray flash drive into a front pocket of his jeans.

***

On the way to the North Rim of the Grand Canyon they saw a herd of bison. "Too bad I don't have my camera with me," Gerd said. "Those buffalo would make some great shots!"

His fellow travelers were sympathetic, but there was nothing anyone could do.

The group stopped at several scenic overlooks and the Grand Canyon Lodge, then hiked down the North Kaibab Trail until they felt they'd seen enough and were ready to turn around.

Gerd lamented losing his camera equipment several times.

"We can find a camera store if you'd like to get a replacement," Alex said. "Our insurance might reimburse the cost. I'll ask."

"Thanks," Gerd said.

Chapter 41

The guys were resting in their hotel room in Kanab after a full day at the North Rim. Alex turned on the television and switched it to a 24-hour news station.

"The search is still on for journalist J.J. Stanfield," the anchorman said. A gritty photo of a dirty and exhausted Stanfield at work in a war zone flashed onto the screen.

"A confidential source has confirmed that Stanfield was ready to publish a hard-hitting exposé detailing the connections of organized crime to law enforcement and high-ranking government officials, not only in Nevada, but also nationwide. His colleagues are concerned that his disappearance is connected to his investigation."

Alex's attention was diverted by someone banging hard on the door. He opened it and was presented with a point blank view of four men wearing bulletproof vests. The black vests had FBI printed on them in large yellow letters.

One of the men said, without any introduction, "Who's the owner of the camera bag?"

"Gerd," Alex said.

"Gerd who?"

"Gerd, uh…," Alex turned his head toward Steve. "Do you remember Gerd's last name?"

"Oh, gosh," Steve said. "I don't know."

Alex turned back to the agent, "Sorry, on our tours we go by first names."

"Which room's he in?" the agent asked.

"Let me look it up," Alex said. He walked over to the desk and shuffled through the papers lying there. "Gerd Leistner," he read aloud. "Leistner is his last name. He's in Room 120."

The agent spun on his heel, and the four of them strode down the walkway between the motel rooms and the parked cars.

"Thank you for your assistance," Alex mumbled to himself in a sarcastic tone.

Alex leaned out to watch until they stopped in front of Room 120, then he closed his door. In light of his own misbehavior, he didn't want any more interaction with law enforcement than was absolutely necessary.

***

Gerd had just undressed to take a shower when he heard loud banging on his door.

"Just a minute!" he shouted, and he pulled on some pants before opening the door.

He was as surprised as Alex had been to find four men standing there with FBI written in large letters across their bulletproof vests.

"We need to talk to you," an agent said, pushing the door all the way open.

"Okay," Gerd said.

"We're looking for something we believe is in your possession," the agent said.

"What would that be?" Gerd asked calmly, mindful of all the encounters he'd had with the secret police in the old days in East Germany.

"We want the flash drive."

"What flash drive?" Gerd asked.

"The one you were carrying in your camera bag."

"I do not have any flash drives. I have never owned one," he said. "I have heard they can carry viruses or spyware from their point of manufacture."

"We know for a fact that there was a flash drive in your camera bag," the agent said, "and we're equally certain that it's no longer in that bag. We want it. And we want it now."

"As I said, I do not have what you are asking for."

The agent turned around to his colleagues, and said, "It's in here somewhere. Find it."

The three men began a methodical search of the room while the lead agent patted down Gerd's pants.

"Hey! What is this?" Gerd said. "Are you allowed to do this?"

The men didn't respond, just continued a meticulous search of every nook and cranny in the room.

While they were tossing the place, Klaus suddenly appeared in the doorway. "What is happening?" he said.

One of the agents went toward him and pushed him out of the room, saying, "This is none of your concern."

"Do you have a warrant?" Klaus asked.

"Are you his attorney?" the agent asked.

The search didn't take long. "It's not here," an agent said.

The lead agent said, "Let's go," and they left as quickly as they'd arrived.

Gerd shouted after them, "What about my camera bag? When are you going to return my equipment?"

There was no response.

He turned around and stared at his room in disbelief.

"What was this about?" Klaus asked.

"I do not know!" Gerd said, "They asked me about a flash drive. They said they were looking for it. I do not have it!"

***

Steve and Alex heard another knock at their door. Alex opened it warily. This time it was Klaus.

"The flash drive that John found, it is mine," Klaus said. "It fell out of my pocket."

"Oh, okay!" Alex said. "Let me look for it. I'll bring it to your room."

"Thanks," said Klaus.

Alex got his laptop and removed the flash drive. Since no one had claimed it, he'd decided to use it to backup some of his own files.

"Here it is," he said. "I'll take it to Klaus."

***

When Klaus opened his door, Alex saw that the lights were off and the curtains were drawn, so he handed him the drive without speaking, in case Tina was asleep.

"Thank you!" Klaus whispered. "When you first asked about it, I did not even realize it was mine," Klaus smiled, and tapped the side of his head. "Just one more sign that I am getting old."

They smiled at each other.

"Gute Nacht," Klaus whispered.

"Gute Nacht," Alex replied.

***

When Alex was back in his own room he fired up his laptop. He'd copied the files from the flash drive onto his laptop's hard drive, to back them up just in case, because he planned to erase the flash drive and use it for his own data. But he hadn't had time to perform the erasure before Klaus interrupted him.

He was glad he hadn't! Now that Klaus had his data back, Alex slid the files into the trash bin.

***

Tina, who'd claimed to be exhausted by the day's activities, was sound asleep. Klaus walked over to the desk and located his computer using the small flashlight the tour company had given them on the first day. He booted up the laptop and inserted the flash drive.

He was surprised that he was able to access the files without needing a password. He was even more surprised when he realized what he had found.

"What are you doing?" Tina mumbled, half awake.

"Nothing," he said, shutting down the computer.

Then he brushed his teeth and crawled into bed.

Chapter 42

When Alex and Steve arrived for breakfast the next morning, Gerd was already at a table with Georg, Elisabeth, Peter, and Frida describing the events of the previous evening.

Steve and Alex sat down at the table next to them. Alex heard part of the story, then moved closer, and asked Gerd for details.

"The FBI searched my room!" he said. "It reminded me of the Stasi treatment I received in the late 1980s. It is really shocking that something like that can happen in modern times and in the U.S. of all places!"

The group speculated about what could be provoking such law enforcement action, but couldn't come up with anything plausible to merit this level of interest.

"Why do they treat the victim of a robbery in this way?" Elisabeth asked.

Everyone agreed that it didn't make sense.

Gerd wondered who he should contact to complain about the treatment and get his camera equipment back. Alex had no idea. Neither did Steve. They didn't know anyone who'd ever had dealings with the FBI.

After breakfast the group boarded the van for what would be the last adventure for the guests on this tour, unless they'd booked an extension trip which would continue to California tomorrow. Gerd, Frida, Georg, and Elisabeth were staying for another week. Klaus, Tina, and Peter were flying back home tomorrow.

On this last day together they'd visit one of the most popular national parks in Utah—Zion. But before they drove up Mt. Carmel, Alex always liked to stop off for fresh coffee.

***

The van arrived at a building that looked like something from a Flintstones cartoon. It was wedged in between a cluster of huge boulders that had rolled to a stop here a long time ago.

The sign said it was *The Rock Shop*, but they stopped there because the store sold something in addition to rocks. Alex loved to surprise his guests with excellent espresso and cappuccino in Southern Utah, an area populated mostly by Mormons.

"Getting such an excellent brew in this area is particularly surprising because Mormons didn't drink coffee," Alex explained.

When they entered the store Steve and Alex were greeted by the owner. The guests shopped the wide selection of interesting geological specimens from the area and bought a few small souvenirs. When they'd finished their coffees, they were ready to go.

"No camera," lamented Gerd, as they drove up the beautiful road.

"I know it will not be the same, but I will email you the pictures we took."

"That is very kind," Gerd said, smiling, despite his recollection of the few photos Georg had taken and proudly shown him along the way.

Georg was the worst photographer he'd ever encountered. Every picture was either over or underexposed, or a finger was blocking the lens, or the head was missing on the person he was photographing.

"We will not be joining you in California, but you can have the pictures I have made so far," Klaus said. "You can transfer them from my computer to yours when we are at the hotel tonight."

***

Meanwhile Butch and Sundance were stuck in traffic, creeping along the highway in the mangled Mustang. Sundance's mind was wandering. He and Butch were just two cowpokes out riding the range on a horse that had been rode hard and put up wet.

His nostalgic western reverie was interrupted by Butch honking the horn and shouting rude remarks at the people nearby who were also hopelessly trapped in the jam.

When Butch called a man in the car beside him a profane name, the man could barely hear him because the windows were rolled up on both cars. He'd heard enough though, on account of the Mustang's missing back glass. He got out of his vehicle, came over, and knocked on Butch's window.

Butch rolled it down, and the man asked, "What'd you say?"

Butch responded to the question by punching the guy in the face. When the guy fell to the ground Butch rolled up his window and inched forward with the traffic.

Almost immediately afterwards he heard a police siren whoop behind him. He glanced in the rear view mirror and noticed the cop car for the first time. It was half a dozen cars back.

The policeman got out and approached the Mustang slowly with his hand on his gun. Butch rolled his window down again and looked up at the cop.

Then he and the cop both breathed a sigh of relief. They knew each other. And, more importantly, their bosses knew each other.

"Hey Dan!" Butch said. "Good to see ya. Howzit goin'?"

"Doin' great," the policeman said. "Doin' great."

The cop glanced toward the man lying on the ground. "Lemme take care of this for yuz. And please give my regards to your family."

Butch nodded his approval.

The cop grabbed the guy by the collar, dragged him back to his own car, and heaved him into the driver's seat. He slammed the door on the slumped figure, waved, and returned to his patrol car.

Butch and Sundance were mightily relieved to have made it back into their home territory where they had lots of associates in the most unexpected places.

***

Alex knew a great hike where the group could see petroglyphs and walk through a hidden slot canyon. The place wasn't well known, and he liked to keep it a secret. The parks were getting more crowded all the time and this spot was one of the few places on the Grand Circle that he could take people any time of year and know that they were likely to be able to walk among the ancient graffiti and red rocks alone.

Their next stop was a nice trail, but this one was well-known. Steve dropped the group near the trailhead of the Canyon Overlook and then drove the van down toward the Mt. Carmel tunnel. He did this because it was always tough to find a parking place before the tunnel, especially when you were pulling a trailer.

The group began their hike by climbing a set of steep stairs when suddenly something jumped out in front of them. Elisabeth screamed, because she thought it was another robbery, but it turned out to be a bighorn sheep instead. The beast's huge horns made it as formidable as an armed robber, but this particular animal continued on its way without any display of aggression.

When it bounded out of sight, everyone laughed with relief.

***

Butch and Sundance reached their destination, then Butch turned down a side street and parked the Mustang in a shaded alley.

"Why don't cha park closer?" Sundance asked.

"Don't want the Boss to get a load of the shape the car's in. This is gonna be a tough meetin' without that bit of info comin' out."

They walked to a nondescript warehouse. Sundance pressed the buzzer beside an unmarked metal security door and both men looked up into the surveillance camera to give the guard a clear view of their faces.

When he heard the answering buzz, Butch shoved hard against the heavy door and the two walked down a dark hallway until they reached another metal door.

Butch knocked on this one with the side of his fist and it was opened by a huge man who looked like a cross between a silverback gorilla and a grizzly bear.

They entered a dimly lit room filled with cigar smoke and stood side by side in front of a heavy wooden desk. The guy behind the desk rotated a computer monitor so they could see the Boss.

"What the frack? You're cowboys now?" the Boss said, looking at their stained, torn, and wrinkled western attire. "You look like a coupla idiots!"

The two men stood with their heads down.

"Do you guys have any idea how hard it was to get you out of that Arizona jail? I had to ask a contact at the freakin' FBI for a favor to get you out! My contact suggested I let you rot there, but I told him I'd rather discipline you myself."

"Sorry Boss! We tried…" Sundance started, but was interrupted.

"I don't wanna hear any more of your *tried* whining. Do you guys have any concept of what'll happen if the info on that flash drive gets out?"

He was red-faced with fury. "Vinnie's a top quality officer. He's got the guy on ice. But I need to get that flash drive to close this out."

The local Boss, Vinnie, stood up, came around the desk, and moved to stand next to Butch and Sundance. He looked into the camera and said, "Permisso, Caporegime?"

The Boss nodded, then Vinnie, a Capo, turned to the cowboys and said, "Wanna know how much it cost me to get that Stanfield guy picked up?" he said, pointing at a closed circuit screen showing a slender curly headed blond guy on a cot in an empty room.

Sundance shook his head.

Vinnie slapped him hard across the face.

"But …" Butch said, and then he, too, got a hard slap across the face.

"I'm sendin' Salvo with you," Vinnie said, tilting his head to indicate the huge guy.

"The item's gotta be with those people. When they leave their hotel tomorrow morning I want you to stop 'em in the desert, turn 'em upside down, and shake 'em hard 'til it falls outta somebody's pocket!

"As long as you're in this area I can see to it that no cops'll bother you. Now get outta here and get some decent clothes you freakin' idiots!"

Chapter 43

When they'd completed the Canyon Overlook hike, Steve picked the group up near the trailhead.

They made one last photo stop, then and went to the Zion Park Deli to buy some sandwiches before continuing on to the George Barker River Park where there were some picnic tables right next to the Virgin River.

Alex decided to call John to see if he'd heard from Deputy Hankins.

"Yep, I talked to him earlier today," John said. "But, just like this whole situation, it was weird. He said he hadn't heard back from the FBI. When he called the closest local office they acted like they had no clue as to who's in charge of the investigation. They said they had no agents working in the area at that time and they hadn't heard anything about a robbery.

"Maybe this is the way they always talk about their work. Lying, I mean. But maybe you should call Deputy Hankins direct. I'll give you his number. Hang on a sec," John looked up the phone number and gave it to Alex.

"Thanks," Alex said. "I'll call him when we get back to Las Vegas."

After a really nice picnic they started the three hour drive back to Vegas. As soon as they entered the fringes of the population sprawl, the group started missing wilderness and the quirky little towns and vintage family-owned motels.

"The United States certainly is a country of many contrasts," said Peter.

"Indeed," said Frida.

Now that they were back in a big city, Gerd asked if they could stop somewhere on the way back to the hotel so he could buy a new camera for the remaining week of the trip.

"Of course," said Steve. He turned toward Alex and said, "Where do you suggest?"

Alex found a place online and Steve took them there. When Gerd came out of the store he was happy. He'd gotten a good deal on a model he'd wanted for years.

By the time they got checked in to their hotel it was 6:30. Alex reserved a table for eight at the Cañonita next to the canal at the Venetian.

Gerd dropped off his luggage in his room and went over to Klaus and Tina's room with his laptop. Klaus transferred the pictures he'd taken to Gerd's laptop.

When they superficially reviewed the pictures to be sure he could see them all, they noticed the group photo that Klaus had been taken at the Forrest Gump scenic spot.

Just before the shutter snapped the group had realized a truck was bearing down on them at high speed. The exposure captured their shocked faces and blurred limbs as they went running every which way to get out of the road.

Gerd, Klaus, and Tina couldn't stop laughing. It was a fabulous group photo to remember the trip by. Perfect, in fact.

***

Steve drove them over to the Venetian where they shared a great Mexican dinner. Everyone but Steve had at least a couple of beers. Some had tequila as well.

It had been a great trip, an unforgettable experience, and they had a wonderful last night together. On the way back to the hotel the ones who were going to the airport tomorrow exchanged e-mail addresses with the ones who were continuing to San Francisco.

When the van was parked for the night, the remaining members of the tour group said good bye to Tina, Klaus, and Peter.

"Are you ready to go back to the monastery?" Frida asked Peter.

He nodded. "I needed a change of air. I got it. And now I am ready to go back."

"Can I make a confession to you?" she said.

"Of course."

"I gave Elisabeth an expensive jar of cream that was not what it appeared to be. It was CBD. I switched the contents. To shut her up."

He smiled at her and nodded. "We all owe you a debt of gratitude."

"I hope you will visit me in Paris if you ever get the impulse," she said. "I have a large apartment on the Île de la Cité, near Place Dauphine. You can have a floor to yourself."

"And we have a guest house," Peter said. "Women are allowed to stay there. We will keep in contact. We must plot our mystery story together. This trip would make a best seller for sure."

"And if you ever want someone to travel with," she said, "I would be happy to go with you. The old maid and the monk."

"A perfect pair," he said.

Frida had tears in her eyes as she hugged him goodbye.

It was midnight by the time the guests finally got to bed.

***

After they'd said goodbye, Klaus told Tina about getting the flash drive from Alex and what he'd found on it. "You can *never* share what I'm about to tell you with anyone. I know some people in Berlin who will pay a great deal to see this," he said. "Our standard of living is about to change for the better."

She smiled and made them each a celebratory drink from the minibar. So Klaus hadn't changed after all. He was still a Stasi. He was still willing to victimize others for his own gain. Then she yawned and said she was going to bed.

He was disappointed that she didn't seem as interested as he'd expected, but it was late and she was probably exhausted, so he didn't say anything else about it.

He smiled to think of all the people who'd come to the American West hoping to make their fortune. He hadn't been one of them, and yet he'd found a treasure without even looking.

Life was strange sometimes. And unpredictable. You never knew what would happen next. He lay down next to his beautiful young wife and went to sleep thinking he was a very lucky man.

***

Steve was conflicted about his reaction to Tina. He was afraid of her, but he'd miss seeing her. And he was ashamed of himself for giving in to her advances even slightly. With this inner turmoil he knew he wouldn't be able to go to sleep.

"I'm gonna go fill up with gas and get some water for the drive through Death Valley," he said. After that he secretly planned to drown his sorrows at one of the Vegas ice cream parlors, like Amorino, or Cream.

Alex had his own guilty conscience to deal with. Aside from the modest tips he'd gotten from the three departing guests, he was totally broke. But the tips wouldn't be enough to live on for a week, especially not in San Francisco where they were headed.

He'd have to tell Steve he'd lost his billfold and his paycheck and ask to borrow money. He'd fudge the date he'd lost it and wouldn't mention the Stanfield cards, but even then it wouldn't go over well. He dreaded saying anything, but there was no way around it.

He swept the van and emptied the trash receptacles, then went inside the store to ask if they'd found his billfold, or if anyone had turned it in during the intervening two weeks. He didn't have much hope, but he had nothing to lose by asking.

The cashier said no wallets had been turned in, ever, in the history of the station as far as he knew, and possibly not in the history of Las Vegas either.

Alex turned away from the counter, dreading having to admit to Steve that he'd been so careless and having to ask for a loan.

He jammed his hands into his pockets and felt a single wadded dollar bill.

This had to be the lowest point of his life. He glanced up and saw a typical tacky slot machine like the ones scattered all over town. He had to smile. Whenever he went to Las Vegas, his wife always asked him to bet a dollar for her. It was a joke between them.

He always did what she asked and sometimes he won a few extra spins.

But with all the chaos of this trip, he'd forgotten to do it. And so far he'd avoided confessing to her about losing all his money.

He knew the machines in a convenience store were a poor choice for gambling, but he made the bet for her anyway. His heart wasn't in it, though. He was just going through the motions.

He inserted the dollar bill and pushed a button. He was so depressed and preoccupied that he turned away before the wheels had stopped spinning. We walked outside and the door closed behind him.

A few seconds later the sounds of bells and sirens. He thought it was an ambulance and looked toward the street. Then he realized it was coming from inside the station. The attendant burst through the door, and shouted. "Hey, buddy, you won!"

He'd won? "How much?" he called back.

"$100," the guy said, smiling. "Your luck is changing!"

This event lightened the mood significantly. Alex took it as a sign that the rest of the trip would be easier.

"Hey, I was going to the Strip to get an ice cream and walk off some of this road stiffness," said Steve. "Wanna come?"

Alex agreed.

On the way they commiserated about the bizarre trip. This one had taken the cake is so many different ways.

By the time they were eating their gourmet ice cream, Steve confessed about Tina.

Then Alex confessed about her, too.

They decided to continue their urban hike to celebrate surviving the previous two weeks. The lights were dazzling and distracted them from their introspective thoughts.

Eventually Alex confessed about losing his billfold. He made it sound a lot more recent than it actually was and didn't mention his use of the Stanfield cards.

Steve commiserated with him and admitted that the guests hadn't actually decided to eat all of Alex's macadamia and white chocolate Clif bars on their own, but that he'd given them out as payback for the drunken escapades.

They were now bonded, true partners in wild west adventure touring. They found themselves standing outside the Bellagio.

"I'd like to make one more bet, for Sonja, my wife," said Alex.

Steve nodded.

He took his fresh new hundred dollar bill toward a Megabucks slot machine. Steve thought, *uh oh*, but before he could stop him Alex won.

Alex kept making spins on the initial hundred, winning and making more spins. He stood in front of the one-armed bandit and felt nothing but a supernatural sort of calm. It was like he was in a trance and couldn't stop himself.

He was oblivious to the large crowd that he was attracting, until he suddenly decided to stop.

He'd won $350,000.

Steve gave him a bone-crushing man hug.

Alex was in shock. He'd gone from being broke to being rich in the span of a few minutes. This trip had gone from being incredibly bizarre and stressful to solving the biggest problem he had in life.

Now his family could have the bigger apartment they'd needed for years. Vegas was a *crazy* town.

He walked to a quieter area and called his wife. "Sonja," he said, "you won't believe what just happened!"

Chapter 44

Klaus had a rough night. Less than an hour after dropping off to sleep he'd been awoken by cramps. He spent most of the night in the bathroom.

He suspected it was the Mexican food, but Tina blamed it on the last of the smoked salami he'd finally finished eating the day before. He'd bought the package of meat on the first day of the trip, two weeks ago, and had been snacking on it ever since.

Tina begged him to throw it away, but Klaus was convinced it was still good. "Now you learn which of us is the smart one," said Tina.

***

The remaining guests gathered at the van at 6:15 in the morning to begin the California portion of their adventure. They missed their other three travelling companions already.

Steve was thinking about Tina in particular. He'd probably never see her again. Their brief romantic encounter had made a huge impression on him.

As a shy person he didn't often have those kinds of encounters. Actually he'd *never* had that kind of encounter before. He kept his thoughts to himself, though, as he and Alex hooked the trailer onto the van and the remaining guests climbed aboard.

They pulled out of the parking lot without noticing a silver subcompact following them several cars back.

Gerd pulled out his laptop to show the others the hilarious group photo that Klaus's camera had taken when the truck was chasing them out of the road. They all laughed when they saw it.

Gerd was happy he'd gone on this trip. Even with all the crazy and bad things that had happened to him. None of it had been his fault. He was a totally innocent victim of forces he had no understanding of or control over.

He glanced at Elisabeth's habitually sour expression and thought that bitterness only perpetuated misery. She tried to spread it around, but her bad attitude blighted her own life more than anyone else's. Negativity was instant karma.

Nobody had experienced the Cold War as deeply as people who lived in Germany, especially the people of Berlin. Both sides feared nuclear war and just wanted peace. Guards had stood on the Wall and looked down onto life on the other side as if it was a zoo.

He'd learned from growing up in East Germany, and especially after reunification, that forgiveness was its own reward. He'd lived through huge changes in his life, unimaginable changes.

He thought to himself that life was an adventure. Every day of it was a blessing. He was thrilled to be alive and out and about in the world, no matter what happened.

***

After an hour and forty-five minutes they reached the Amargosa Valley and the Area 51 Alien Travel Center and Brothel. It was a unique rest stop that was a combination gas station, café, and whorehouse.

Steve stopped at the pump that had a view of the so-called *Alien Cathouse*. A sign offered free tours of the brothel. When Frida read it, she said, "Oh, that would be interesting!"

"Sorry Frida," Alex said, "I believe the tours are for men only."

Frida looked at the two scantily clad women who were standing in front of the building smoking. She waved, and called out, "Gute Morgen, meine Damen!"

The two women smiled and waved back.

Everyone was so preoccupied with the exchange between the old maid and the hookers that they didn't notice the men who'd held them at gunpoint four days ago sitting in the silver rental car watching them.

***

They'd finessed the rental saying the people in the van had made the Mustang so they had to ditch it. Salvo was crammed into the back seat of the little car with his knees nearly touching his chin.

"I need ta get outta here," he said.

"No way!" Butch said, "You'll draw too much attention."

"I'm getting cramps," he said. "I can't keep sittin' like this!"

"Shuddup!" Butch barked.

***

The tour group took a restroom break and bought some snacks at the store. When they congregated back at the van Georg was missing.

Elisabeth said, "This man is killing me! Always late. Where is he this time? Has anyone seen him?"

Frida glanced at Alex, and whispered, "Maybe he is on a free tour."

Alex couldn't help but laugh.

Then Frida added, "I can certainly understand his interest."

Elisabeth marched back into the store. A minute later she came out with Georg. "Hurry up," she said, in a shrill voice. "We have been waiting."

***

It was time for Tina and Klaus to leave for the airport. Peter's flight wouldn't be departing until later in the day, so the couple took the short taxi ride without him.

When they arrived at McCarran airport, Klaus had to run to the first bathroom he could find. It was ten minutes before he was able to return.

Then, while standing with Tina in the line to check their luggage he became really ill again. He was sweating profusely. As soon as they'd dropped off their checked luggage he ran back to the restroom leaving all the hand luggage with Tina.

When Klaus was out of sight Tina unzipped his backpack, searched it to be certain the flash drive was inside, then zipped it back up, put it on, and walked away from the rest of their carry-on luggage.

She smiled to herself. The drugs she'd put in his food last night were working perfectly. She went to the nearest courtesy phone and dialed 911. She talked for less than a minute, then left the area.

Chapter 45

The Wild West Adventure Tours van was on its way through the desert headed for the entrance to Death Valley National Park. Just before they reached the California state line, though, a little Toyota Yaris with a car rental bumper sticker suddenly zipped by, then slowed rapidly and turned sideways in front of them.

Steve had to slam on the brakes to avoid a collision. He did a great job of defensive driving and had didn't hit the small car.

Steve turned around to the guests, and asked, "Are you okay? Is everyone alright?"

They all nodded. They'd all been wearing seat belts this time.

Some crazy stuff had been happening during this trip, but this took the cake. Steve was furious. He leaped out of the van and walked rapidly toward the driver's side of the little car.

When the window rolled down he found himself looking into the barrel of a pistol. Whatever he'd been planning to say, died before escaping his lips. It was those crazy cowboys again, but now they were dressed in modern clothes.

The guests wondered why Steve was standing there, frozen, then they saw Sundance get out of the passenger side. He ran back toward the van, jerked the passenger door open, and pointed a pistol at the guests.

"Not again!" Alex said.

"Get out!" he shouted. "All a ya!"

He looked around behind him, and called out, "Hey, Salvo! Get ova here and gimme some help!"

"No can do," said a voice from inside the Yaris, "My legs ain't workin' no more!"

"Get the frack outta the car!" Sundance shouted.

The men had been forced to abandon the Mustang due to the extensive damage and they'd blamed it all on the tour group. Vinnie and the Boss were suspicious, but they'd let it go, for now.

While the group was scrambling out of the van, Salvo managed to extract himself from the back seat using his considerable upper body strength. The lower half of his body was numb.

When he finally managed to squirm his way out of the two-door car, he fell on his face. He lay there on the pavement holding a pistol.

The black asphalt was radiating the temperature of a frying pan and Salvo screamed. He rolled over and flailed at the pain.

Butch forced Steve to unlock the trailer and open it while Sundance held the group at gunpoint. "Hey, Salvo, you look like a cockaroach. Get up and get over here and help me out."

The big guy made it over onto his knees, then stood up, and hobbled over.

Steve and Salvo dragged the suitcases out of the trailer and tossed them onto the pavement. Then Butch tore each one open, and searched it, flinging the contents off into the desert. He pawed his way through everyone's belongings.

"Salvo, search the inside of the van," Butch said.

"The rest of ya empty your pockets and turn 'em inside out."

When neither the luggage nor the contents of their pockets nor the interior of the van yielded any results, Alex asked, "What exactly are you looking for?"

"One a them things for a computer," Salvo said.

"A flash drive," Sundance added. "Which one of ya has the flash drive? You'd betta hand it over or some very unfortunate things are about to happen. To *all* of yuz."

"A flash drive?" Alex said. "We did find one. Is that what you're looking for?"

Sundance nodded.

"It belonged to a passenger and I gave it back to him, but he's not with us anymore."

As soon as he said it, Alex realized that it must've been far more than an ordinary storage device.

"Who offed him?" Sundance said, looking at the men with fury.

"He's not *dead*," said Steve. "He and his wife left to fly home."

"No! No! No!" Butch shrieked, while stomping and kicking his way through the jumble of clothes and toiletries lying around him on the ground.

He and Butch jumped back into the Yaris. Butch ground the gears noisily and the little car didn't go anywhere for several long moments, then he finally found a gear but released the clutch too fast and the car died.

He had to restart the engine, put the car in first, execute an agonizing three-point turn, and drive away accelerating as quickly as possible as he attempted to hold onto the shreds of his dignity.

The group stared around in shock and exchanged traumatized looks. The huge man, Salvo, was standing there beside them, open-mouthed, holding his gun loosely at his side. He was as startled as they were.

They heard the squealing of tires, then an engine screaming as Butch came wobbling back toward them, reversing at high speed. He skidded to a stop, and shouted, "Get in!"

Salvo squeezed into the back seat and they drove away.

Once they'd disappeared from view the group looked in dismay at their stuff being spread across the desert by the wind.

***

Klaus flushed the toilet, then staggered to the basins, washed and dried his hands, and exited the restroom. He was immediately confronted by an armed security officer who shouted, "This way! Everyone this way! Right now!"

Klaus saw that his luggage was surrounded by security officers. He scanned the crowd for Tina, but couldn't find her. A man with a dog was approaching the scene. Klaus guessed it was a bomb sniffer. If it had been a drug dog, they wouldn't be forcing people to move away.

"Sir," Klaus said, to one of the policemen.

"Go! Go!" the man told him. "Get back for your own safety!"

"Sir, this is my luggage!" Klaus said, wondering where Tina was.

"Then I need you to come with me," the agent said, lifting his pistol and gesturing the direction he wanted Klaus to take.

***

While Klaus was busy trying to explain that he was not a terrorist, but rather a retired German businessman, his wife was at a different ticket counter.

"I would like a ticket for one to Moscow," Tina said. "First class if possible."

"When do you want to fly?" asked the woman behind the counter.

"Now," Tina replied.

"Alright. Let me take a look and see what we have," the agent said, looking at a screen and typing on her keyboard.

After a few moments, she said, "There's a flight at 10:20 with layover in L.A. From LAX it's a direct flight to Moscow, but First Class is full. Boarding will begin in a few minutes. You'll have to hurry."

"Great, I'll take it," Tina said.

"When do you want to return?" the agent asked.

"I need only one-way," Tina said.

"I'll need a credit card and your passport," the agent said.

"I'll pay cash," Tina said, then reached into the backpack and pulled out a thick roll of U.S. currency.

"It's $962.54," the agent said.

Tina counted out ten $100 bills onto the counter then dug around again in the backpack and found her German passport, but hesitated for a moment, then put it back. She turned away from the agent, jerked open a seam in her jacket, and removed a Russian passport from the lining.

"Is this the only luggage you have?" the agent asked, pointing at the backpack.

"Yes," Tina said.

"Let me see if I have the correct change."

"Keep it," Tina said.

The agent typed a bit more, then printed a boarding pass. She returned Tina's passport and handed her the boarding pass.

"How do you pronounce your name?" the agent asked.

"Jekaterina Iwanowa," Tina replied, pronouncing it *Yekaterina Ivanova*.

"You're at gate A13, Ms. Iwanowa. Have a good flight!"

Tina rushed through security and to the gate. Her name was already being announced as she arrived and she was the last person to board.

The flight was totally booked and there was no space in the overhead bin near her seat to store the backpack. She tried to shove it underneath her seat, but it was too large to fit, so she kept it on her lap.

When the stewardess walked the aisle to prepare for takeoff, she said, "Ma'am, you can't keep a bag on your lap. Let me put it in an overhead bin for you."

"No, I wish to hold it," Tina said, holding on tight.

"I'm sorry ma'am, I *have* to store it for you," the stewardess said, grabbing of one of the straps on the backpack.

Tina wouldn't let go.

"Ma'am, you're delaying the takeoff. You *must* allow me to stow the bag in an overhead bin. Or you will be removed from the aircraft."

Tina reluctantly let go and the stewardess walked off with the bag heading toward the rear of the plane. Tina watched her place the backpack in an overhead compartment and close the door.

Moments later she returned to say, "It's above seat B22."

The plane started moving and the stewardesses gave the safety instructions. The flight crew took their seats and the plane taxied and took off.

Tina smiled because she knew that nothing could stop her now. All the years she'd spent with Klaus would finally pay off. Handsomely.

When she'd been sent to Germany, she'd been a kid, a Russian of German ancestry. Most of the young German-Russians, *Deutschrussen*, as they were called, were Germans who'd emigrated to Russia in the late 19th and early 20th centuries, some of them Jewish, who could still claim German citizenship, but most of whom no longer spoke German.

Tina's family was very traditional, though, and they'd spoken German at home, so Tina could speak the language without an accent.

It had been an easy matter to encounter Klaus seemingly by accident. He was celebrating his 60ᵗʰ birthday with a party on his yacht in Palma de Mallorca, Spain. She'd slipped aboard by pretending to be the DJ's girlfriend.

The Foreign Intelligence Service of the Russian Federation, Sluzhba vneshney razvedki Rossiyskoy Federatsii, or SVR for short, knew that Klaus still had ties to functionaries of the old East German regime, former Stasi officials. And even more importantly, he had connections with agents of the west German intelligence agency *Bundesnachrichtendienst*.

After the wall came down the west German agency had hired former east block agents to get access to their knowledge. The western intelligence community was keen on using the Stasi to gain insight into the power structures of the former eastern bloc.

When the SVR sent Tina to Germany, they had every reason to hope that someday she'd be able to deliver confidential information back to them.

It had been a wise wager. Now she was about to collect her winnings.

Chapter 46

"I need ta use the restroom," Salvo said.

"We'll stop at the next gas station," Butch said.

"I need ta find one pretty quick," Salvo said.

"The quickest one is if I stop right here and you go," Butch said.

They were in an area where you could see for miles in every direction.

"Thanks, but I'll try ta hold on til we get somewhere," Salvo said.

At the first station they saw, Salvo wormed his way out and ran inside. It was clearly a genuine emergency.

"If we make it to the airport in time, who are we lookin' for?" Sundance asked.

"No idea," Butch said.

"If the garage can't get the Mustang fixed and we have to show up in this rental and tell the boss we don't have the thingamajig, he'll kill us for sure," Sundance said.

"How far's Mexico?" Butch asked.

"Dunno," Sundance said. "Why're ya askin'"

"Iddn't that where Butch and Sundance went?"

"Yeahhh…..I think so," Sundance drawled, trying to remember what the outcome of the trip had been. He tried to pull up a map on his phone. "I can't get a signal, so I can't tell ya how far it is."

"Then there's only one way find out!" Butch said, starting the engine. "It's gotta be south of here, right?"

"Right," Sundance said.

When Salvo came back outside the Yaris was gone. All that was left was a faint cloud of dust in the distance.

Tina had finished congratulating herself and was relaxed enough to be watching the movie when she was startled by a huge bang. She looked out the window and saw that one of the engines was on fire.

The seat belt sign came on, and the captain said, "We're experiencing a problem with one of our engines. Please give your attention to the flight attendants. They'll instruct you on the proper procedures.

"There's no need to worry. These planes are designed to handle situations a lot tougher than this. It'll get us back to Las Vegas safely. We might have a bit of a rough ride, so stay in your seats with your seatbelts fastened at all times."

In addition to the flaming engine, Tina could see that part of the wing was damaged as well. And storm clouds were clearly visible coming toward them from the west.

The aircraft was vibrating significantly and the passengers were freaking out. Nobody was screaming but she could hear some people praying while others tried to call home.

They had a bucking bronco ride all the way back to Las Vegas. The captain had a tough job landing the plane, but he did it.

When the wheels touched down the plane tilted to the right and the wing on that side made contact with the ground. The dragging wing tip caused the plane to rotate toward that side, but it came to a stop without further incident.

The evacuation procedure began immediately. Tina wanted to run to the back of the plane to retrieve her backpack, but that was not going to be possible. She was being shoved forward toward the closest emergency exit.

Then smoke started building in the cabin. No question. She had to get out of the plane. She made it to the slide and to the ground without injury.

Once she was on the runway airport personnel led her away from the plane. All passengers and crew made it out safely. From a distance they watched as the fire spread until it engulfed the entire aircraft. Then it exploded and everything inside it went up in smoke.

Epilogue

It was all over the news. J.J. Stanfield was still in hiding, but he had escaped from his kidnappers and made contact with his news organization. According to the news story rogue or counterfeit FBI agents were involved in his illegal detention.

Stanfield had lost custody of a flash drive containing the proof he'd amassed of corruption between the Mafia and high level government officials, but he retained hope that it was out there somewhere and he could find it.

A request for assistance was issued. If anyone had any information as to the whereabouts of the flash drive, they should contact his news organization immediately via a web address or an 800 number.

Sketches of the fake or corrupt FBI agents who were involved flashed on the screen and Alex recognized them from his own unpleasant encounters.

Oh no.

Maybe these guys were the ones who'd broken into the trailer, in addition to the open harassment they'd been dishing out. Suddenly all this craziness was starting to make sense.

Alex knew he was innocent and he felt confident that Gerd was innocent as well, but he had no idea how the flash drive had gotten associated with Gerd's camera bag in the first place.

Still, some of the pieces were coming together. The picture it was painting was much worse than Alex could've imagined. The Mafia, the FBI, politicians, and God only knew who else, were involved in a massive conspiracy.

It was only a matter of time until somehow one or more of them circled back to him and Gerd. He wondered how long it would take. He tried to organize his thoughts.

He got a bad feeling about the info on that flash drive that John had found and given to him, that he'd started to use, but then given to Klaus. He checked his computer to see if he still had the data he'd copied off it.

Nope. He'd trashed it.

He didn't know whether to be disappointed or relieved.

Then he checked his trash. He hadn't emptied it. The files were still there.

He looked at a few of the images and documents. *Holy moly…*

And he still had a week to go on this tour before the group made it to San Francisco.

THE END

HOW YOU CAN HELP

Your reviews are extremely important in helping other readers locate this book. If you enjoyed this book, please share information about it and leave a review on Amazon or GoodReads. Thank you!

ABOUT CAROLYN JOURDAN

Carolyn Jourdan is a *USA Today*, Audible, and 5-time *Wall Street Journal* best-selling author of memoir, medicine, wildlife, and mystery.

Jourdan's trademark blend of wit and wisdom, humor and humanity have earned her high praise from Dolly Parton and Fannie Flagg, as well as major national newspapers, the New York Public Library, Elle, Family Circle Magazine, and put her work at the top of hundreds of lists of best books of the year and funniest books ever.

Her books have been honored with citywide reads.

Carolyn is a former U.S. Senate Counsel to the Committee on Environment and Public Works and the Committee on Governmental Affairs. She has degrees from the University of Tennessee in Biomedical Engineering and Law.

She lives on the family farm in east Tennessee with many stray animals, including a rescue Havanese named Jimmy.

Visit CarolynJourdan.com to hear her read stories from her books.

To be notified about free books, special discounts, and new releases join Carolyn's mailing list at http://carolynjourdan.com/mailing-list/

Carolyn will never send you any spam or share your email address.

Make friends with Carolyn on Facebook
https://www.facebook.com/carolynjourdan

Follow her on Instagram
https://www.instagram.com/carolynjourdanauthor/

ABOUT LUDGER DOMINIC BRACHT

Ludger was born and raised in the industrial center of Germany, but at the age of thirty decided to make the beautiful bicycle town of Münster his home. His first trip to the U.S. was at the age of thirteen when he came to San Diego, California, to live with a host family for three weeks. Since that time he has returned to the American West every year.

He worked for an Austrian ski school when he was eighteen, then went to a town near Barcelona, Spain, to work at his first job as a tour guide. After that he worked as a guide and ski instructor in Austria, Switzerland, and Utah.

He received two and a half years of training as a travel agent.

When he discovered he was a passionate foodie, he took jobs as a cook on 19th century Dutch sailing boats repurposed for hire and at a hut in the French-speaking part of the Swiss Alps. His freelance job as a chef also took him to Croatia, Sweden, and France.

Ludger tries to spend the majority of his time with his wife and his two daughters in Münster, so for almost ten years he ran a catering company that specialized in catering bands, comedians, and their crews when they were touring near his home.

As founder and owner of the company Personal Scout Tours he offers and guides tours through the American West and ski trips to the U.S., Canada, and Japan.

Visit Ludger at
https://personal-scout-tours.de
https://www.schneesatt.com
info@personal-scout-tours.de

BOOKS BY CAROLYN JOURDAN

Memoir
Heart in the Right Place * *Wall Street Journal* Bestseller * Chosen by 100s of librarians for their book club collections * Read by 100s of religious-based book clubs, including Protestant, Catholic, Jewish, and Muslim.
https://www.amzn.com/B001FA0G9E/

Medicine
Medicine Men: Extreme Appalachian Doctoring * Wall Street Journal Bestseller * Amazon All-Star *
https://www.amzn.com/B00A9L3E62/

Nurse: The Art of Caring
https://www.amzn.com/B01JGQB5P2/

Radiologists at Work: Saving Lives with the Lights Off
https://www.amzn.com/B016PCQM1M/

Talking to Skeletons: Behind the Scenes with a Radiologist
https://www.amzn.com/B016PCQZLY/

Mystery
Out on a Limb: A Smoky Mountain Mystery * *USA Today* Bestseller * Best Kindle Book of the Year *
https://www.amzn.com/gp/product/B00B9FKLS6

School for Mysteries: A Midlife Fairy Tale Adventure
https://www.amzn.com/B00K0VPMTI/

School for Psychics: A Midlife Fairy Tale Adventure
https://www.amzn.com/B00LYTZMQS/

Bears
Bear in the Back Seat: Adventures of a Wildlife Ranger Vol. I * *Wall Street Journal* Bestseller * Audible Bestseller * A Top 50 Must Read for the 100th Anniversary of the National Park Service with Edward Abbey, Nevada Barr, and C.J. Box * https://www.amzn.com/B00EW8TTQW/

Bear in the Back Seat: Adventures of a Wildlife Ranger Vol. II * A Top 10 Must-Read That Could Save Our National Parks and the Environment with John Muir, Henry David Thoreau, Lewis & Clark, Bill Bryson, and Ken Burns * https://www.amzn.com/B00J7XP6CI/

Bear Bloopers: True Stories from the Great Smoky Mountains National Park
https://www.amzn.com/B00Q3NB3Y0/

Dangerous Beauty: Stories from the Wilds of Yellowstone * A Best Book About Yellowstone and A Top Must-Read About Yellowstone * https://www.amzn.com/B06XZYNXLS/

Waltzing with Wildlife: 10 Things NOT to Do in Our National Parks
https://www.amzn.com/B01LWEAVSX/

Writing
How to Write, Edit & Publish Your Memoir: Advice from a Bestselling Memoirist
https://www.amzn.com/B07FC8TPWJ/

www.ingramcontent.com/pod-product-compliance
Lightning Source LLC
Chambersburg PA
CBHW051415170626
46809CB00006B/2168